REQUITED

a novel

Kimberlee Liu

REQUITED

Cover design by Roderick Brydon

I know that I found it beautiful. But I cannot recapture its beauty.

—BERNHARD SCHLINK, *THE READER*

Chapter 1

An eight-year-old boy attending the elementary school in my neighborhood stabbed his teacher with a steak knife recently. He'd received a B+ in precalculus. It was devastating, as he had no hope and no other options; the woman single-handedly wrote his future a death sentence. According to the school's policy, students who failed to earn at least an A- in the class were not allowed to join the honors program starting in third grade.

I was annoyed by the frequency with which this piece of news was broadcast in my area. Since I had no children, the school system didn't concern me much. More importantly, it was disrupting the movie I was mentally invested in.

As my mood steadily crumbled, I turned off the projector altogether. Sensing a sudden darkness, a lamp nearby switched on, immediately followed by the warm yellow lights mounted on the hallway walls. I walked barefoot toward the kitchen area, across the heated floor. The temperature had dropped significantly in the past few days. Tonight, the wind blew with exceptional relentlessness. Sporadic rain drifted through the sky for hours before dusk. But the sharp strikes of lightning were new to my ears.

Fortunately, the weather outside had no ability to harm me. Inside my multistory shelter, the weather was always perfect.

I opened the refrigerator to search for the two bags of cherries sitting in the produce drawer. They were plump and juicy, and they glistened after a quick rinse under the faucet. It was too far into fall to consume fresh cherries grown within the country, but shipments from Japan ensured they could be acquired in any season.

I returned to the couch with a glass bowl and a paper towel for the pits. When I popped one into my mouth, its sweetness and sourness burst on my tongue simultaneously. As a loud crack of thunder shook the house, I contemplated what I wanted to order or cook for tomorrow's dinner. I was envisioning seafood, either prawns or lobster.

Earlier during the day, one of the peacock statues in the front yard had fallen over in the wind. The gardeners were coming in two days; in the meantime, I could walk around the debris.

I threw the cherry pits into the biodegradable part of the trash can and began walking toward the main bedroom.

The door monitor rang. The marble stairs turned cold beneath my feet. My heart thumped once loudly. It was well past midnight.

I slowly turned and laughed at the way my body jerked.

The computer system was smart enough to recognize motions created by different weather conditions. Before I had time to think of what the alert could possibly be, other than what I didn't want it to be, forceful pounds penetrated the front door.

I checked the projection in the air, rubbed my eyes, and opened them again. I saw her standing in a long black raincoat in the corner of the porch.

Confused, I wondered if what I was seeing was real, or if robbers were intelligent enough nowadays to hack into people's door monitors before breaking in. However, the necessity of opening the door as soon as I could felt like a reward which easily outweighed any consequences.

I twisted the door handle. The metal lock clicked.

She looked drenched. A droplet fell from the hem of the hood onto her face, making it look like she was crying, though her eyes conveyed otherwise. A few strands of her dark brown hair had turned black and were glued to her cheeks. She tilted her head upward, looking at me silently.

I didn't dare raise my voice. I quickly stepped aside and gestured for her to come past the overhang. When she stalled on the doormat, I walked over and helped her out of her raincoat. I was surprised to see her fully dressed underneath: boots, a blouse, and a pair of wide-legged pants. At this hour, I imagined she'd be wearing pajamas instead. Her pant legs had darkened and were halfway stuck to her legs.

"Your shoes," I said. I could only see the tips of her leather boots. I assumed her socks were wet as well.

"I don't want to ruin your floor." She shook her head

3

lightly. "I'm not staying long."

"Is everything all right?"

A nerve pulsing in my neck told me things were far from all right. I hadn't seen her in months. The first thought that entered my mind was that Chris had died, or gotten entangled in trouble due to his overly engorged ego. It wasn't a thought I felt proud of.

"Edward?"

"Yes?" I wondered if Chris had cheated on her.

"I'm sorry." Her eyes met mine, now holding back tears.

"What?" I frowned. From the way she spoke, it didn't seem as if she was delivering me a piece of bad news; she said it like she, personally, was apologizing to me. But she hadn't done anything wrong.

"I'm sorry for being a jerk to you."

I let out a little laugh of embarrassment as tears began pouring out of her. She raised a hand to cover her mouth. The sniffling sounds escaped through her fingers.

"No, no. Don't say that." I scratched the back of my head.

"I'm going now. Bye." She reached for the raincoat in my arms. I was holding it too close to my body; a large, wet surface was pressed against my chest. When I shifted its weight, a chilling stain of water marked my thin undershirt.

"Where are you going?" I asked.

Her fingertips clutched the slippery material. "Home."

"No. You're not traveling through the night."

"It has nothing to do with you."

I suppressed my annoyance to the best of my ability. She was being selfish to the core, to think she could pull away without offering me an explanation.

"I'm calling Chris to pick you up."

"No!" She raised her voice suddenly.

"If you come inside and talk to me about what's going on, then I won't." At this point, I was certain there was friction between them. As worried as I was, a seed of joy sprouted within me. It was so minuscule and weak that there was no need to hide it.

She hesitated. I pushed her on the shoulder, attempting to lead her inside. She mouthed an *ouch* and flinched dramatically, as if I were really hurting her. I retracted my hand and grabbed her wrist.

Inside, we sat at the kitchen island.

"Your shoes," I said.

"Can you get me something to drink?"

"Yeah—tea?"

"Tea."

Once the kettle was whistling, I poured the water into a black-and-white mug. The small tea bag drowned itself and began gradually releasing silklike strands of brown until its hue tinted the rest of the water. I reached for the milk pitcher in the refrigerator.

Whiteness swirled against the darkened liquid and eventually blended into one.

I turned around and pushed the mug toward her. Her boots were already lying on the floor, and her socks were folded on top. Her pant legs covered her feet. She frowned at the sight of the mug and wrapped her fingers around it to warm her hands. The many diamonds on her engagement ring, paired with her wedding band, glowed under the pendant lights.

"How did you get here?"

"The car," she said. "I don't want milk."

"Sorry." I thought about pulling the mug away and drinking it myself later, due to the fact that she had once held it in her hands. Afraid of her seeing through my intentions, I threw the entire drink down the sink and quickly made her a new one. "How did you get this wet? Do you need a change of clothes?"

"No, thank you." She inhaled, looking like she was trying to say something, but eventually swallowed her words. I waited with more patience than I thought I had in me. Sitting in the kitchen with her wasn't entirely horrible. "I was just standing outside. I wasn't sure if I wanted to come in."

"No. There's an overhang, and my monitor didn't see you."

"I know. I stood away from your camera."

"Why?"

"I came here to tell you that I'm sorry for being a jerk to you."

"You already said that." My eyes landed on my phone, resting comfortably on the counter. "I'm calling Chris."

"No! I'm going now." She slipped off her seat, charging for her shoes.

"You drove all the way here in the middle of the night to stand in front of my house, say something irrelevant, and dash afterward?"

"I'm sorry for disturbing you. Pretend I didn't come."

"Too late," I snapped. "I've already been disturbed."

I couldn't pinpoint what she was planning on doing once I let her go. As annoyed as I was for having a restful night of sleep taken away, I couldn't let stupidity control her when she was alone.

"Sit. You're not leaving."

"I'm just gonna go sit in the car," she said coldly, but she didn't take any steps toward the door.

"You're soaked." I raised my voice. "You need a change of clothes."

She looked at me briefly. "I have a bag in my car."

"If you stay put at least for tonight, I won't call anyone."

I couldn't trust her to leave the house, so I took her keys and went to retrieve the bag myself. Her car was spotless and smelled brand new. A blue duffel bag sat in the back seat. If she hadn't brought extra clothes, I'd be obliged to offer her something from my own closet. I couldn't imagine the level of discomfort it was going to bring me.

"Your house is different," she commented when I came back. Her mug was now empty. "How have you been?"

"I've been good. I redecorated it a while ago." I led her through the living room and another hallway on the first floor, holding onto her bag. I opened the door to a guest room with a bathroom attached. "You need to be here in the morning. When I come downstairs, if you aren't here, I'm calling Chris right away."

She didn't answer.

"Make yourself at home. Do I need to scrub down the bathtub, or are you all right with a shower?"

"A shower is fine. Do you have to go to work tomorrow?" she asked weakly. I could see her eyelids starting to shut on her.

"I'm working from home. Signing in at nine. I'll come find you before that." I placed her duffel bag in the guest room.

She went inside obediently, then rested her hand on the wall. "Night, Edward."

"Night."

She locked the door from the inside. I turned, caressing each button on her key fob. The metal grooves felt warm, having been nestled in my palm. The trail of water on the floor left by her entrance was still visible.

I climbed back up the stairs and retreated to my bedroom. I loved the feeling of being under the same roof as her. To cherish it even further, I popped two caffeine pills before lying down.

I stared at the ceiling light. Its softness warmed me from the inside, knowing how we were both sharing the same current of electricity. Sleep could happen any other time. Tonight, I only wanted to be aware of her presence.

Chapter 2

She had a beautiful name I wasn't accustomed to using. In my head, I had always labeled her as *she* or *the person who floated in and out of my consciousness, day and night*. Names were meant to distinguish people from each other, but since she was the only one who consumed my mind, she didn't need one. I was painfully aware of the wrongness of my desire; only her husband was allowed to harbor the same feelings toward her. For years, I'd wrestled with self-loathing and guilt over how I wasn't able to think in the way of a normal human being. Recently, though, I'd found acceptance in holding onto thoughts that were strange to others.

From my window, I watched the sun slowly crawl up the horizon. I squinted my eyes and stared at it. The movement was almost imperceptible. Each second was as still as a photograph. Yet when I shifted my eyes, even for the briefest moment, I was stunned by its progress. The beams of light first bathed the trees nearby; a golden glow seeped through the yellow leaves, then slowly dulled itself until the entire sky turned a transparent shade of blue. I opened the window. The air was exceptionally fresh, having been washed by the rain the night before.

I dressed in my standard attire for a work-from-home day: suit and tie on top, sweatpants and socks on the bottom. Whenever we had meetings, our legs weren't shown on camera. I considered coming down the stairs obeying my full work dress code so that I wouldn't look funny to her, but it would have been too pretentious and, unfortunately, pointless. Letting her stay past morning meant actively searching for trouble myself. I needed to send her home.

She had dug through the kitchen without me and eaten the chicken-and-spinach dish I'd made for my lunch today. The container wasn't rinsed; she'd pushed whatever she couldn't finish into its corner and left it in the sink. The sauce was stuck to the sides and showed itself in a ring of brown scabs. She'd carelessly left a greasy fork on the countertop, along with a used piece of napkin scrunched into a ball.

I disliked her sense of entitlement.

"Hey." I knocked on her bedroom door and waited for a response. "Alicia?" I spoke louder.

Upon my second attempt to get her attention, she groaned unwillingly. When she opened the door, she stood in front of me in a set of pajamas. Strands of hair puffed up from her head. A swipe of greenish-blue sat underneath her eyes.

"I just fell asleep," she murmured.

"Well . . ." I hesitated. "I need to go upstairs and do work. Are you going to stay put?"

"Yes." She closed her eyes and looked like she was about to pass out in the next second.

"Give me your phone." I already had her car keys and had collected her boots earlier. Without her phone, she had no chance of leaving unannounced by ordering a ride. Even if she were to run out on foot, how far could she go on a post-rainy morning without shoes? "Your breakfast is in the kitchen," I said. "I'll see you at one o'clock."

The next four and a half hours were unbearable. I trusted she was getting some well-needed sleep, but I couldn't help but keep the door monitor close to my computer after setting it to the highest sensitivity level and turning the notifications to the loudest volume possible. It alerted me once; I was about to bolt down the stairs before I realized it was a delivery drone dropping off a package. I let out a loose breath and went back to work.

My eyes took in every word, but my brain refused to piece them together to form any sort of meaning. I raised my screens and switched to a standing position. The thought of her sitting in a car for a whole day only to then stand in front of my house puzzled and excited me at the same time. I made up imaginative, colorful scenarios explaining her behavior.

I placed an order for what I remembered to be one of her favorites for lunch. When I went downstairs, her bedroom door was still shut, and her breakfast plate remained untouched. I pushed on the door handle. It was stiff. This wasn't a problem; I had control of all the locks in the house, but breaking into her room was an invasion of privacy. Yet the silence worried me. I leaned against the doorframe and closed my eyes in an attempt to calm my newly gained headache. I needed to shove her out the front door and command her car to take her home. If I had a choice, I wanted to pretend like she had never shown up.

Life had not treated me poorly. For the sake of familiarity, I wanted to maintain my current state of being neither happy nor unhappy.

"I need to know you're all right!" I begged before giving her one last warning. "I'm coming in if you don't answer!"

My panic felt out of place as soon as I pushed into her room. She was lying on her side and sleeping soundly, the comforter draped diagonally across her body. The hem of her long shirt and pants peeked out from underneath. Her legs were curled up, clutching a spare pillow between her knees. The top two buttons near her collar had fallen loose, exposing the deep crease of her breasts pushed together.

I watched her for a little longer, then advanced further into the room. "Wake up!" I pushed her shoulder.

She stirred and swatted my hand away in a semiconscious manner.

"Wake up!"

"Go away." She finally budged, moving her wrist on top of her forehead. I cleared my throat. "Give me two more hours."

"You can go back to bed after lunch. I need you to come out now."

"No."

"Okay." I shrugged. "I'll just make a quick phone call."

"I hate it when you threaten me."

We went into the kitchen. I heated and served lunch on ceramic plates.

"Hope you still like this," I said.

She nodded and then looked at the red lump of pasta on my plate.

"You can have both. I'll eat whatever you can't finish."

She lowered her head and toyed with her fork slowly. "That's not right."

I laughed. "You had no issues eating my food last night."

"That wasn't me." She squinted. "Your house is haunted."

"It wasn't Daria. She would've washed the dishes right after."

She glanced at me from one barstool away. The slight distance gave her the perfect opportunity to examine me without turning her body completely. Her eyes were piercingly sharp. I felt like I had just committed a heinous crime. "It hasn't been a full year yet, has it?"

"A little less than a month till a full year," I said. "You don't expect me to cry every time her name is mentioned, do you?"

"No, but you must still be grieving."

"Of course I am!" My voice sounded a little louder than I had intended.

"Don't you think it's a little too soon to be allowing other people here for sleepovers?"

I reached for my glass and took a sip of water. "But you're my family," I said.

"Right. How are you adjusting?" she asked. "I haven't

gotten a chance to talk to you one-on-one."

"I'm doing great!" I paused to change my stance quickly. "It's certainly very difficult. But moving here helped a lot."

She put her fork down.

"So," I said gently, "is everything all right with you?"

"Yeah."

"Are you sure?"

"Yeah. I'm fine."

"I'm not saying this in a mean way, but are you good enough to go home by yourself? I don't know if you two were in a fight or something like that. It's probably the right thing for you to tell him you're here."

"Not really, but I understand." She threw her leftover food into the appropriate section of the trash can, then rinsed her plate in the sink and loaded it into the dishwasher.

"You know I can't help with anything if you don't talk to me, right?" I said from behind her. "What did Chris do? What did you do?"

Her strides to the guest room came to a halt.

"Did he cheat on you?"

"I don't know for sure."

I exhaled a breath of relief. It wasn't the worst scenario possible. "I'll go ask him."

"You don't need to do anything about it. I'm here to say goodbye to you, not to talk about him. I'm going now."

"What? Why?" I yelled, catching up to her. "Why are you saying goodbye to me? It doesn't make any sense!"

She kept her mouth shut, her lips pressed into a tight

line. A clear discomfort boiled inside of her.

"If you continue not to talk, I'll call Chris," I menaced, hoping she would give in.

"Edward, don't. It's me." Her voice was so low, I wasn't sure how I was able to hear her. Yet every word in the following sentence was etched with remarkable clarity. "I had a miscarriage. That's all," she finished with a careless shrug.

The sound of a roaring train surged from the back of my head, rampaging through my skull. Before my next heartbeat, its deep echoes turned into a high-pitched ringing, which lingered at a constant volume despite my best effort to speak over it. "You're pranking me."

"Why would I do that?"

"But . . . no." I blinked harshly, trying to repel the moisture in my eyes.

Before I could weave together a coherent sentence, she stepped toward me and pulled up a corner of her pant leg. A black, leather-sheathed monitor clung tightly to her ankle. It was compact and strangely elegant. A small green light jumped in the middle of the screen. "You can also look up my record online," she added.

"Take it off," I demanded. "If you want a reaction out of me, you have it now. Please take it off. Jokes like this aren't funny."

"I can't just do that." There was irritation in her voice. "I actually got arrested."

Dizziness crawled over my head, inch by inch. Even though her behavior finally fit into a reasonable narrative, I still hoped that she might break out in laughter and tell me how stupid my expression looked. Growing up, she'd been keen on tormenting me with fictitious scenarios. Even after I finally stopped taking them seriously, I played along to keep her and her other friends happy.

This time, the anticipated moment of relief never arrived.

"What's Chris doing about it?" I asked.

"He's filing for divorce. It doesn't align with his image."

"Why do you give me this?"

"I don't see how this concerns you." She seemed unbothered.

I chased after her toward the guest room.

"I'm just going to get more sleep."

"Can you just tell me one thing right now?"

"What?"

"How many more days do you have left until the final decision?"

"Seventy-two."

Chapter 3

I knew their marriage had been strained, but I'd underestimated Chris's capacity for coldheartedness. Two years ago, their son was eight months old. They lived in Europe for a year and a half to prepare for the baby's arrival; she'd gotten pregnant there and moved her art studio over. Chris traveled back and forth on chartered planes, of course. The amount of time and energy they devoted to family building was insane to me. It was during a time when most people prayed not to get pregnant. They handpicked the doctors, newborn care specialists, physical therapists, and so on. None of the house staff were allowed pets at home.

After the baby was born, they moved back to New York. It wasn't that life abroad was treating them horribly, but there was a certain aspect of privilege in the States that they couldn't give up.

James had been coming back from a walk with the nanny. A few blocks away, a man in his thirties walked out of a job interview in a skyscraper. He'd taken off his cheap, paper-like suit jacket and unbuckled his belt, then swung it over his head like a cowboy swinging a lasso. The waves of pedestrians were his herd of cows and steers. Eventually, his pants fell to the ground. He stepped out of them and walked on in his underwear. No one paid him any attention until he brought out a box cutter from his briefcase. The blade had been sharp, but it was thin, brittle, and not meant to be used as a weapon.

Clumsily, he attempted to slash anyone walking by, especially those who "looked happier than him." Two or perhaps even one stronger person would have been able to tackle him or pin him down, but no one found it a wise decision to put themselves in more danger for the safety of others. People began running in all directions. A civilized street soon turned into a human stampede, which spread to the next and the next street in no time. The stroller lost its balance and was assaulted by the many square and pointy heels of the adults nearby who were merely trying to break out of the swarm themselves for a chance at survival. The harness eventually broke loose on James. But I didn't know if, at that point, it was still relevant.

Fortunately, the nanny recovered after only a few weeks in the hospital. The rest, I could not say.

I went back up the stairs and canceled my afternoon, along with the next day. Seventy-two days weren't enough. Perhaps I would have felt slightly better if she'd said something along the lines of thirty thousand days, but even that wouldn't be enough. I wished for a few hours to breathe, and then immediately slapped myself for my lazy mindset. How could I breathe if she was going to die?

I had very little legal knowledge regarding miscarriage

cases, but it didn't take a genius to figure out how nearly impossible it was to turn a sentence of capital punishment into a verdict of no imprisonment at all. She was not the type of hardened woman who could make it out of prison alive. She was too weak; she lacked the basic resilience that the "commoners" possessed.

A few moments later, I opened a private browser to search for information on how to cross the border into Mexico, which had political refugee programs. Abundant walls of text appeared. Just like this morning, I couldn't comprehend a single sentence. I slouched in my chair and stared at the search engine. The cursor flashed in the search bar, waiting for me to ask the next question.

Before the sun went down again, the room turned a deep shade of blue. I sat in the dark and disabled the room lights. The computer screen calmed me slightly as it adjusted itself to match the darkness of the rest of the environment.

Eventually, I walked away. I was neither hungry nor thirsty, or even fatigued. The gears in my brain were completely rusty. I had always been a rule follower, not a rule breaker. Whether I agreed with the nature of certain rules had no impact on my tendency to obey them.

She was still in bed. I found her lying in exactly the same position as last time.

"I'm bored," she said without looking up. "I couldn't figure out your TV, and you have my phone."

"What if you run once I give it to you?"

"You still have my car keys and shoes. Where am I gonna go without shoes?"

"I'll go get your phone."

Her voice pulled me back. "If you're so concerned about me running out, why put me on the first floor when you have other rooms upstairs?"

I shook my head. "We need to talk about it at some point, whenever you're ready."

"There's nothing to talk about," she said mildly. "There's nothing I can do about it. And it really isn't that bad. Hopefully, the line will move fast. For the last few months, they'll even give you your own room. And it's not going to be boring. I heard there are activities you can do, like furniture assembly, construction, or grounds maintenance for the facility. They keep you busy until injection time." Unbothered by my silence, she pushed herself up against the headboard and said airily, "Wanna hear my ideas for my last meal? They will literally serve you anything, if you know what I mean."

"No, I don't want to hear what your last meal will be," I snapped.

Abortions were regarded as first-degree murders—no doubts, no exceptions. A miscarriage may not have been intentional, but it was still a form of failing to sustain another life. Anyone who ended a life had to give their own in return under an unyielding principle of fairness.

In medieval times, those who already existed had more value than the non-sentients. A woman was a full-grown member of the laboring force, while a baby faced slim odds of surviving past five years of age. A woman could produce other children in the future, but a newborn couldn't take care of itself without a parent. But we'd evolved and become better than our ancestors. A progressing society had to stay away from utilitarianism; in the present day, equality reigned above all other ideologies.

Her indifferent attitude intensified my hatred toward Chris. Through her words, I saw her protecting him. Chris was not defenseless. He must have brainwashed her—or worse, raped her. With no form of contraception, very few sane women voluntarily had sex. Even if she had been out of her mind, Chris, as her husband, should've known better than to put her in danger.

At the same time, it was likely that he'd committed adultery. And when she was charged with murder, he'd left her.

I dug through the deepest grooves in my brain without finding a single good quality in his character. In fact, someone who was willing to intentionally hurt their loved one most likely didn't have any good qualities at all.

"You know I have to go home at some point, right?" she said.

"You're going home to someone like that?" My eyes flickered in disbelief. Her lack of self-respect made her unrecognizable.

"I haven't seen him in a whole week. Thanks for having me. But I really can't stay in your house forever." She smiled at me.

"There has to be a way to get you out of it."

"I don't want that." She shook her head, then dropped her gaze to the comforter. "You need to let me be."

"I'm sorry. I truly am." I put my arms around her. As expected, she neither reciprocated nor resisted.

"Thank you." She put her palm in the middle of my chest and pushed me away. I heard a sharp hiss of her breath, as if she was in pain.

I was shocked by my own reaction speed. I grabbed her wrist and rolled up her sleeve, searching for any traces of bruising or cuts. After seeing nothing but pale skin, I reached down to the hem of her pants.

"Stop," she said with belittlement in her voice. "You're not gonna find anything."

We sat in a stalemate, my heart racing. After I calmed down, she stood to face away from me.

Her fingers moved deftly, unbuttoning her shirt. Various bruises unfolded in front of my eyes as the fabric rolled down her bare shoulders. They were almost entirely covered by wounds of different shades and causes; I couldn't find a clear area larger than the size of my hands. There were scrapes, like she had been dragged against a harsh surface. In the middle of her back, multiple eerily long lash marks ran down her spine, extending all the way to her waist. Under the newer marks, which still had trails of clotted blood, older and fainter scars peeked out.

Nausea quickly built up and boiled inside my stomach. The sight itself was appalling; the fact that she'd been treated in such a gruesome manner stimulated an intrinsic fear inside me. None of the wounds had been produced without precision; a simple T-shirt could have covered them all. Excluding the top of her arms, every commonly exposed area remained clear.

"There's more, but you get the idea." She re-dressed herself and looked at me with a blank face.

I couldn't bring myself to lift my head. Long streams of salty tears poured out of my eyes and pried their way into my mouth. Mucus thickened in the back of my throat. I choked and panted. "I—I didn't—" I squeezed a few words out. I couldn't bear to face her. Irrational guilt consumed me. All I could think about was how I had failed her by not finding out sooner, even if there'd been no way for me to find out sooner. We were each married to different people. I'd been ordered to stay away from her.

She lifted my chin. Through my blurred sight, I saw her carefully wiping my cheeks with the tips of her fingers.

"Don't cry," she whispered. "You're gonna get me started."

"Why didn't you say something?"

"It's embarrassing."

"It's not embarrassing for you, it's embarrassing for him!"

She stepped away. "You gotta get over yourself sometimes."

"You're not letting me!" I shouted at her. "None of this is my problem. It's just that—" I buried my face in my hands. "All I wanted was for you to be happy. And now you're not. I don't know what to do."

"I don't need you to do anything about it. I can take responsibility for my personal choices." I felt her judging me again. "Look. Stop this." She pulled my hands away from my eyes. "I'll stay another night."

Chapter 4

The next morning, I stood in front of a gray skyscraper in Manhattan. It was the address of one of Chris's companies. Despite the construction work in progress, the building seemed to be in full operation. Since the day was early, only a handful of homeless people leaned up against the concrete. They each sat on a piece of cardboard or thick clothing. The sky was once again ocean blue, and the air was fresh. Regardless of the effort put into environmental cleanups, the ground of New York City grew so filthy that even the homeless couldn't bear to sit directly on it.

The few parking slots were occupied by trucks and cars with different miniature flags posted on their roofs. My car turned itself around and searched through a few other equally crowded streets before parking nearly six blocks away from the building. I swore at the length of the walk. Even roughly a year after Daria's passing, I was still fearful of being a pedestrian in a big city.

I carefully avoided the clumps of tourists who stopped in the middle of intersections to take photos. Luckily, I arrived in one piece after a terrifying ten-minute journey. The construction workers spoke to each other at the maximum volume possible while standing on ten-foot-tall scaffolding. Each of them blasted their own hip-hop music from speakers hanging by their belts, different rhythmic patterns stacking on top of each other, overtaking my sensory spotlight at different times. People wearing three-piece suits entered and exited the building without looking up from their phones. I tilted my head up and looked at where the tip of the building met the skyline. I couldn't recall the floors the company rented.

"You fired?" one of the homeless women shouted at me. She was wearing an oversized winter jacket, which was slightly too warm for the weather. "Have some of this, man. It'll make you relax." She extended her arm, holding out a small bag of off-white powder. "Come and try. Don't be shy. You don't have to buy." Instead of standing to approach me, she chose to scoot her body forward, moving her legs on the ground like a crab crawling on sand. The cardboard under her had stuck to the bottom of her pants; it moved along as she hurried, rubbing harshly against the ground. "It'll make you feel better." She smiled at me.

Her gums were receding badly, exposing the thin roots of her yellow, decaying teeth. One rotten front tooth was barely intact, hanging from her upper jaw bone. The powder she had offered me must have been more than effective, as she seemed to be suffering from no pain whatsoever. When she opened her mouth to speak again, a rancid odor mixed into the air.

"No, thank you." I shook my head.

The homeless woman was persistent. She stood, pulled the cardboard off her pants, and ran after me into the building.

The security guard was hiding behind a big counter with a marble finish. When we entered together, he stared straight into the revolving door but ignored our presence.

I cleared my throat.

The guard looked up at me impatiently. "Can I help you?"

I gestured toward the woman, who had advanced further into the lobby.

"Ugh," the guard whined, then reluctantly left his chair. "This is private property. I'm going to have to ask you to exit the building."

The woman plastered the same smile onto her face. She raised her arm with the powder at the guard this time. He crossed his arms in front of his chest. There was a small gun clipped on his belt. After a few moments of insistence, the woman finally turned around. She cussed and spat on the floor.

"Can I help you *now*?" The guard sat back in his chair as fast as he could.

"I'm here to see the CEO of Leon Enterprise."

"Hold on." He scratched his nose and made a few clicks on his computer. "Your name?"

"I'm not on the visitors' list. I'm his sibling."

A glance brushed over my body. Luckily, the suit and tie earned me an automatic pass. "Let me call up for you."

The elevator door opened on the thirtieth floor. A young, blonde receptionist greeted me at the front desk.

REQUITED

She couldn't have been more than twenty-two or twenty-three years old. She wore a traditional blazer over a nearly sheer blouse that was unbuttoned to the middle of her chest. Her breasts were squished together and lifted to an unnatural height by dark undergarments under her white shirt. I tried to look away, but the way she was dressed was meant to show off her figure. To add the final touch, she wore a silver necklace, the pendant dropping into her cleavage.

"Good morning! How can I help you?" Her blood-red lips moved on her powdered face.

"Is Chris Franklin in the office today?"

"Do you have an appointment?"

"No, my name is Edward. I'm his sibling. Do you mind?"

"Do you have an ID?" The receptionist stood and leaned forward, putting her disproportionally large breasts on the counter.

I took out my driver's license. She examined it carefully and slowly slid it back to me.

"Please give me just one minute," she said with an upward inflection before pushing a single button on the phone. "Good morning, Chris! I have a person, Edward Franklin, wondering if he could see you right now." She paused to bite her fingernail. "Yes . . . okay . . . okay . . . I'll be sure to do that."

The receptionist emerged from behind the desk. On her feet, a pair of black stilettos clunked loudly. Her skirt followed the same style as the rest of her professional attire; it was barely long enough to cover her glutes. With each step she took, her hips swayed from left to right, revealing a small corner of her panties.

All companies, including my law firm, were bound by law to require a certain level of "self-expression" in their female employees. But the way the rules were enforced at Chris's company seemed more like an exaggerated joke—or a pornography set.

I was left at the end of a series of mazelike corridors. Out of courtesy, the receptionist knocked on the door for me.

Chris sat behind a large desk, facing three different monitors simultaneously. His black suit jacket hung on a spare chair close to him. Near its chest pocket, a long row of pins was embedded into the fabric, each representing a cause the company advocated for. He didn't bother to move his gaze when I walked in. His weight was shifted forward, his back upright and perfectly aligned. As usual, it was impossible to detect a single trace of laziness in him.

He reached for a cup of espresso sitting on the desk. His fingers knew exactly where it was; they brought it to his lips without him needing to look. The saucer was embellished with golden flowers glazed with a blend of thin and thick strokes, like the work produced by a fountain pen with an open nib. Despite its glossy surface, the cup couldn't have been real porcelain; it barely made a sound as it landed back in its saucer.

I gave the idea of throwing the rest of the coffee in his face some thought.

"Is everything all right?" Chris asked with genuine care in his voice. It agitated me. I wondered which acting studio he attended in his free time.

I yanked his twiglike body by the collar and drove him forward onto his desk.

Surprisingly, he didn't resist in the slightest. Growing up, he had always been a lanky figure towering over me. Now that we were no longer children, our height difference had closed to almost nothing.

My fist landed on his chiseled jaw. His head flung backward without a fight. I grabbed him by the hair and forced him to look me in the eye. When he chose not to explain himself, I slammed his face against the desk and pinned him down by the arm, twisting it at an unnatural angle. A streak of blood drew from the corner of his forehead.

I thought I was hallucinating when, instead of begging me to stop, I heard gentle laughter escaping his thin lips.

"Nothing about this is supposed to be funny," I said.

He groaned in pain, pushed himself up, and managed to call me a creep. "You need to learn to be normal," he added.

Perplexed, I watched him collect himself. Since his perfectly ironed shirt was now seeing wrinkles for the first time in its life, he spent nearly a whole minute fixing his collar and sleeves to perfection. The blood and sweat on his forehead became an afterthought. Only when the red line was about to drip into his eyes did he pay attention to it. Using the smallest range of motion, he finally wiped it away, almost as if the act was an inconvenience.

"Did you throw the vase at your wife too?" he mocked.

Heat rose on my face. It wasn't that I had done the deed, but his speculation brought me great discomfort.

Chris coughed twice. He tried to speak again, his voice raspy.

To stop his incoming insults, I pushed him down on the floor and punched him until more bleeding broke out beneath his skin. At first, it appeared in minuscule dots. When I was finished, they'd connected themselves into a solid splash of color under his eyes. His face became puffy. It was the first time I had ever seen a fat-looking version of him, the hollowness in his cheeks now rounded. I found the sight oddly comical.

"What's with you and other people's—"

I felt ashamed, so I locked both my hands around his neck. Blood first tinted, then seeped through his teeth. The more pressure I put on his airways, the harder he tried forming incoherent sentences with guttural noises.

I let him go before he looked close to fainting.

He flipped over and quietly gagged out a long gob of saliva infused with pinkness. A couple of chipped teeth fell from his mouth without their roots.

When I walked out of the office, he was still on the floor. Luckily, no one was by the door when I came out. The walls must have been soundproof, probably making it easy for him to take advantage of the "professionally dressed" women he hired.

I hid my bruised hands inside my pants pockets and walked out.

Chapter 5

I thought about the ways she was going to thank me. She would look at me with shock in her eyes, maybe even cry a little for my pain. I wanted her to kneel in front of me and kiss every inch of battered skin on my knuckles. She could also slide her tongue over them like animals do for their kin. And then I wanted her to press my hands against her cheeks. No words would be necessary.

When I returned to the house, she was asleep. The lamps and the TV in her bedroom were still on. Her fear of the dark pinched my heart in a way I couldn't describe. If she would allow me, I would have held her for an entire night so whatever scared her in the dark had no chance of getting close.

In my defense, certain thoughts were reserved for our minds only. As long as I didn't reveal or act upon them, I would remain righteous.

My brain insisted on playing ostrich against my will. I couldn't bring myself to type a single word relating to crossing the Mexican American border. Going to Canada would be an easier solution in many ways. However, once Alicia's circumstances were revealed, she would be sent straight back. Mexico, on the other hand, kept a refugee program running. When I was younger, I'd often heard about illegal South American migrants risking their lives, passing through the desert on foot to enter the United States. Within the last ten years, the direction of travel had reversed. I'd never imagined that one day, I would also become part of the scene.

The stinging pain on my skin offered me great gratification. I quietly applauded myself. Though it was far from enough, I was happy to serve Chris a small portion of what he had enacted onto her. I despised how certain people intentionally hurt others but stayed free of external and internal repercussions themselves. I imagined Chris moaning in pain on his expensive carpet, only to be found by his employees in the most undignified position possible. His handsome complexion was going to look distorted. I imagined him holding a bag of melting ice and trying his best to articulate words through the blackened gaps in his teeth. To everyone else, he would be uttering nonsense.

What happened? they would ask.

It's nothing.

It doesn't look like nothing.

My brother beat me up.

That's horrible. Why would he do that?

Because I hit my wife, and he found out.

Chris wasn't someone willing to admit his own faults. I knew he wasn't going to talk.

I kept myself busy with work until early afternoon,

when she sent me a text. I looked at the small,
concentrated beam of light from my phone, which diffused
evenly to cast a series of letters into the air: Alicia Franklin.
Silently, I let her name roll off the tip of my tongue—her
first and my last. How convenient.

Where are you? I'm out of clothes.

She had made the bed sloppily. But I was happy that
she woke up early enough with some time of the day left
for us to spend together. A large corner of the top sheet
was exposed, and the comforter itself, though stretched
over the mattress, was covered in wrinkles. She was finally
out of sleepwear and now wore an oversized sweater and
flared jeans. Her ankles were, once again, hidden. A pile of
laundry, including a few pieces of her underwear, had been
thrown on the floor. It resembled a small mountain.

"I couldn't find your laundry room," she said.

"It's in the other hallway. I'll show you."

She squatted to pick up her clothes in one swoop. The
stack of garments reached a height nearly covering half her
face. To keep the pile compressed, she secured it by
clamping down her chin, clearing her line of sight at the
same time.

She frowned deeply when I showed her which buttons
to press on the washing machine. "What's wrong with your
hands?"

"It's nothing," I said.

"Wait." She chased behind me into the kitchen. I
turned my back to her as I poured myself a glass of chilled
water, momentarily concealing my hands from her
view. "Oh my God!" she gasped. "Please tell me you

didn't—"

"Don't worry about it." I smiled at her.

"What is wrong with you? Is he okay?" Her lips parted, her eyes widening. She scanned the room, then turned her hateful gaze back to me. I could see her trying her very best to stop tears from running out of her eye sockets. The spiderweb-like blood vessels around her irises swelled. She was indeed crying, but in a completely different way from what I had hoped for.

I couldn't bring myself to comfort her. Her concern for Chris made me unable to breathe. I locked myself in my bedroom and lay down. There was a pulsating sensation in the corner of my skull, as if someone was pressing on and releasing my nerves steadily and calculatedly. The pain was both too dull and too slight to grant myself the permission to moan for help.

When I lifted my head from the pillow, the silk covering was drenched. Dampness had seeped through the worm's cocoon and into the duck's nest linings. The bird was known for its snow-white necks and coal-black stomachs. The females were ugly-looking, yet they were the main contributors to the down harvesting as they plucked at their own bodies with their bills to keep the eggs warm.

Someone had gifted the bedding set to my mother, who then gave it to me. The house had originally been owned by my parents. I didn't deserve it. My salary as a salary partner at Montgomery Sterling wasn't enough to purchase a residence like this. Without what had been given to me by my parents, I would have been living in the city and devoting the rest of my life to student loans. The interest rate went up yearly, or so I had heard.

I'd attended an Ivy League university because my father had attended an Ivy League university. I had never been particularly bright myself. My father was the father; I was the son. Chris could have been the father but was lucky enough to be born as the son. I couldn't explain this without sounding comical.

My father had been born in a poor area in Alabama. Meemaw had been a prostitute. My father never knew who his father was, as Meemaw often saw multiple men at the same time. Many of them traveled quite a bit of distance to avoid being recognized by people in their lives. My father had attended a private high school in an affluent district on scholarship. He was then accepted into a top-tier university but finished horribly. During the first three years, he struggled to navigate the environment and the differences between traditional schooling, which he breezed through, versus higher education. By the time he understood the system, it was too late. With a 3.1 GPA, he was internship-less upon graduation.

He had a suitemate named Matt, who had been a biology major. Matt had the idea to make a nutritional powder, advertising itself as "maximum wellness for the everyday person." It consisted of different minerals and essential vitamins. The instruction label told people to take it first thing in the morning with eight to twelve ounces of water, preferably iced. Although not harmful to the human body, the extra nutrients Matt selected were entirely indigestible. Surprisingly, the product fulfilled its promised functions: the people who rigorously consumed the powder also drank the water. In the end, it turned out that the powder was nothing but a placebo. While no study supported the powder's contribution to health, many showed that drinking fluid on an empty stomach was proven to provide people with more energy during the day and, generally speaking, made them feel "better."

Matt was the brain and my father acted as the muscle, taking care of everything from packaging, shipping, and product surveys to after-sales. Instead of a wage, Matt paid him with equity to the LLC. Right before the company took off, Matt drove his car into a tree, holding on to a photo of his ex-girlfriend. In his will, he wrote where he wished to be buried and a lengthy clarification of how he firmly believed his nutritional powder, though ineffective on its own, would significantly improve the healthcare system if made widely available. He went into detail about how powerful the human mind was, and if we believed the supplement was going to work, with the smallest amount of help (the water), we were going to become much healthier. After everything, he left the company to my father.

A lie couldn't sustain itself for too long. People were curious and always looked for scientific explanations for both good and bad occurrences. My father earned a large lump sum of money when he sold the powder to a much bigger company, which later drove it into the ground. With that money, he went on multiple business ventures of his own and eventually delved into finance. Classmates whom he had never spoken to all returned to him, claiming to be his best friends. Making connections as an already successful person was easy; with only a bachelor's degree, he managed to lecture at the best business schools in the country. No one remembered his not-so-glorious years in college.

Chris had outperformed my father by far. Not only was he financially more successful, but for a long time, he was extremely well-rounded. He was constantly three steps ahead of me, and every step he took guided him in a better direction. He was a piano genius and a horse whisperer, and later on, he became a robotics captain. I was a failure in all of those areas. To an adult, these activities were minor, but I remembered them clearly because it was how I learned to navigate the world: by being a counterfeit version of my brother. With my mother's genes, he was tall, effortlessly lean, and, objectively speaking, beautiful.

Next year, he planned on running for Congress. At thirty-seven, he would be the youngest candidate in the country. The average age of his competitors was one hundred and three. He was a true miracle.

I, on the other hand, was slightly unlucky. Without my mother's genes, I devoted an endless amount of time at the gym to avoid blowing up like my father, who was unpleasant-looking. To this day, I was adamant about counting the calories in my daily meals.

I didn't see myself as intelligent either. The resources my parents had poured into my education had landed me a conventionally well-to-do yet dull career. Unlike the group of people I'd entered Montgomery Sterling with, I had no intention of using the firm as a springboard to venture elsewhere. The repetitions—with minor differences—at my job made me feel safe, and the tight schedules made me feel fulfilled. My father often claimed that lawyers and doctors were nothing but decorated servants. He was not proud of my career.

Later that day, I felt the vibration of Alicia's footsteps traveling up the stairs. She searched through the hallways first, then ran through every other room on the floor beside the main bedroom.

I was battling a familiar sensation of hunger; I'd waited for her to have lunch together. But when I heard her, I wasn't sure if I wanted to see her face. She was known to take my acts of kindness for granted. However, I held on to the hope that she might appreciate that someone was willing to stand up for her.

"Hello?"

"There's food in the fridge."

"I didn't mean it like that." She stalled in the doorframe. "I was worried about you."

"What about me?"

"What if you get in trouble for doing that? What if he presses charges?"

"He won't," I said.

"You didn't have to do that for me."

"He doesn't care about you."

"I understand that part," she said defensively. "It's just that . . . why didn't you talk to me about it first before going to find him?"

I sighed. "Because you wouldn't let me. If you knew about it, you'd be partially taking responsibility for it. You don't need to feel guilty for something that's not your fault."

"You don't think I feel guilty now?"

"Actions have consequences."

"Is this your way of keeping me here?" she murmured. "I can't go home now. What if I accidentally run into him?"

I blushed. I suddenly became very happy. I was going to live in the same house as her. It felt surreal.

"You don't need to go home," I said as calmly as I could. I had defended and protected her from Chris's horribleness. I had to keep the appropriate demeanor of a savior.

"So, are you still keeping me on house arrest?"

I shook my head. Inside my closet was a special row of drawers with locks. I got up and pressed my index finger on the top one. A compartment wheeled out, holding her car keys and boots.

"You're not mad at me, are you?" she asked.

"I think you're actually trying to say thank you."

"Thank you." She lowered her head. "Do you care that I'm stuck here?"

"Stay."

From that day, I took over a moral high ground. For the first time in my life, I'd won against Chris. When he hurt her, I saved her. I was determined to continue to do so. Perhaps her feelings were still swaying toward him at the moment, but morals were the foundation of a person. I had enough time to watch him crumble. If my father had been alive, he would realize how wrong he was in the way he saw us. And he would finally spare a little bit of his love for me.

Chapter 6

I know what you're thinking," she said when I finally pried her mouth open. "Chris didn't hit me when I was pregnant. You can't blame the miscarriage on him."

Although she could have been intentionally protecting him, I realized I had made a fatal mistake. My anger in beating up Chris had almost cost us the loophole we might be able to pursue.

It was going to be unethical. And perhaps I should have sat down and thought about it earlier. But if Chris had the tendency to physically harm her, it could also imply the miscarriage was a result of his abuse. She would be able to walk away free. Because I had acted too early, if we were to shift the blame onto Chris, he would undoubtedly retaliate against me. The only reason for him to keep quiet was to keep his image clean. People didn't hurt others without reason. Anyone with a brain would question why he'd been assaulted by me. If curiosity was raised, investigations would be made, thus exposing his less-than-ideal family life.

Unfortunately, all the effort he put into maintaining his image would be useless if more severe accusations were made toward him. It would make sense to go after me at that point, even if it was solely for the purpose of revenge.

Physically assaulting someone would get me fired. In my case, I wouldn't be wronged. And even if I were stripped of being able to practice law somehow, there were still other career paths for me to explore. It would be complicated but not unfeasible.

The thought of leaving Montgomery Sterling saddened me. It wasn't the top law firm I had initially wished to work for, but over the years, it had grown on me. Since my first day of being a summer associate, everyone had met each other with a smile on their face. Unlike other firms, there was little sabotaging between offices. Secretaries and paralegals voluntarily shared their knowledge. Inconveniently, I was already a nonequity partner. Carrot on a stick or not, the real partners put a tremendous amount of trust in me. I should resign beforehand.

Alicia didn't have other options. If I were fired or received other penalties, it would at least be my own doing. Though what I did to Chris was morally justified, it didn't mean I could remain unpunished by law if he decided to pursue it. Ironically, if he thought physical beatings mattered in the slightest way, he wouldn't have hit his own partner. Knowing how aggressive and defensive he had become in recent years, he was certain to attack anyone.

Between Alicia and Chris, one of them would be paying with their life. There was nothing else we could do.

I wasn't sure if I wanted to turn the tables on Chris.

The solution was extreme. We might win, but I couldn't imagine what would become of me if I pushed my brother to his death with glee. I had secretly wished it upon him multiple times in the past, for how he was the better version of me and for how I could never outargue him even in the most minor disagreements. I wanted to see him locked under the cold ground, alone. Insects biting him. Maggots wriggling their small white bodies over his neck, eventually digging into his skin. I wanted to see his bones softening, corroding the flesh around them. With time, he would turn into a puddle of grease mixed into a putrid-smelling liquid.

I couldn't admit this to anyone, not even to myself, on a typical day.

But it was uncharacteristic of Chris to get into a muddy situation and be unprepared for the possibility of change. I couldn't understand the logic behind his actions. He couldn't be certain that she wouldn't frame him in court.

***

According to Alicia, I lived in one of the "scariest places on Earth and the Milky Way combined." She demanded I volunteer as her bodyguard in case the spirit of my wife planned a brutal attack on her. I slept on the couch downstairs, which was only a short hallway across from her guest room. Her fear of my late wife stemmed from not understanding who she'd been as a person. Daria had been the kindest and gentlest person I'd known, and, at the same time, beyond cowardly. Even if she turned into an all-powerful entity, she could never muster up enough courage to hurt anyone.

I drove to Alicia's apartment in the city alone. I thought about bringing her along for a day out, but I didn't want her to feel triggered by the scene. Chris could be there. It was not going to end well if he saw us together. I put an empty suitcase and folded cardboard boxes into the trunk while she was still sleeping. Her TV shows lit up her room and half the hallway throughout the night. She intentionally kept the door open, supposedly so I could run to her rescue faster. I was no spirit whisperer myself. My plan was to simply beg it to go away, or attack me instead.

A private elevator shot up in a tall building overlooking Central Park. They didn't quite live on the top floor yet. A sterile, minimalistic path led me to a slender, gray metal door.

When I entered the great room, I realized the entire place had been emptied. A few abstract paintings in deep colors leaned against the lower half of a nearby wall. I wasn't sure if those were by Alicia or had been purchased. Otherwise, the space seemed completely abandoned.

I saw a full-figured woman who looked to be in her late fifties. She wore all black with a white apron tied around her hips. Her platinum-blonde hair was pulled back neatly into a bun and secured by a blue hairnet. The compact pockets sewn on her apron held various common cleaning supplies. Two cloth shoe covers were wrapped around her sneakers.

"Are you Mr. Franklin?" she greeted me warmly, in an old-fashioned way. Her voice echoed in the room.

"Yes, and you are?"

"My name is Priscilla. I clean the apartment," she said

in a Southern accent. "Chris told me someone might be coming to, uh, pick up a few things. We've been waiting for you for a few days already."

"Is he moving out?"

"Mm-hmm." Priscilla nodded. "He'll be putting this on the market soon."

I hesitated. "He's not here, right?"

"No, he has a doctor's appointment."

Probably a dentist appointment, to be specific.

When my mother was young, she'd worked as a dental assistant. She made sure we understood the fragility of human teeth from as early as I could remember. They weren't like other parts of the body; once damaged, they couldn't heal or grow back. One small decay was the catalyst for a lifetime of drilling, filling, and curing.

"Just wait here for a minute. I'll go get the boxes for you," Priscilla said.

"I can help."

"I'm sorry." She put on an apologetic smile. "Chris said you can't come in any further."

I walked to a row of floor-length windows. His apartment dominated the landscape. The trees and foliage were transitioning from the usual emerald green to a blend of orange and dashes of bright gold. From this height, the city's imperfections were more than adequately hidden. The open areas of Central Park no longer looked like a drug hub for the homeless. Chris must have stood in the exact spot and congratulated his peers on how well-managed the city had become.

Out of curiosity, I leaned forward to look through

every crevice of the view. I was determined to find a flaw in the scenery. After a few minutes, I spotted someone wearing an oversized blue jacket. He swung his arms up and down in slow motion and skipped from bench to bench. The man seemed to be under an uncertain influence. At the very least, he looked happy.

I tilted my head up to relieve the tension in my neck. It took me less than a few seconds to lose the jumping man and regain a breathtakingly perfect view of the deep blue sky. The horizon felt within my reach. A handful of cottonlike clouds floated in the distance. Without reservation, the sun gleamed over the city.

Priscilla came back, pushing a small hand truck with three large cardboard boxes stacked on top of each other. The openings had been sealed by lines of meticulously straight tape.

"Thank you," I said. "I'll load them into the car."

"Let me help you with the door and elevator."

"It's all right. I got it."

"Can you come back when you're done? I need to go get the mail for you. They're important ones too," she added.

Priscilla handed me a thick stack of envelopes when I returned through the elevator.

"Will you tell Alicia I said hello?"

I nodded. "Of course."

"And tell her I said I'm sorry this horrible thing is happening to her."

"Will do. Thank you."

I glanced over the various letters under Alicia's name.

One of the orange envelopes was from the court.

Priscilla frowned at me. She tipped her head and opened her mouth but immediately pulled herself back.

Seizing the opportunity, I spoke first. "I know I'm not supposed to ask, but if you happened to know anything about the situation—"

"I wasn't here," she retorted.

"I'm sorry."

"No, no, I'm sorry. I wish I could help, but I wasn't there. That's all I can say."

"Chris made you sign an NDA, did he?"

Priscilla didn't respond. I took her unswerving gaze as an affirmative.

"You have to go now."

Chapter 7

She was lying in the same position as before I left for the city. Her thumb brushed over the physical screen of her phone as she scrolled through a long sequence of mindlessly entertaining videos.

I knocked on the doorframe. "I got your things. Wanna open them?"

"Thank you."

"There's mail for you too."

She immediately shuffled through them, tearing open the one from the court.

"You sure you don't wanna look at them later?" I frowned.

"It's my divorce hearing. It's on Tuesday," she said calmly. "Chris must have expedited it somehow."

"Would you like me to go with you?"

"It's okay."

"I won't go inside if you don't want me to. But I can drop you off and pick you up."

"This has nothing to do with you!" she yelled without

warning, then tried to slam the coarse paper onto my face.

I blinked and dodged out of reflex. "It's okay." I softened my voice. "It's going to be okay."

She covered her face with her hands and sucked in a deep breath. When she released herself, her voice turned raspy. "I'm sorry. I just had no idea it was going to be this fast. It must have been sitting there for a while. I hate him!"

"It'll be for the best." I sat next to her on the bed.

"What do you know about anything? I love him!"

I retracted the hand that was making its way around her shoulders. She screamed again about how much she hated Chris. Her body shook in pure anger. I knew it was physically impossible, but her movement gave off an illusion that she was about to explode into pieces.

"Listen," I said. "Chris doesn't need anyone besides himself. He doesn't deserve to be with anyone, period. It's a good thing you're separating. Really."

"I hate you, too! Leave me alone!" Her fingers dug into the creases of my shirt until her fingertips turned white. With what little strength she had left within her body, she shoved me toward the corner of the bed.

I took a peek at her before I left the room. She'd dropped again, facing away from the door, and grabbed a spare pillow to bury her face in. I heard her moan, sniffle, and pant with every inhalation. I felt like a spineless stack of meat at her disposal when I realized that I was worried about her passing out due to a lack of oxygen, even after she had screamed at me and favored Chris over me. It had very little to do with me, but the pain in my chest prevented me from being a bystander. I felt as if she had taken a blade and cut me open from within, severing each layer of my lungs and breaking my sternum with a loud crack.

Chris leaving her was more destructive to her than her own death. I wondered if, to her, I was worse than a domestic abuser. It was the same as leaving a torture dungeon. A normal person should've been jumping up and down in celebration.

I was annoyed by her lethargy and the incoherent phrases she yelled in pain. There were two hopeful paths laid out in front of her, one physical and one emotional, but she chose to go down neither. She spent the majority of her day sleeping or crying; both were done in bed. I wanted to shake her awake, force her into productivity, and take control of her life. It was beyond easy: all she needed to do was forget about the grievances of the past and let herself be helped in the future. I wanted to tell her there was still a bright side to her situation. Conveniently, it involved me from the very beginning.

It was my own self-deception. In the past, I'd found endless excuses for the way she treated me. Very rarely did I let her take responsibility for her own doings. This time, there were no excuses. If our places were swapped, there was no guarantee I would be as enthusiastic as her right now; I didn't think my coping mechanisms would be any better than hers. If I was able to take any frustrations away from her, it was better than letting her hurt herself. I tried to decipher the torment she had gone through during her marriage. There was likely a form of codependency between her and Chris. I wanted to know what strategies he used on her to make her stay obedient. Abusers often gaslit and manipulated their victims, sometimes by pretending to be the weaker ones themselves.

I left her alone to restore some normalcy in myself. When I entered my office, I turned around. I went into the kitchen and poured her a glass of water with a clear ball of ice. I put it on her nightstand, along with a box of tissues.

I should have taken it as a warning when she woke up before two o'clock in the afternoon. Nothing good ever followed when she woke up early. I imagined the day to be a happy occasion. We were going to unbox her things and make her sterile room more welcoming. I considered putting a baby monitor in her room so I wouldn't have to worry about her hurting herself, but that would never be appropriate. She was neither a baby nor an old person who needed help during the nighttime.

She didn't sleep at night. From my office, I heard waves of faint whimpering, and each noise tugged at me. I would have thought the distance between the rooms would make that physically impossible; I was beginning to question my sanity. The pain in my chest worsened. The only form of relief hid in rushing back to her. The same sentence ran through my head over and over. I envisioned myself saying it to her each time, delivering the words in a slightly modified way: *Forget about Chris. This is your new home.*

I didn't force myself on her, since she had made it unreservedly clear she did not want my company. To salvage my image, I buried myself in work.

I supposed she was only propelled by an innate desire

for food. When she finally made her way out of the guest room, the sky had already turned dark. Blue and purple veins crawled under her eyes. The rest of the area was pink and swollen. My eyes lingered on a thin streak of tearstain by her lips.

Without a word, completely ignoring me, she went to the refrigerator and examined each compartment. After shutting the door in dismay, she dug around in my pantry and searched through the drawers. When she knocked over a box of pasta on a shelf, she kicked it out of her way instead of putting it back where it belonged. She stood on the balls of her feet, reaching for a tall cylinder filled with cereal.

"Hello?" I waved my hand in front of her face.

She stepped aside and then resumed the tasks at hand with a blank expression. She took one of the biggest bowls and filled it to the top.

"You know, I need dinner too," I said.

"You didn't eat without me?"

"No . . .?"

"I'm sorry. I thought you were mad at me."

"I'm not mad at you."

She tilted her gaze to meet mine. A bright dot of white light flickered against the warm brownness. The inner circles carried a lighter hue against the obsidian rims, locking all the colors inside.

Perhaps I sounded too gentle.

"It's understandable," I added as sternly as I could. "Special circumstances."

"How would you feel if I randomly started trash-talking Daria and telling you it's a good thing she croaked in the middle of the street?"

"You're right. I was wrong." I laughed.

Chapter 8

The delivery drone from McDonald's slowly descended over my front porch. It hovered for about thirty seconds to dispense a small parachute, which guided the bag downward. After I paid the tip, it went on to the next house in the neighborhood.

For a woman, Alicia wasn't particularly tall. With the bags placed on the counter, she inserted her arm into them with greater difficulty than I imagined. Her eyebrows scrunched together as she searched through the bottom of each bag. The paper rustled. As usual, there were no sauce packets, straws, napkins, or ketchup for the fries. She rolled her eyes in defeat.

"Don't worry," I assured her. "I saved extras from their physical locations."

"I know they don't give out sauce packets anymore in the cities. But I thought the ones in your area would be better at it."

"It's free, so it's optional. There's a component of luck to it."

Her naïveté made me chuckle. The stores near my house never provided sauces for deliveries. In fact, when someone went to the counter to ask for sauce packets, they were almost always met with dirty looks, the same ones every employee gave the homeless people sitting outside. How dare people demand more work from them?

I hid a small mountain of McDonald's sauces in the refrigerator door. They were saved and cherished. I always thought that one day, I might need them en masse, so it was better to keep them around. The day never came, except for today. The neon green of their sweet-and-sour sauce was the most noticeable.

"I know you want sweet and sour for sure. Anything else? I got their ranch, spicy buffalo, and honey mustard. Of course, I have my own ketchup."

"You're funny."

Though I knew what we were eating was only partially food, dinner was strangely calming.

She immediately jumped to the couch where I kept my pillow and blanket stacked on top of each other. Due to the space they took up, I sat closer to her this time.

"Do you really hate Chris?" I asked. I had another idea—an afterthought, really. If Alicia had been the one wanting to pursue it, I would have helped her and thanked her for it.

"Do you?" she asked softly.

"I can't answer that."

"Well, I hate him. I hope he falls into a pit of anteaters."

"Anteaters. Interesting."

"Yeah."

"I think we should take some photos of you. In case you want to bring it up."

"I'm already going down. Why tank him?"

"Because how dare he leave you? How dare he finally free someone from his wrath?"

"Edward," she begged. "Please don't make fun of me. I don't know how I'm supposed to feel right now."

"I think it's ultimately a good thing because he is truly a terrible person. It's not just you. I mean it when I say he doesn't deserve anyone. On the other hand, I guess leaving your spouse is supposed to be sad."

"You guess?" Her tone sounded sourer and crueler than necessary.

I subconsciously dodged her gaze, even though she wasn't looking at me. "For the time when you felt happy about the divorce, did you ever consider other options?"

"Like what? Claiming that he was the cause of the miscarriage?"

"You just said you hate him," I objected. "It's not impossible. Just say he abused you so much that he caused the incident, and you were too afraid to speak up when you were arrested at the hospital. It's completely coherent."

"No one asked about them at the hospital in the first place. It's my right to privacy."

"Mental abuse counts too. Like high levels of stress, for example."

"What are you trying to get at?" She licked her lips.

"I'm being completely honest here." I sighed. "I don't know if I want him to die. But he can't do terrible things and receive zero consequences. That isn't right."

She shifted her weight on the couch and crossed her arms in front of her chest. "We can take the photos if you want to," she mumbled. "I don't really care. But what are you gonna do if he comes after you for beating him up?"

"I'm a lawyer. I can deal with that."

"I thought that's not what you deal with."

"It doesn't matter. I can deal with it better than you."

She switched on the TV. The entertainment channels were replaying the newest live-action films. Her hand stalled in the air as she contemplated between the live action version of *Cars 2* versus the live action of *Cars 2: Mater's Adventures Around the Galaxy*. We watched twenty minutes of the latter.

Then I followed her to the stack of boxes by the garage. With two of them in her arms, she wobbled toward her bedroom. In the same way she dealt with her laundry, she clamped her chin down on the top one. A few steps later, she dropped them to the floor and pushed them forward instead. It was an interesting sight.

"How's nighttime treating you?" I asked.

"Meh."

"The couch is hurting my back."

"Oh, sorry," she said politely. "You should probably go back to your bedroom, then."

"That's not what I meant." I blinked quickly, trying to find an appropriate explanation. "Why don't we move you upstairs? I can put an actual mattress by the door."

"That's fine by me, if you insist."

The hallway wasn't wide enough to fit an entire

mattress without it becoming a safety hazard. We dragged one from a spare room into my office, which sat right across from the bedroom she was going into. When both doors were open, the placement provided easy viewing access to a large portion of the other room.

"You know, I do think you're a jerk sometimes," I said. "You first forced me to couch surf in my own house, with plenty of actual beds for two people. And now you've downgraded me to the floor. Remind me why I deserve this treatment again?"

"Because your house is scary?" She looked at me with great skepticism, as if I should have known the answer beforehand.

"What are you actually scared of?"

"What if Daria hates me?"

"She doesn't hate you. She was friendly to you, remember?"

We sat together on the floor. She used scissors to pierce through a strip of packing tape.

"I didn't have a list from you," I said. "So I just took what I thought you wanted."

She picked up a shirt and shook her head. "No. These were folded by Priscilla. It's her way of folding things."

"I'm sorry," I said, though I could have built on the first lie by saying someone else helped me fold them. I didn't want her to find other evidence and be even more upset later.

"Priscilla told me to say hi, and that she's sorry this is happening to you."

"I liked her. She was nice." She tried to ask the question

using the tone of small talk, but her shaking arms gave her true mentality away. "Did you see Chris?"

"I think he went to get fitted for dentures."

A light laugh escaped her lips. She reached for the last item in the very first box. It was a photo framed with chestnut-colored borders, not larger than a standard paperback. A group of children around eight or nine years old smiled in front of an overly inflated Santa balloon. It was an obvious snapshot of the Macy's Thanksgiving Day Parade. My mother had called it a near-death experience. Alicia split the middle with another girl in pink who might have been her cousin; I couldn't remember. Alicia wore a purple jacket with a matching headband. Her hair was slightly lighter than the present and was kept in pigtails. I scanned the other children in the background; they were mostly old family friends. I clearly remembered being in the photo with the rest of them when it was taken. But I was nowhere to be found.

"Something's off," I said.

"You were in this one. Chris had you digitally removed."

"Why?" I frowned. "Wasn't this from a long time ago?"

"Yeah. But he had a sort of manic episode last year and erased you. It's not just you. But he was upset when you made partner."

"I'm not a real partner. And I'm not the only one."

"But you're the only one he knows."

"What is wrong with him? It doesn't make any sense."

"You were doing well. He felt threatened," she said

calmly.

"What?"

I disregarded her explanation. I felt like I had accomplished something monumental. It was finally something worthy of being put on the fridge. After all, it was the only place my father had paid any attention to. Logically speaking, Chris had zero reason to feel threatened by me. Nevertheless, the thought of it made me happy.

Childhood with Chris was a suffocating experience I didn't wish to look back upon. He wasn't always a bad person; the lack of flaws took away my right to vent or complain. Even during moments of friction, he rarely raised his voice. He held my hand through math homework, reading projects, Lego League, and eventually FRC. The inadequacy he imposed was rightfully deserved. Statistically speaking, he was better than me in every way possible. My father's favoritism was apparent. My mother hid hers better.

"I think I'm just gonna throw it out," Alicia said.

"Keep it."

She shook her head adamantly. A few moments later, she spoke again. "Do you love Daria?"

I had two options laid out in front of me: to say yes with unusual determination, or to act like she was completely out of her mind for raising the question. I was losing either way. I could feel her demanding an answer more thoughtful than a simple retort.

"What sort of question is that?" I exclaimed.

"Sorry, Daria!" she tilted her head up and half yelled into the air.

"Stop it!" I said sternly. "I do love her."

"Then why did you beat up Chris?"

"What do you want me to say? Give me an answer that will make you happy, and I'll say it for you."

"See? That's why I'm scared of her."

I wanted to tell her I could explain. Eventually, I would be able to find a coherent answer that justified all of my actions without making myself look like an ungrateful, coldhearted person.

She was no longer interested in the conversation. She moved in and out of the closet, settling her clothes in different drawers. There was no dismay written on her face, yet I could feel her openly judging me.

"Is it something I did? Did I do anything suspicious?" I asked from the floor.

She refrained from answering and began humming a little tune.

"You realize people can cope with traumatic incidents in different ways, right?" I chased after her. "Just because I'm not acting obviously depressed doesn't mean I'm not sad about her."

"You are not."

"What gives you the impression I'm not grieving?"

"If you're actually grieving, then you wouldn't be so worried about whether you look like you're grieving."

"Alicia." I exhaled. "I truly cared about her. And I was beyond desperate when she first passed. I understand I moved on a little too fast. You have to believe me. I was very much enraged and upset about the vase incident. But there's nothing I can do about it anymore. So, I have to move on at some point. And I'm sure she doesn't want me to be drawn in."

"You speak so fast." Her voice was solemn. "I know it's none of my business. But it sounds like you put in all of this effort to move into this empty house and play hermit just to prove to people that you're sad about her passing."

"It is pretentious," I confessed. "But at least I understand I need to be grieving."

"The bar you set for yourself is really low."

"I did love her," I said, this time with honesty. "I just never deserved her."

I remembered kissing Daria goodbye the morning she walked out of our apartment. Her black, six-inch-tall heels clicked in the same rhythm as every other day. She was smiling at me. To help with carbon emissions, she took it upon herself to travel to work on foot. The distance itself was supposed to take less than ten minutes. I received a call from the police in less than five. When I arrived at the scene, she still had the same smile plastered on her face, except it had gone to complete paleness. Through the gaps between people, I gained a glimpse of her body. A long edge of porcelain stuck out from her neck. Dark red blood oozed endlessly out of the incision. From afar, it looked like a long scarf was wrapped around her neck and hanging from her shoulder. The paramedics had reached her with shocking speed, yet they were no longer in a hurry to save a life, as there was none to be saved.

After the initial wave of sadness, I tried to cling to the feeling and immerse my daily life in it. When the tears were scarce, I forced them. It was what a good partner should have done, regardless of my real thoughts. Within a week, I had a stark realization that, with or without Daria, my life was just as mundane, effortless, and lonely. Within two weeks, I found myself imagining how my future relationships were going to pan out. I began working through the logistics in my brain of when it might be appropriate to officially move on, free from the weight of other people's judgment. During the rare occasions when I was consumed by guilt, I lingered under scorching showers, hoping the heat would ignite some basic morals in me.

That night, I lay on the floor of my office. I watched the lights flicker and change patterns on Alicia's TV. For my sake, she kept it at a barely audible volume. I turned away. I had taken working from home to a new level. Theoretically, I would not need to leave the room for almost an entire day.

"Did you know you're wasteful?" Her voice rang across the empty hallway.

I kept my mouth shut.

"I know you're awake!" she added. "Talk to me!"

"What do you want me to say to that?"

"You know people would die to be with her, right?"

I told her that she wouldn't understand.

Chapter 9

She insisted on attending her hearing alone. I came home late that night. Work had stalled me. Once again, I found her in bed. She lay on her side. I could see where her legs were curled under the comforter. With the wounds on her back, it was probably the only comfortable position for her to be in. The clothes she wore in the morning were scattered across the floor: a gray blazer, black tank top, pants, and socks. Their sheer modesty spelled out her status as a woman away from the traditional workforce.

"It's over," she murmured as I approached the hallway.

"Are you all right?" It was an unnecessary question. I didn't expect her to say yes when she looked absolutely distraught. But if I didn't ask her, I wouldn't know how else to speak to her. "Do you wanna talk for a bit, or do you want some alone time?"

She refused to engage.

When midnight approached, I knocked on her doorframe again. She had not moved an inch on the bed. I

63

spotted a relatively empty space next to her feet and sat down. "Are you hungry?"

She shook her head.

"Do you wanna talk? You might feel better if you talk about it."

"Chris looks bad."

I laughed. I imagined how air must have flown uncontrollably through the gaps in his teeth every time he tried to speak. Perhaps there was even spit. And others were disgusted by it.

"He looks really bad," she added, "and I'm happy."

"Do you want me to make you something for dinner?"

"No, thank you."

"Do you want me to order something instead?"

"No, thank you." She twisted her head toward me without turning her body. "You wanna guess how much money they decided to give me?"

"Very little, I assume?"

"They said they were being generous, considering I only have two more months left and anything given to me will go to waste, so they decided that it would be more economically appropriate to give the majority to Chris. I only got some because my name was already on a few things before we got married."

If her own partner was cruel, strangers had no obligation to treat her any better, although it was likely the judge had personally sided with her. However, their personal stance couldn't trump what was written on paper.

"I think I do things without thinking about their consequences," she said.

"It's not your fault. You don't need to interact with him again."

She clapped off the lamp by her bed. The hallway light suddenly showed itself. A splash of creamy-white glimmer poured onto the floor, blocked off by the edge of the bed frame. Her face was hidden in the shadows. Thin strips of moonlight squeezed past the window. They outlined her compressed frame, turning the outer shell of her head golden.

I wondered if Mexico had automatic lamps. It wouldn't be a normal immigration case; once we left, there would be no visiting and no room to change our minds. Every piece of memory, good or bad, was going to be left behind. We couldn't stay there forever; the real destination lay in Europe, perhaps the UK, with my limited linguistic abilities.

I sat with her in silence, staring back into my office. Time was ticking slowly, steadily, accompanied by my existential dread.

There was no guarantee our future would pan out as I wished. I feared leaving my life behind for her to face the same eventual separation in another country. If I were to help her and take responsibility for her, it would be too cruel for her to deprive me of what I had always wanted. She had known for years.

I desired her in a way that easily transcended a simple biological craving. I deemed myself better than an animal that never understood gratification beyond what could be received by the body. I longed for genuine companionship, closeness, and the ability to have my most honest thoughts understood and accepted. Sex and intimacy had little to no correlation, or so I thought.

As most partnerships I witnessed eventually ended, a worry grew in me. If we were to spend the rest of our lives together, what would happen to us if we began hating each other for whatever reason? What if the mundane killed our passion that was yet to be built and made us indifferent? I couldn't imagine a world where I didn't love her. I wouldn't be able to recognize myself that way.

I mentally slapped myself for making my help an exchange. How disgusting I was to hold her hostage. I couldn't imagine a world where she pretended to love me as a form of payback. I wouldn't be able to recognize myself that way either.

After a while, she took out her arm from underneath the comforter and reached in my direction. Up to the point of her collarbones, it was free of any clothing. It occurred to me that, instead of changing out of her court attire, she'd simply taken it off and was lying entirely naked. She held onto the sheets with her left arm and clutched them in front of her chest, high enough to cover her breasts. Our fingertips touched. I watched hers slowly crawl their way over mine. She rested her small palm on my healing knuckles.

"It's not the end," I said, attempting to comfort both of us. "We can get out and go somewhere else."

"What do you mean?"

"Go down to California, cross the border there."

"Stop—" She was forced to cut her sentence short, overtaken by a series of coughs.

"You want some water?"

"No. And I'm not going to Mexico either." She rolled away from me.

"I—"

"I need you to go," she said sternly.

"Okay." I shrugged. "I'm going into the office tomorrow, just for a little while. Are you going to be okay?"

She nodded.

I told her food was prepared for her in the refrigerator. All she needed to do was to put it in the oven or the microwave.

I stayed awake for the majority of the night.

Chapter 10

The bottle of water on her nightstand was left untouched. She had taken a bite out of the chocolate bar without following its pre-carved grids; the grooves on it followed the shape of her teeth instead. When I saw her the next morning, she had managed to throw on a teal T-shirt. The fabric was thin. I could trace the shape of her breasts with a short glance alone. She half leaned her shoulders against the wooden headboard. A few spare pillows were cushioned behind her lower back. Rosiness dominated the tops of her cheekbones. Otherwise, her complexion was gray. Her lips were lightly parted with a half circle of chapped skin.

"Can I get a few Advils?" she said as I walked past her room.

"What's wrong?"

"My head kind of hurts."

I rushed over while fixing the collar of my dress shirt. I pressed the back of my hand first to her cheeks, then under her chin. Her soft skin burned against mine.

Scanning the time shown on my phone, I became impatient. "You don't have a headache," I said. "You have a fever. How long has it been?"

"Yesterday. Since I got back."

"Why didn't you say anything then?" I raised my voice.

She lowered her head but lifted a pair of glistening eyes at me as if she were about to burst into tears from my harsh words and relentless scolding. I was happy she was willing to give in to her childish side in front of me, but sometimes I wanted her to behave like a functional adult.

"Does your throat hurt too?" I asked.

"Yeah."

I grabbed the nearby bottle of water and pushed it into her arms. I walked back into the main bedroom and to my medicine cabinet. After a few minutes of digging through shelves and drawers, I found a box of NyQuil still within the expiration date. When I came back to her, the bottle of water was still full; it flopped on her lap.

"You need to drink this."

"It's unopened," she whined like a mosquito.

I snatched the water from her, twisted off the cap, and took the opening to her mouth. I raised the bottle slightly, and a thin splash of water moistened her lips.

She turned her face away. "It hurts my stomach."

"You need to eat something, then."

I went downstairs, grabbed a can of chicken noodle soup, and dumped it into a small saucepan on the stove. When it came to a boil, I poured it into a ceramic bowl with handles.

She refused the steaming-hot liquid in front of

her. "Just put it down. I'll eat it later."

"If water hurts your stomach, then you need to eat this first so you can take the pills."

"It smells bad."

"It doesn't," I said. "You can't be picky right now. I need to go to work."

I dunked the spoon inside, scooping up some soft noodles and a piece of chicken. I blew on it, cooling it slightly, then brought it to her mouth. The edge of the spoon was thin enough to part her lips. I thought about the logistics of how the content would go in without her loosening her jaw. "Open up."

She looked at me with skepticism and reluctantly complied.

I carefully slid the spoon into the small opening between her parted lips without letting the metal hit her teeth. She chewed for longer than I would've liked but eventually emptied the bowl. I offered the pills to her and watched her swallow them.

"Sleep for a bit," I said. "I'll be back as soon as I can." I pulled her forward by the arm, trying to remove the pillows behind her back.

"Stop!" she yelled. Her face was flustered. She looked like she was thinking hard.

"Are you okay?"

Before she could answer, her body fell forward. With a slight moan, she vomited all over my lap. Hot, sticky liquid warmed by the lining of her stomach fell in front of my eyes and onto my pants and shirt. She was struggling to breathe, so I patted her back. She vomited again, this time next to my feet.

Her faint apologies were combined with loud coughs. I told her it was okay, though I wasn't sure if she heard me. I held her body upright as she whimpered in discomfort. A loose strand of hair fell in front of her face. With two fingers, I wrapped the strand around the back of her ear.

"Here." I gave the water to her, not letting go of the bottle until she had a full grip on it. "Rinse your mouth with it. Just spit it out on the floor."

My impatience had backfired on me. The rancid smell of undigested soup and acid gave my clothes a sharp stench. What had been intended to be appetizing was now offensive. As I moved away from the bed, chewed-up carrots, celery, and chicken fell from my shirt and pants. In the bathroom, I scraped off as much vomit as I could. Luckily, none had gotten on her own body or the sheets around her. I asked myself why I couldn't have been less ambitious and given her saltine crackers instead to line her stomach. She would have been asleep by now, and I would have been close to my office.

When I wiped the floor around her, I felt her looking at me, watching my every move. Whatever gears turning in her brain were most likely generating a fundamental flaw of mine. Our dynamic was making me severely uncomfortable. Between the two of us, I didn't know who was more shameless. Was it her, for expecting me to wait on her hand and foot while degrading me in every waking moment? Or was it me, for letting her treat my genuine care like a piece of dog crap while wagging my tail at every chance I got?

"I'm sorry," she said.

"You don't need to keep on apologizing. Next time, if you don't feel well, don't wait the whole night. Try to get some sleep. I'll be back as soon as I can."

"Can you skip?" she mumbled.

"I have to go. I can't just skip."

"Please don't go to work." She pinched my sleeve. "It'll be the only time. I really don't feel well. Don't go to work."

I couldn't stand begging. Her whiny voice tugged at me, destroying my ability to think rationally in a matter of seconds. It was an obvious trap. She was back to using and manipulating me, and I felt compelled to give in. It was almost as if I had wanted this to happen. I wanted to put an end to her tormenting me. I couldn't do so if I continued to let her run rampant.

"I'll stay," I said.

I saw her eyes light up, then stall in disbelief. Soon, redness took over her sclera. Tears swirled around her warm brown irises, eventually streaming down her cheeks. She sniffled in front of me. Her face was torn.

I was taken aback; I bent to look at her from a closer distance. She began sobbing loudly when our eyes finally met on the same plane.

"I already said I'm not going anymore. You don't need to cry."

"For real?" she whimpered.

"Yes, for real. I'm staying."

"I'm cold. Can you come in?"

I lifted a small corner of the comforter. From the gap, I could see her bare legs and the edge of her pink underwear. Her thighs were covered in goose bumps despite being under the heavy bedding.

I felt like a thief. But I couldn't blame myself. It wasn't my idea to begin with. I didn't need to be condemned for the enjoyment I was going to gain from pressing myself against her.

I pushed her forward and sat behind her, leaning against the headboard. I wrapped my arms around the trunk of her body. She was overheating, yet shaking with uncontrollable chills. I wondered if my normal temperature was warming her up or making her even colder. She fussed with the metal buckle of my belt. I took it off and threw it to the side. Her head slumped toward my shoulder. Her breathing had smoothed, but the faint sniffles remained. I felt dampness in front of her shirt. It seemed as if all the water she drank went to her tear glands.

I raised my palm to her face. "Stop this," I cooed at her. "I already said I'm not going to work."

"Is it because you pity me?" she asked. Her voice was coarse.

"No," I said. "You have to think positive thoughts."

"I can't think of any."

"Try really, really hard."

"I wanna go on a trail ride," she murmured.

"No can do."

"We met at the equestrian school, remember?"

"Of course. You were super brave, and I embarrassed myself."

My father had an obsession with raising Chris and me in a very particular way. His own childhood was a wound he never recovered from, therefore he built us a fantasized version of it. When he paid attention to us, he enrolled us in pretentious activities that served little to no use. We had to learn how to ride horses, sail, and play golf and piano. It was what he envisioned children of established parents should do. To him, it was insulting when the people around him didn't reflect the material privileges he was able to offer them. He controlled how my mother dressed, the products she used, and the accessories she carried. Her clothes were required to be tight and expensive. When the men they interacted with didn't pay attention to my mother's beauty, my father behaved like he wanted to pry their eyelids open so they could see what he was able to keep next to him in his house.

The day I had met Alicia, I was six years old. I lay facedown on the ground. It smelled like feces mixed with dirt. I clutched my mother's ankle, refusing to mount the giant gelding standing calmly in front of me. I now understood how I didn't make the best first impression on Alicia. No matter how hard I cried, I didn't have a way out of it; my lessons had already been paid for in a package deal. My parents never asked if I even wanted them; one day, I was strapped in a booster seat and driven there with Chris.

Eventually, my father grew agitated. He dragged me off the ground and walked toward the mounting block. My legs shook from the height of the top step. As I stalled there, he threw me onto the horse's back. They had given me an English saddle; I thought I was going to fall and die.

"I don't remember you embarrassing yourself, I just

knew we met there. I don't really remember seeing you there either."

"You might wanna rest your throat if it's sore. We'll talk more when you feel better. Give me five minutes, and I'll be right back."

I called Henry. I was supposed to have lunch with him, another associate, and a client. He was a young attorney with a towering frame. He had a head full of red curls and an accent similar to Meemaw's when he spoke. He tried to hide it, but it was apparent to anyone who grew up around it.

He was the hardest-working person I knew. I wasn't sure if he genuinely enjoyed work to the degree he presented to others, but on the surface, he was constantly energetic. He spoke very little and never asked questions.

I didn't want to explain to people why I couldn't be there, nor did I have any interest in making up a believable story. Maybe Henry was waiting for this moment to please me and show his reliability.

"Hello, Edward," he yelled down the line.

"I'm so sorry to put this on you at the last minute, but I can't come to lunch today."

"Oh no."

"I have an emergency."

"Should we still go . . .? They mainly wanted to eat with you I think."

"Don't cancel. The restaurant is too hard to book." I hesitated in embarrassment. "I'm not gonna be able to answer my phone. So, um—"

"Are you all right?"

"Yeah."

"I hope everything is okay."

I hung up the phone and went back to her room.

She moaned when I kissed the crown of her head. I sat behind her. Her body burned like a small furnace on top of mine.

"I'm really upset," she said softly.

"Don't be."

She teared up again. I was unprepared. I didn't know what to do when women cried, or how to make them feel better. Daria almost never cried. In fact, I'd rarely seen any form of negative emotion from her. I could let Alicia express her feelings until she tired herself out. I could also try to soothe her; I wasn't sure which path was going to be better.

I helplessly watched her wince nonstop. Every time I told her how things were going to pan out all right, she rejected the idea. When she needed to flip over, she pressed her hand against my chest, her nails digging into my skin. She sniffled, took a corner of my shirt, and dabbed underneath her nose. I didn't know if I should laugh or frown.

Her body felt bonier than I had imagined. She was now close to being rail thin. As a teen, I remembered the plump and healthy parts of her, which had now almost diminished entirely. She'd been sunnier, more athletic, and, generally speaking, happier than the average girl. I missed the roundness of her cheeks when she smiled and the slight protruding of fat on her lower belly.

She'd started show jumping around the same time I was

finally allowed to quit. It was what she truly loved doing. Her favorite horse was a chestnut-colored gelding named Rashad. He was the nicest horse I had ever met, calm yet powerful. I used to watch her in awe, wondering how she was utterly fearless of a creature ten times her size. His body leaped with her in the air, hooves tightly tucked into his chest. I could see each group of muscles and tendons bulging and extending upon landing. She'd leaned into his neck, her knees and feet gripping his stomach.

When it became illegal to own horses, Rashad was led into a box and electrocuted.

Chapter 11

During the next few days, I received many texts and calls from people who were genuinely concerned about my well-being. One of them was Ben. He was by no means using his seniority to force me into giving an explanation, but I felt compelled to speak to him over anyone else. The man's attitudes and behaviors sometimes resembled my father's on a good day. I never mentioned that to him, though.

I had known Ben since before I was a summer associate. Recently, he'd become half a friend and half a guiding figure. I labeled him this way in my mind due to the sheer difference in our age. There was only so much common ground we could find.

In comparison to the other sets of moving lips at the office, Ben's would be the easiest to stuff.

He occupied one of the bigger offices on the forty-third floor. I walked out of the elevator, took a right into a short hallway paved with dark green carpet, and arrived in front of a tall wooden door. My hand halted in the middle of the air, but with enough courage, I knocked.

"Come on in!" Ben yelled from the other side. All the rooms in the building were decently soundproofed; talking through doors always required effort.

The door handle was thin and lengthy, with a fine point at the end. It felt cold. He was sitting at his desk, his body filling every inch of the boss's chair. His fingers were interlocked, both of his hands resting comfortably on his stomach. He was a corpulent man in his early sixties with about half a head of platinum-blond hair. Luckily, his sides were long enough to cover the top of his head, which was barren, making it seem like he suffered less from balding.

The office itself had great lighting. The walls were painted a light cream color, with two tall wooden bookshelves against the wall next to the entrance. They were filled with old-fashioned leather-bound legal doctrines. I found them pretentious. Searching through actual books was so much more strenuous than pressing Command+F on a keyboard. I doubted Ben had ever read anything from his big collection.

I had a choice between a plastic hardback chair and a delicate, soft-looking red velvet chair that rolled. I chose the plastic one.

"They have barbecue in the lounge today. I figured you haven't had food yet." Ben's mustache flared upward.

I looked at the plate in front of me and shook my head. There were three ribs glazed in a brownish-red sauce. The ends of the bones were charcoal black. Next to the main dish was a juicy sausage link and a handful of overly marinated pickles. The oiliness made the meat reflective in the ceiling light. Two years ago, Ben had suffered a stroke, but his love for rich foods remained.

"Well, I guess I'll wait too."

"What exactly did Henry say?" I asked.

"He said you were on your way to work. You ran into a group of advocates protesting for the removal of plastic on shoelace aglets, and you felt the need to join them because you were deeply moved by the cause. You ended up walking with them and couldn't think of anything other than saving the planet."

"That's not realistic . . ."

"It's realistic to him. Isn't he, like, nineteen?"

"Twenty-five, I think."

"Same thing." Ben threw his hands in the air. "So . . . how are you doing?"

I looked around the space. I liked his office far more than mine. It was decorated with care and enthusiasm.

"I'm—" I was about to answer *fine*, but I quickly stopped myself. Although it was what people usually started with, it couldn't have been further from the truth. Alicia had drained me. My appearance must have represented my state of mind to a certain degree.

When I tried to put myself in her shoes, I arrived at two drastically different conclusions.

Sometimes, I felt the horribleness of the chain of events she was going through. There was nothing but betrayal and anguish. I wouldn't have known what to do. To lose a child, be hurt by the person she loved, go through a failed pregnancy, face the death penalty, and be divorced immediately? I was surprised by the degree to which she was able to hold herself together. A person who was remotely weak would've harmed themselves, or worse, random people they'd never met before.

Other times, I had to use all of my self-control not to raise my voice at her. She was beyond entitled, immature, and unnecessarily mean to the only person who was trying to help her. She had a hopeful path paved in front of her; all she had to do was step onto it.

I blamed her entitlement on her father. She was an only child, and he'd been the type of parent who would rather drain every single pool he owned than send his daughter to swim lessons. Her mother had died when she was a toddler, and he'd never moved on or acquired a life of his own outside of her. Now he lived in a facility for patients with Alzheimer's and other health issues, and he could no longer intervene.

"You know, this really is none of my business. But as someone who's known you for a while, I just feel like I needed to check up on you. Granted, I know a lot has happened in your personal life during the past year, but workwise, you seemed fine. So, is there something I can help you with? Did anything new pop up?"

"I'm sorry."

"I've heard that, for some people," Ben continued, unwilling to let me off the hook with a simple apology, "when they first lose a spouse or a loved one, they experience some form of shock that blocks them from the pain for a while. And when that shock is over, they experience the pain all at once, and it can be pretty hard on them. So, I just wanna let you know that you have my full support."

"I appreciate it." I smiled. "But it's a little more difficult to say than that."

"So . . . what were you doing?"

"I can't say."

"Well." He shrugged. "Then I guess—"

"It has to stay confidential."

"Of course."

"There's . . ." I looked down at the tips of my shoes and inhaled deeply. I knew of no appropriate words to describe my relationship with Alicia. I was going to make myself look creepy and taint both our reputations. Not that it mattered. I shook my head, gave myself a little more energy, and started over. "There's this woman who lives in my house. She caught a fever and threw up on me. I don't know why I didn't just give her saltine crackers in the first place, but I chose to feed her a whole can of chicken soup instead. It just made her feel horrible, and she had to retake the pills from earlier."

"Okay?" Ben smiled with his mouth open. It stalled in the air. I wished for an interjection that unfortunately did not come, despite the obvious question marks indicated by his raised brow.

"I couldn't come to work because she asked me not to, so I didn't. Even today, I feel bad for leaving the house because she's supposedly better, but she's only surviving on deli meat. I think she should eat less sodium. And she couldn't stop coughing the whole night last night. I was trying to sleep, but I couldn't. I also can't stop her from being depressed—for valid reasons; her ex-husband treated her badly and divorced her last week. I'm not sure if she's mentally well enough to be left alone. I'm constantly worried that she's going to hurt herself. And now I just remembered the hunting rifle I have in my bedroom, which she kicked me out of. I'm sleeping on a mattress on my office floor. She should know about the rifle because my grandmother loves weapons. She gave the exact same model to my brother and me last year for Christmas. If she really wanted to, she could probably find it. Now I wish I'd locked my bedroom door before I left. And I couldn't look at my phone that day because I wanted to watch her sleep when I really should've been doing something more productive, like researching about the UK."

"What are you smoking? Can I get some too?"

"I'm not smoking anything."

Ben studied me. There was amusement in his eyes that he couldn't hide. "I'm not sure I follow everything, but here, in case you need it." He pushed a box of tissues toward me. "If I may ask—first of all, how long has this woman been living with you? Second of all, why would she know about the rifle that was a gift from your grandma?"

"About a week. And she should know about the gift because her ex-husband is my brother."

"Are you sure you're not smoking anything?"

I grew annoyed. I shook my head adamantly.

"How much of what you're saying is true?"

"All of it. I probably haven't said enough. But I don't think I can stay at Montgomery Sterling anymore. I have to go before I get fired."

"W-why?"

"Because my brother hit her when they were married, so I went to do the same to him. He might come after me at any time."

"Please don't tell me you did it with cameras around."

"I did it with cameras around."

Ben let out a thoughtful laugh. "Let me attempt to put your words into normal people's language—"

"Don't. I can't bear to hear it."

"Edward, I know this is personal." His voice suddenly dropped to a whisper. "If I remember correctly, didn't your wife just pass last year? From the vase incident? Right? And now you've moved on to your sister-in-law? I mean, obviously you're free to do whatever you'd like in your own life, but . . ." He began rambling. His words blended into the white noise of the room.

My face burned in shame. I clutched the armrest as hard as I could. It was the only way to stop myself from bolting out the door. I wanted the building to crumble, fall, and bury me inside the heaviest pile of broken concrete so I couldn't be seen, heard, or judged.

"I'm sorry. You know I take things seriously. I'm just afraid I won't have much time left with her. She had a miscarriage."

That finally washed the awkward smirk off Ben's face. His eyes sank. "If you want to, why don't you come over to my house sometime, and we can talk more about it." After a long pause, he opened his mouth again. "I promise everything stays safe with me. You know my stance on this type of issue."

"Thank you. I appreciate it. I really do." I stood,

84

roughly collected myself, and walked toward the door.

"You don't wanna stay and eat with me?" Ben called out, disappointed.

"I have to get going."

"But the barbecue!" He pointed at the now-cold meat on the plates. "Take one with you."

"No, thank you."

Chapter 12

It would be difficult to accomplish the task alone. When extreme confidentiality was involved, the fewer the people, the better the outcome. I wasn't sure if I wanted to throw the burden on the people I trusted, and as for the people I didn't trust—well, they might've been tremendously helpful, in fact, but smuggling a criminal out of the country was not something people voluntarily involved themselves in. It was so dangerous that only close, blood-related family members should've known of it, and I didn't have much faith left in my family.

I contemplated never reaching out to Ben again. My spewing was unforgettable, but I doubted he would chase after me. Rationally speaking, he was a good candidate; he *had* made his stance clear more than once, and he had cousins living in Europe. But even if he had no intention of reporting us, it wasn't fair for me to drag him down with the burden. If I asked him for concrete help out of empathy and morality, was I really giving him an option to say no?

When I got home, I reached into the mailbox with shaking hands. I closed my eyes and begged the universe not to let me be served. My palm warmed against the metal lining of the box. A wave of chillness crawled up my arm. I had received nothing.

Alicia looked better. It wasn't yet two o'clock in the afternoon. She sat on a barstool in a set of pink silk pajamas. Her hair was draped over her shoulders. An oversized mug sat on the counter, and steam rose in the air. She stared at it. A few inches away was a box of tissues. The used ones were scrunched into one big ball despite the trash can being only a few feet away.

"How are you feeling?"

"Better," she said with a deeper voice than usual. "I found these tea bags in your cupboard. They're supposed to help with your throat. Hope you don't mind."

"I told you to make yourself at home." I shrugged. "Is there anything that interests you for dinner?"

"Hot pot." She cleared her throat. "Can we find a way to get some hot pot?"

"We can go to a fondue place instead."

"No, like an actual hot pot with frozen tofu in peppercorn broth."

"How are we gonna get in? The restaurants won't let us in."

"Can we get it delivered?" She took a small sip of tea.

"They can't deliver a pot. How are they gonna get it back?"

"Never mind," she said quietly. "I'll just starve, I guess."

"Seriously?"

A good alternative would be to order the individual ingredients needed for hot pot online and put it together at home. But recipes and some trial and error would be expected. At that point, she would faint from being without food for too long.

"Is that the only thing you actually want?" I asked.

Her head bopped up and down. For a split second, she looked exactly like the girl who bullied me into letting her have her first dips from my lunch box every day. Little did she know, it was never the bullying that made me budge.

"Are you still friends with Ian?" She blushed. "You can call him and see if he can scoop some out for us."

"He's on the robotics trip. Techno Penguins made it to the final round at regionals." Ian was half Chinese. He could go inside an Asian restaurant without too many issues. "I know someone else who can get in. My office assistant is Asian too. You won't go hungry for long."

She turned her head sharply. "Is she pretty?"

"No . . .?"

"I didn't know you were the type of person to call other people ugly."

"Fine. She is pretty."

"Okay, have fun." She looked away from me.

"Stop," I said firmly. "She's a kid."

"How old?"

"I'm not sure. Like, twenty-something?"

"Do you always call her after working hours?"

"First of all, stop." I felt myself on the edge of losing my temper. "Second of all, most people's working hours haven't ended yet. I left early. Third of all, I'm only calling her to get you what *you* want."

Fortunately and unfortunately, Leah had never said no to anyone or anything. And just like Henry, she never asked questions.

I handed my phone to Alicia. "I'm putting her on speaker, if you care so much."

"No, it's fine. I don't care."

"This is about to be embarrassing," I whispered under my breath. "But since you don't feel well and it's the only thing you want . . . I'm taking one for the team."

I scrolled through a long list of contacts before finally seeing Leah Lee's number pop up on the screen. After hitting the call button, her sharp upward inflection blasted through the phone. Alicia cocked her head with a smirk on her face.

"Hey. This has nothing to do with work, but, um, I need a favor from you. Whenever you're off today, do you mind picking up something for me from a hot pot place? If you're free, of course. Yeah . . . sorry to bother you. It's for my grandma, she's in town. . . . She has Alzheimer's. Thank you so much! I really appreciate it!"

Alicia's mouth gaped, no doubt in awe of my ability to fabricate such a natural, effective, convincing lie. It was the best kind of lie, one that was based in reality and consisted of more than fifty percent truth.

"Yeah, so if you can maybe cook it there and scoop out some in a container, that would be greatly appreciated. The content doesn't really matter, she's not picky about that. Can you just make sure there's one or two servings of frozen tofu in a spicy broth? . . .Yes, yes. Thank you so much. And let me know how much I should send you . . . yes . . . perfect. Thank you." I hung up the phone. "She said she's happy to help. And I can meet her in front of Happy Happy Sheep at sevenish. Problem solved."

"You're so good at lying," Alicia commented, looking concerned. "And apparently I'm Meemaw? I'm pretty sure she doesn't have Alzheimer's."

I chuckled. "No, you are not Meemaw. And I don't think she has Alzheimer's, either, but she *is* ninety-seven years old. Yes, I did lie, but it was a harmless lie. I didn't force her to do it, and I'm going to pay her back."

If I had asked a friend of mine, I'd be bombarded with questions and forced to explain the reasons behind my stupid request. Using Meemaw as a facade wouldn't; she was somewhat famous among the people I knew. Plus she'd made it clear that she could only eat "strictly American" and would contract an eating disorder otherwise.

As a so-called superior to Leah, it was harder for me to be rejected.

"Do I need a supervisor?" I asked. "Do you wanna come with me?"

Chapter 13

During the car ride, Alicia poured another batch of tea into a thermos. She leaned the passenger seat back and turned on the heating underneath the cushion. I sat in the driver's seat and typed the restaurant's address into the car. The SUV had ample space in the back seat. She suggested we both take a nap until we got close. I declined.

"You're not gonna manually drive, are you?" she asked.

"Of course not. I always sit in the driver's seat, though."

"Why? There's less space. And it doesn't make sense since the car is driving itself anyways."

"I'd like to feel like my efforts didn't completely go to waste."

"How many times did you fail again?" She smirked at me.

In her senior year of high school, she took the test in the suburbs. It was the same year I learned to drive. My father made passing the driving test within the city a rite of passage. Chris had passed it on the first try. I shouldn't have listened to him. The first time, I was driving too slow and couldn't keep up with the rest of the traffic. The second time, I was driving too fast. The third time, a fire truck rang behind me; I panicked too quickly before pulling over. Looking back, it was by no means embarrassing for an inexperienced driver, but to my teenage brain, my confidence and self-esteem took great damage.

She rolled down her window as we traveled through the quiet neighborhood streets. The previously ocean-blue sky had been washed out to a shade of white. The breeze hit her gently, blowing a few strands of her hair away from her face, revealing some to be darker, while others were golden. She looked to be in a reflective mood, the palm of her hand pressed against her chin. I gazed out of my own window and didn't disturb her.

It was a beautiful day. The sun was slowly descending, and before blending with the horizon, it burst with a last few rays of bright orange mixed with shades of gold and red. A long row of faux trees looked extra green, despite the changing season. It was an entirely normal occurrence, as plastic leaves were never known for welting. Each tree was manicured in the exact same shape; not a single crown was bigger than the other. They had absorbed some of the sunlight and, strangely, cast a few different patterns of shadows that quickly disappeared out of my sight.

When the car approached the freeway entrance, she reluctantly rolled up the window and looked back at me. She cleared her throat with a few deep hums.

"Why would she go out of her way to do this for

you?"

"Because it's part of her personality. She never says no to anyone. Plus, it's harder to refuse someone with more power or authority than you. I don't necessarily like these dynamics, but that's how things work sometimes."

"It's not just that," she teased. "I'm betting one whole million dollars she likes you. At least a little bit."

"Stop it. We're picking up the container from her and heading right back."

"You aren't *too* ugly, and you shower regularly."

"So I'm not completely horrible?"

She paused for a few seconds, then spoke again. "I guess not."

There wasn't a single car parked in front of Happy Happy Sheep. The small restaurant had a green overhang with an obese sheep printed on it, grinning eagerly from ear to ear, as if it felt genuinely ecstatic to be sliced thinly into sheets of raw meat and cooked in a boiling broth within a matter of seconds.

Leah said it was one of the best places she had ever been. After we arrived, she sent a long text full of apologies, asking if I could wait another thirty minutes. I let Alicia know and began logging my hours.

"Excuse me. I don't see you doing any work."

"I'm thinking about work. Thinking counts too," I said with my eyes closed. "And if I fall asleep, I'll be dreaming about work. Dreaming definitely counts."

"Didn't you hear about the two people who got caught because they billed more than twenty-four hours in a day?"

I nodded. "Yeah, that was pretty funny."

"I didn't think you were someone who did this. I had really high standards for you."

Once again, I followed her gaze out of the car window. The two glass doors allowed a perfect view of the restaurant's interior. Only two tables had customers despite the hour being prime dinnertime. They chatted with each other. I couldn't see a single server. An Asian man in maybe his fifties was standing outside the entrance. He wore a black T-shirt with the same eerie-looking sheep printed on it. A cigarette rested between his index and middle finger. He brought it to his mouth, his lips clutching the tip as he carefully lit it with one hand, protecting the small burst of flame. He looked toward our car. His eyebrows furrowed as he let out a deep exhale of gray smoke.

"If everyone stuck to every rule ever written, we'd all be dead by now," I said.

"But you wouldn't even lie about community service hours."

"That was a lot fewer hours. I've learned from my mistakes. And unfortunately, people change. I think you've changed too."

"For better or for worse?"

She kicked off her slippers, which she'd worn into the car, pulled her knees to her chest, and looked at me with curious eyes. My eyes stalled at the edge of her ankle monitor, which peeked out from her pant leg.

"Worse," I confessed. "I didn't think you're someone who lets other people walk all over you. But if I were in your situation, I'd have no idea how I'd manage."

"You don't know everything about me. And vice

versa."

Her voice was calm. I agreed silently. It was possible that she had turned into someone I despised. Perhaps I didn't know her anymore. We saw each other multiple times a year, but our interactions consisted mostly of holiday wishes or distant small talk. I had a strong feeling that she couldn't have turned into a bad person. If she did, I wouldn't know how to face it. I refused to consider the possibility of her having ill will toward other people. She didn't want to frame Chris; that alone was evidence of her stance on morality.

A while later, she alerted me with a tap on the shoulder. Leah had switched out of her work attire; she was now wearing a long green jacket that covered her from head to toe. In her hand was a medium-sized mesh bag. With an anxious look on her face, she stood a few feet away from the green overhang, her eyes scanning the pedestrians passing by.

"I think that's her!"

"Stay inside. I'll be quick."

I walked toward Leah. She looked in my direction, acknowledged me, and then turned her head away. With curled fingers, she re-tucked a strand of hair that was already behind her ear.

"Thank you so much! I really appreciate it. How much do I owe you?"

"Oh, don't worry about it." She took a step back with each step I took forward. "We ate here. They let me take these out for free, too."

"Are you sure? You wouldn't have had to come all the

way here if it wasn't for me."

"Hey, Edward?" She tilted her head up. It was one of the rare occasions where she didn't speak to the floor. She continued, "I was going to have dinner with my parents somewhere else today. But I told them about your grandma, so we came here instead. They, um, they've heard about you, and they were very impressed. So . . . they wanted me to ask you if it was okay for them to meet you?"

"What did I do?" I was dazed.

"Oh, it's just that they were asking me about who you were, and I mentioned where you went to school and stuff. They've always looked up to things like this, so they wanted to talk to you . . ."

I watched Leah's face slowly turn the shade of a ripened tomato. I didn't know how to respond. Though I found it bizarre, it couldn't hurt to say a quick hello, especially after she'd deviated from her family's plans.

"Is that okay with you? It's okay if it's not, I was just wondering—"

"Of course."

"Just give me one second." She turned away quickly and stopped in front of a white sedan parked nearby. She knocked on the passenger window lightly. A few moments later, a middle-aged couple slowly emerged from the car. Leah walked to each side of the car, helping them out one by one by letting them grab her arm. Her parents were far too young to be immobile; Leah's arm seemed more like a status symbol rather than a real helpful gesture.

The woman approached me first with another bag in

hand. She wore a big red puffy jacket and a pair of insanely tall platform shoes covered in silver glitter. Her lips were painted bright red to match the color of her jacket. The perfume she wore was so potent that I quickly acquired a headache, despite being outdoors. It was hard to imagine this woman being Leah's mom. The man who was presumably her husband was dressed modestly in all black.

"Hello!" I said. "I go by Edward. Nice to meet you."

"I go by Judy. Nice to meet you too!"

Her husband initiated a handshake in a much more timid manner. "I go by Thomas."

"We're visiting from out of state!" Judy said. For someone in maybe her late fifties, her voice sounded exactly like a teenage Valley Girl's. She continued in the tone of a rehearsed script, "Leah said you were trying to get some hot pot for your grandma. Did you know there's a famous saying, 'Filial piety comes before all forms of kindness'?"

I took a moment to try to understand what *filial piety* was supposed to mean. Perhaps it had something to do with religion. The bag was shoved into my arms. Underneath the soft fabric was what felt like a cardboard box.

"It was invented by Rosa! Have you heard of her? Isn't she just brilliant and amazing?"

"Yes, I have heard of her."

"We were so moved by how much dedication you have toward your grandma, so we thought you might like this pot too! You can boil your own hot pot for her at home! It's a mandarin duck pot!"

Partially dazed from the floral perfume, I didn't understand how the orange-like fruit and ducks had anything to do with each other, or what they had to do with the cookware.

"It's basically one pot where you can have two different-flavored broths. There's a built-in divider on the inside. It just happens to be called a mandarin duck pot," Leah added.

"Thank you so much. I'll definitely look into how to use it," I said politely, searching for my line of exit.

Thomas stopped me and took a pointer finger to his daughter's face. "We hope Leah is doing all right at her job."

"If she isn't doing a good job, just let us know. We are her parents, and we'll definitely keep her in check!" Judy grabbed Leah's sleeve, pulling her closer to the group. Funnily enough, the daughter, without any high heels on, was still considerably taller than the mom, who seemed to wish to stand on stilts.

"We'll beat her into submission," Thomas added.

I wasn't sure how to follow that up. My eyes danced among the three of them. No one gave me any hints on how to appropriately respond. Both Judy and Thomas stood in front of me with their mouths open, excitement and anticipation written on their faces. Leah, on the other hand, looked completely mortified.

"She's doing absolutely amazing!" I said. "She's always responsive and great at communicating. She's really putting in a lot of effort, especially compared to others."

"Oooh." Thomas exhaled loudly. A deep vertical line

formed between his eyebrows, which were now scrunched together. "If she is putting in a lot of effort, that means she's lacking in capability. Are there any skills she needs to improve?"

"No, no." I shook my head quickly. "I meant that even though Leah is skillful and capable, she's willing to put in a lot of effort despite being a lot more competent than her colleagues in the first place."

The couple looked at each other and nodded at the same time. "Not bad, Leah! Very not bad!"

"Super not bad! My daughter is not useless!" Thomas patted Leah on the back, so hard and loud that her entire upper body shook with his palm's rhythm.

Judy pulled her daughter down to her height and planted a big kiss on her cheek, leaving a crimson mark in the shape of two swollen sausages, which Leah didn't dare to wipe clean. "Look! An Ivy League person gave you a compliment! I knew my daughter was better than a dog!" she screamed.

"Better than a big dog!"

"Golden retriever!"

"Saint Bernard!"

"Uh, it was very nice to meet you both. I think I should bring this back to my grandma now," I said.

"Can we keep you for just one more minute? We've never seen someone who went to an Ivy League school in real life. Is it all right if we get a picture with you?"

"I'm sorry, I'm not sure if this is—what?"

"You went to an Ivy League school, didn't you?" The smile froze on Judy's face.

"Yes, but I—this—"

"So is it okay if we get a picture with you?"

I was completely drained of any cognitive ability. Leah's body had frozen in sheer embarrassment, but she still had enough mobility to mouth the word *please*.

I put the bags on the ground and out of frame. Thomas and Judy both closed in on me. I was wearing sweatpants. They clutched my arms. Leah used her phone and took photos from nearly twenty different angles until her mother ordered her to stop. "Our neighbors are gonna be so impressed! And one last thing."

Judy gestured to Thomas, who brought out a pen and a piece of neatly folded paper from his pocket. "Leah has a little brother. He's in eleventh grade. Is it okay if we get your autograph? We want to put it in his room so he can absorb as much intelligence as possible for his college application."

"I appreciate the opportunity, but I'm just a regular person—"

"No!" she shouted. "How can an Ivy League graduate be regular? You are young, handsome, and successful, and you have so much filial piety! You are anything but regular!"

There were stars in her eyes. Her red lips parted, unveiling a row of glowing-white teeth. I felt a sudden chill running up my back. She carried the expression of a predatory animal fondling its prey before sealing the air supply near the trachea. She looked as if she wanted to bite into my skin and devour me alive, piece by piece.

I quickly realized the ridiculousness of my imagination

and shook off the uneasy feeling. What did *filial piety* mean? I gave up all forms of objections and cooperated by scribbling my name on the paper.

The couple looked at it and finally seemed satisfied. They each ran their fingers over the signature.

When I returned to the car, Alicia was staring at me. My cheeks burned with fire. From the window, I could see the family still standing under the overhang. Judy and Thomas were taking turns sniffing the piece of paper.

Chapter 14

"Wow. That was such a *quick interaction*," Alicia said, mimicking Judy's voice. She was still fully invested in the scene, her body turned completely toward the window.

"I'm sorry. I have no idea what just happened."

"They were treating you like a circus animal."

"It was all weird."

"Look. She's crying." She pointed to the family.

"What? Why?"

Leah's shoulders were slightly hunched forward. She took her long sleeves to her face, dabbing underneath her eyes. Her mother had lost her joy from the useless signature and was now pinching, pushing, and slapping Leah on the arm. Thomas stood a few feet away from the woman. He placed both of his hands against his lower back and seemed perfectly undisturbed by his wife's actions.

"It doesn't make any sense," I muttered to myself.

"Are you stupid?" Alicia glared at me. "Let's just go."

I swallowed my rebuttal and commanded the car to

navigate back. I half threw the bigger bag with the pot onto the back seat and handed the smaller bag with the food to her.

"They gave me a special pot for us to make our own hot pot at home, if you were wondering what that was," I said. "Do you want to try the tofu now, or do you wanna wait until we get home?"

"I'd rather wait until we get h—" She caught herself and immediately rephrased, "I mean, get back to your house, where I'm currently crashing."

I laughed. "I don't care if you call it home."

"For how long? Two more months?" She pressed the button to darken the windshield so the glaring headlights from oncoming traffic didn't blind us both. Even though cars didn't need lights to drive themselves, government regulations still mandated that their headlights be on at night for the safety of pedestrians, despite the fact that there were no pedestrians on the freeway. "Do you think her parents were all over you because they're disciples of that Rosa lady?" she asked as we entered the freeway.

"Yeah," I said half-heartedly. "They said so themselves. It's not really a surprise, though, since they're from California. That's Rosa's home state."

"So what ended up happening with the vase-throwing lady?"

"Nothing."

"Nothing?"

"It was an accident."

"But it's not like the vase jumped out of her window on its own. She actually threw it with intention," she objected.

I mentally noted how she had no trouble bringing up events from the past that hurt me. I didn't mind her doing so, but I felt like I should be offended by her double standards. No one else in the past year had dared mention anything remotely intimate or sensitive to me. Some were fearful of deepening my wound; others were fearful of being reported to the police for intentionally triggering speech. Even my best friends walked on eggshells. As a result, I had no one to talk to.

"To be honest, her parents looked exactly like the type of parents to hit their kids when they got a B too."

"Alicia . . ."

"What?" She turned to me with a playful smile on her face. "Will you report me to the police for saying that? Maybe they'll execute me faster."

"No. You're just so—" I shook my head and gulped down the following word. *Defiant.*

A year ago, a Californian woman named Kathy Han had moved to New York with her family. Her daughter had failed to perform well in the most competitive district, so she chose the second most competitive one. When the first round of report cards was released online, Kathy was distraught. She found it completely unacceptable for her daughter, who was a sophomore at the time, to have a B+ in abstract algebra. She became furious after a verbal argument escalated—or so I had heard—and had hit her daughter repeatedly using various objects in the apartment. The daughter ran to a corner near the window. A few pieces of furniture blocked Kathy from unleashing more damage, so she found a white porcelain vase on a shelf and threw it at the daughter's head. The poor girl ducked next to a half-opened window. When the vase made contact with the window frame, it broke into sharp pieces and dove down from the fourteenth floor. Daria was walking down below.

I remembered watching people march for the woman's freedom on the news. Their mentor, Rosa herself, had come out and spoken on Kathy's behalf, along with her other disciples. Their uniforms filled up street after street.

Rosa was an educator to millions of parents wanting success for their children in the most desperate ways possible. Her biggest achievement was where her children had gone to school. I'd briefly known her oldest son, Ethan, in college; he barely spoke to her. She wrote a book on her parenting style and encouraged others to copy her. The first group of disciples emerged from Purple County and quickly spread across the entire country. She was soon on her way to becoming a global sensation, powered by pure greed.

"Didn't the woman say in an interview that she was gently hitting her daughter for educational purposes and for her own good?" Alicia said.

"I'm sure she did. I'm just happy we grew up before Rosa became famous. Imagine being raised by her devout disciples."

"Is being successful really that important?"

I hesitated. Neither of us had enough authority to condemn other people's desire for success. Alicia had never been the biggest fan of school, but she'd had a proper education after her dad made subject tutors line up in front of her room every day after school. If I had told Leah's parents how I was rejected by more than ten schools the first time I applied and was only accepted the second time, after my father used his connections, they wouldn't have been so keen to let their son absorb my "intelligence."

"Life is hard without money," I said, "so it makes sense for people to want to climb the success ladder, since it usually leads to money."

"But if everybody is climbing, there has to be a group that ends up on the bottom, right?"

"Well, since you can't change other people, the only thing you can do is change yourself. There's nothing wrong with not being successful, really. Everybody is dealt a different hand at birth—some people are luckier or unluckier than others. For example, Chris has fewer grooves on his brain than the rest of us."

She giggled. "Rosa has an interesting ideology. Maybe I'll add reading her book to my bucket list."

The last two words bothered me immensely. Kathy Han's motivation was unusually similar to Chris's case with domestic abuse. No one knew whether she had truly been trying to hurt anyone when she threw the vase; it could have been planned or entirely unintentional. As for Chris, whether he had caused the miscarriage was something only he and Alicia knew. But the concrete evidence was that he did hit her. With the wounds on her body as proof, it could be easily argued that it was within his intention to terminate the pregnancy.

Throughout the past few years, there had been many

cases where men chose death and prison time for their partners' lost pregnancies by claiming to have performed forced abortions in different ways. A lot of them told incoherent stories, yet ultimately got their wish. I wondered why some people were willing to give up their own lives to have offspring genetically represent them. My mother, to whom I had no relation, had treated me far better than my father ever cared to. At the same time, there were probably more men who were more than willing to risk their partner's life in order to obtain offspring with their genes. In a sadistic way, the second option sounded more like a win.

I waved my hand in front of Alicia's face to get her attention. "What if there's a way for you to not need a bucket list after all? Chris could've easily—"

"I already said I'm not framing him."

"It's not the same as framing. You have no idea what goes on in someone else's head."

"I told you he didn't do it. I need you to drop this." She looked at me with disappointment in her eyes.

"Not all forms of abuse require concrete evidence to be proven true. What about emotional stress? Things he said to you, perhaps," I insisted. "You could say you really wanted the baby, et cetera. Make yourself sound innocent. The end result might not be as bad as a straight-up death sentence."

"I . . . never mind." She turned her body away, crossed her arms in front of her chest, and closed her eyes as if she were about to nap.

"What?"

"I'm not sure if they would believe me. I've had a legal abortion before."

After a notable shake in the middle of my chest, I felt a blockage inside my airways. Had she been promiscuous in the past? I didn't know what emotion was causing me to feel the way I did. It could have been anger, sadness, or a combination of both, though my conscious brain told me I had no right to feel those emotions.

"How come I didn't know about this?" I heard myself ask.

"Why would you know about this?" she asked, as any other sane person would. "It had nothing to do with you."

I didn't speak.

"See? We don't know everything about each other," she added.

"Let's go home and eat the food."

Chapter 15

She dumped the liquid inside the container into a pot on the stove. The broth had a thick texture, with pieces of red chili peppers floating on the surface. She swirled a spoon inside the pot to reveal what was hidden under the oil: a handful of mushrooms, bean sprouts, quail eggs, lotus roots, and two big pieces of yellow pumpkin. The tofu was soaked and had sunk to the very bottom. Due to the prolonged duration of being drenched in the soup, some had crumbled into much smaller pieces. The main portion consisted of many slices of fatty beef or lamb, I couldn't pinpoint which without tasting it.

"Is it better to microwave this, since boiling it again might overcook everything?" she asked.

"I'd say it's already overcooked. Just bring it to a soft boil and dish it out."

The amount of oil accelerated the cooking process. Within a couple of minutes, a spicy, aromatic steam rose from the pot.

I pulled out two salad forks and placed them next to the bowls. The new dish sitting in front of us looked nothing like the original. It was a spicy, undrinkable, oily soup stuffed with meat. I waited for her to dig in.

"I'm not getting the numbness on my tongue," she said.

"They're missing the peppercorn." I remembered that when I had it in the past, sometimes the numbing sensation was so strong that it left my mouth tingling for hours afterward.

She dabbed the oil off her lips and headed toward the sink. When my phone dinged, she dashed back immediately.

"Leah texted," I announced unwillingly. It could have been ignored, but for some reason, hiding the text felt wrong.

"See, I told you she likes you." Alicia rolled her eyes. She stole a glance at the long blocks of text messages.

"Here. You can read it." I pushed my phone to her. "I don't have anything to hide. You can have my passcode, too, if you want."

"I'm not trying to spy on you. And I don't want your pass—"

"One, one, two, five, one, six."

"Isn't that your birthday?" She seemed unimpressed by my lack of creativity.

"Read the text."

"Okay." She began reading in a high-pitched voice: "'Hey, Edward! Hope you enjoyed the hot pot. I specifically made sure not to include any Szechuan peppercorn, as my

parents said they're not good for older people like your
grandma. And thank you so much for meeting my parents;
they were very happy with me afterward. My dad was too
shy to bring this up to you in the moment, but they were
wondering if you'd be willing to write a recommendation
for my little brother next year? It's okay if you don't wanna
write it, they were just pressing me to ask you. Please let me
know! Thank you again! Have a good night! Tee-hee!'"

"Let me see that."

Everything she read out was accurate, except there was
no *tee-hee*.

"You have options," she commented coldly. "That's
one long text message right there, written like an email."

"Please stop. I do not like her. And she does not like
me!" I exhorted. "On top of that—" I brought my voice
down to a whisper. "One, she's way too young. Two, I can
get reported easily for cultural appropriation, even if I'm
not saying there's something going on between us. Three,
even if no one reports me, it's not like marriage is an
option, so why string some innocent person along when
there's no end goal?"

"See?" She gave me the middle finger. "You're already
thinking about marrying her?"

"I'm not—look, she's not living in my house. I don't
make food for her. I don't pick up her trash. I'm not
sleeping on the floor for her. She doesn't do anything with
me. There's no reason for you to be jealous."

"I'm not jealous. I'm just pointing out facts."

I went to bed with half a smile on my face that night.
Quitting my job suddenly became a rather enticing option.

I thought about what I could do after arriving in the UK. Many people I knew went into consulting. It was a viable option.

I heard her voice echoing from across the hallway, which disrupted my picturing myself working in a differently decorated office. I found my undershirt, pulled it over my head, and went to her. The room was pitch black. A positive of being sick was her sleep schedule returning closer to normal. At the very least, she was able to fall asleep before sunrise.

She was standing by the bed. I pressed the back of my hand against her neck. It felt colder than it had been in the past few days. I switched on one of the lamps on her nightstand. A gentle glow covered about half of the room, giving us both a very large shadow on the wall. "What's wrong?"

She didn't answer.

I retrieved the thermometer gun and scanned it over her forehead. "Ninety-eight point nine. You're not running a fever. Do you want a cough drop for your throat?"

"No. I just can't sleep."

"Okay?"

"Get in." She lifted a corner of the comforter and crawled in herself, expecting me to follow.

The fabric of our clothes rustled against the sheets until she settled in a comfortable position. I lay on my side, facing away from her. She hugged me from behind and draped one arm over my stomach. I felt her foot brushing against my calves. When she found a spot uncovered by my pants, she drew long strokes with her toes. The coldness made me shiver, but I managed to stay in the same place.

"You wanna link?" she asked.

I frowned, bothered—offended, even. She used a word that was more than casual, colder and more emotionless than all the more vulgar counterparts combined. It was a word only teenagers used. "No, I don't wanna *link*."

Her hand crawled from the bottom of my shirt up the middle of my chest. She pressed her palm against my skin.

My hesitation was received. She plopped onto her back. She looked at me playfully but spoke in a serious tone. "Why not?"

Crassness screamed easiness. Sex was far too accessible when I invited it toward me; emotional connections were not. With the way we were designed by nature, anyone was almost bound to be able to mate with anyone else. It was how humans and other animals survived and passed on their line of DNA. I had spent a considerable amount of time envisioning what it would be like when Alicia finally offered herself to me. In my mind, if I were ever to have a bond with her, it would transcend basic biological reflexes and reach a level of near spirituality.

From my late teens to my mid-twenties, I had gone to bed with far too many people I felt no desire to wake up next to. The only person I'd cared about other than my late wife was the first woman I had been with—the rest, I didn't quite remember. Her name was Gerdy. I had been almost nineteen at the time, and she was more than a few years older. In a way, she resembled a blue-eyed version of my mother. I didn't know whether it was more or less acceptable for me to be attracted to people who looked like my mother when we weren't related by blood.

Gerdy had told me about her ex-husband's fetish for women in different types of socks. He was a man with a rigorous skincare routine and a hairline that was too far pulled back on his forehead. Our relationship ended when I found out that her ex-husband wasn't her ex; he was just her husband at the time. I didn't care enough to fight for us. The man was a multilingual PhD professor with more than three passports. I was an infantryman at the time.

"If you feel fine, I'm going back to my office," I said.

"Whatever. No linking."

I was careful around her hair, which tickled my face. It smelled like the shampoo in the guest bathroom, along with a tint of natural human scent.

"I can't sleep," she murmured after a long pause. "It's still a little early."

"Try counting sheep."

"Do you really value boundaries, or are you intentionally trying to prove to someone how much you value boundaries?"

"I haven't looked into it too much." I changed the topic. "But I've heard about people going to California or Arizona to cross the border into Mexico."

She propped her body up. Her eyes gained a sudden alertness. "I told you, I'm not doing that."

"What else are you gonna do?" I turned to look at her. All that I could see was the shape of her facial features, a continuous line traced over her forehead, eyes, nose, and lips. "It'll be okay," I said, comforting her and myself at the same time.

"I know I'm freeloading here, but I have morals."

"What does that even mean?"

"It means I'm not trying to destroy anybody's life."

"I don't care."

"What is *wrong* with you?" She raised her voice.

"There's nothing wrong with me."

"You are creepy."

"I know you've been hurt by previous experiences, but I'm not Chris."

"I need you to seriously stop trash-talking other people at every opportunity available. It doesn't make you look any better in comparison. I thought you grew out of it." Her voice was trembling; I could feel her crying silently into the corner of the bed. Her shoulders heaved up and down. The reason behind her tears was arbitrary. Once again, I found myself unable to hold her accountable.

I lay on my back, putting my hands against the back of my head. "I wish I hadn't been kicked out of the Marines," I said.

The story was simple. I had failed to get into my dream school. Neither the second nor the third choice. I enlisted in the military at eighteen, in a field that Chris had not tainted, to avoid his relationship with Alicia and my parents, who had carelessly informed me that year that I was the result of an affair.

It was the best time of my life. The uniforms and shaved head concealed my guilt of familial privilege and the fact that I was a knockoff version of my brother. Tiredness washed away my thoughts of inadequacy and the thoughts of *her* nestling in Chris's arms. At the time, I wanted to get an education and eventually become a commissioned officer, only I was honorably discharged after a year. The reason was also simple: I had accidentally seen too much I shouldn't have seen, and heard too much I shouldn't have heard.

A loud sniffle escaped her throat through the clenched sheets, followed by a whimper. She turned over and slowly crawled her body onto mine. She cried into my neck, the softness of her breasts and stomach pressed tightly against me. I was thoroughly provoked, yet the thought of owning a heartless version of her felt so wrong, I couldn't do it in a time of distress. It wouldn't have been what I wanted.

I ran my fingers through her hair and gently patted her back. "We are gonna get to Mexico. It's gonna be fine."

"No." She sucked in a large amount of air as if she was about to choke on her own spit. "Please. Don't. Bring. This. Up. Again."

"I won't," I cooed at her. "I won't."

Chapter 16

I spent less than thirty minutes on the road before seeing the infamous fifty-five-plus community sign. Ben was someone who didn't enjoy sharing his private space with people from the younger generations. The security guard at the gate was nearly as skinny as Daria had been. She checked my ID without an ounce of enthusiasm, but she managed to put on a smile after I selected how much to tip her. The guardhouse must have been well heated, as her cropped uniform barely covered her breasts. It was essentially a small piece of black fabric with the word SECURITY printed in white.

After arriving at the neighborhood roads, I felt lost, like the last time I visited. All the houses were close in size and structure. The only slight variation was the colors of the roofs. Even so, there were only two choices: a light brown or a light maroon.

The car stopped itself in front of a house with a brown roof. It was close to the center of the community. An off-white ramp led to the front door. Before I found any doorbell to ring, Caroline had already opened the door for me. She was a mixed-race woman in her late fifties with tan skin and a pair of eyes too big for her face.

"We've been waiting for you!"

Caroline smiled and pointed me toward a set of wide marble stairs secured between brown railings. Ben's house was significantly smaller than my own, but it was far more thoughtfully decorated, with European-style faux leather furniture and Rococo paintings. I wondered if it was all that the couple could afford, especially given the amount of time they'd spent in the workforce. Had my father not passed, I wouldn't have come close to owning my current residence.

Once again, I was greeted by a heavy wooden door. Caroline skipped knocking and led me into Ben's study. He sat behind a big desk, which supported a trapezoid tray filled with various bite-sized desserts. Two white porcelain coffee cups embellished with golden floss sat in the middle of the desk. There was no computer monitor to be found, which made the desk look even bigger. The very tall ceiling held a round glass chandelier directly above him. Like his office at work, there was a considerable number of books standing on even bigger bookshelves. Instead of work-related tomes, they were the most well-known literary works in human history: Homer, Shakespeare, Hugo, Austen, Dickens, Tolstoy, Hemingway, the Brontë sisters, Twain . . .

It boggled my mind. Had Ben really read every book on the shelves, or were they just book covers purely for the purpose of decoration and elevating the owner's sense of taste? Many of them were high up on the shelf and only accessible by ladder. As far as I could see, from the way Ben walked after his stroke, he was not effective on ladders.

"Hey!" He waved at us. "Sorry! I figured you were going to come up soon anyway, so I didn't want to walk to the door and right back. Take a seat!"

"Let me know if you guys need a refill." Caroline turned around. She closed the door behind her.

Ben spoke with a warm smile on his face. "There's no need for you to be concerned. The room isn't bugged, and there are no recording devices anywhere. I swear on my life, everything you say stays with me. I won't tell anyone besides Caroline. But I can guarantee you she won't tell anyone either."

"Thank you. I appreciate it. Frankly, I don't know where to start—and I'm not sure I remember everything I told you last time."

"Don't worry, I have all day today. I'm not going into the office tomorrow. Are you?"

I shook my head. "I'm surprised I haven't received anything from my brother's lawyer yet."

Ben tore two packets of artificial sweetener into his cup and reached for the milk. "Feel free with the pastries. There's more downstairs."

I looked at the trapezoid tray again. The top shelves were the savory bites: smoked salmon, beef tartare, caviar on different crackers, and various dried meats. The bottom three layers were filled with brownies, mini cheesecakes, mousse, puddings, macarons, chocolate-covered strawberries, and a couple of items I failed to recognize.

"So, when are you leaving?" Ben asked after sending half a piece of brownie into his mouth. The stroke apparently hadn't been strong enough to weaken his love for what was poisonously unhealthy. I related to his struggle.

"I was honestly expecting you to warn me against that," I said wryly.

"Well . . ." He began chewing on the other half of the brownie. A few dark crumbs dropped onto his crimson T-shirt and went unnoticed. It reminded me of when my father ate anything that had the slightest chance of breaking apart. "As jaw-dropping as your speech sounded the other day, based on how much I know you, I'd say you're a very smart person. So you should naturally know what the 'right' thing to do is in your ex-sister-in-law's situation. It seems like you just don't wanna do it that way."

"There's two different 'right' things—one for me, one for her. The most logical plan to *me* is that she hires an attorney in the hopes they'll help her lighten her sentence as much as possible, I move her out of my house and into her own place, and I stay away from the situation as much as possible. The right thing for *her*, though, is to leave the US and get into a refugee program. Prison time destroys people—even if she evades the death sentence, we don't know how long she might serve. There would be no way for her to be fully reacclimatized into society after ten or twenty years. Even five years, or a single year, is undoable."

"See? You do know what the easy, safe route for yourself is. And it's obvious you don't wanna go down that path—if you wanted to do that, you would have done it way earlier!" Ben exclaimed. "Now, normally, I don't condone cheating the slightest bit. But at the very least, you didn't just knock someone up and leave them to die alone, and you're actually willing to put your own life in jeopardy, like how you did to hers. So, morally speaking, I'm leaning on giving you some necessary leeway."

Regardless of the situation, it wasn't his place to be judgmental.

"I'm not the father," I explained. "It has nothing to do with me."

His eyes widened. He mouthed, *What is wrong with . . .* in disbelief. "Then do you care to elaborate a little?"

"First of all, we met first—"

"Yeah, yeah, that's what they all say," he interjected. "Please excuse my crassness, but you realize your situation could sell big on sex fantasy websites, right?"

"I wish I could laugh about it. But it really isn't funny," I said. Still, I laughed. "There isn't too much to say. We met riding horses. My parents became friends with her dad. We went to high school together."

Ben swallowed a long piece of prosciutto. "And then what?"

"And then she asked my brother out."

"That's it?"

"That's it."

"Wait." He licked his mustache. "You're talking about the one who's running for Congress?"

"Yes. He's my only sibling."

Ben reached for his phone. He projected the screen

into the air for me to see. He squinted as he pulled up the search engine.

"Christian Franklin," I prompted him.

A confused look appeared on Ben's face. His eyes danced between the photo of Chris and me. It was the same reaction as everyone else who learned we were siblings for the first time. "You . . . kind of look alike . . ." he said.

"Same dad, different mom. He's better-looking than me, I'm aware."

"He worked for Blake Moore?"

"Let's not read his entire biography. He's basically great at everything except being a decent person."

"You haven't had anything yet. Are you not hungry?" Ben began working on the top section of the trapezoid. A small chunk of beef tartare fell off the cracker and onto the desk. He immediately picked it up with his fingers, reunited it with the rest of the beef ball, and then sent everything all together into his gaping mouth. He hummed with satisfaction. "No regrets on your end?"

"There's nothing I can do about it."

"Can I give you some advice, coming from an older person?" He leaned forward. His stomach pressed against the edge of the desk, giving it a harsh crease that didn't seem to cause him any discomfort. "I obviously don't know about your relationship with your sister-in-law. But this is what I would tell every couple if I could—don't allow your partner to do something you resent and later turn around to claim how tolerant you were."

"What does that mean?"

"It means don't sacrifice yourself and then turn around expecting something in return."

"I'm not looking for gratitude or reciprocation."

"Are you really looking forward to leaving us at Montgomery? I guess most people leave at some point, anyway, so it's not that big of a deal."

"You know I'm one of those who wanted to stay."

"It feels like I just met you yesterday. And now you're about to become a criminal. It's truly unfortunate. Everything is. Anyways, I'm just saying"—he dropped his voice sternly—"you are making a huge sacrifice. And let's say your relationship doesn't end up working out. You'll lose everything. How are you going to prevent yourself from blaming her?"

"I just won't," I retorted.

"It's one thing to have faith in yourself. But let's be realistic—it's human nature to blame others."

I was left with very little to defend my own standards of morality. In all fairness, even though I knew how I could never in a million years blame her, to an observer like Ben, my attitude, paired with the most drastic measures, made me look like someone who would be seeking large repayment in the future.

"How should I fight that nature?" I asked, paying close attention to the tone of my words, infusing them with politeness and sincerity.

"What if you don't have to . . ." He didn't finish his sentence. His eyes met mine. There was an obvious heaviness written on his face, yet the corners of his lips flickered upward into a barely noticeable grin. For a fleeting moment, he looked terrifying in my eyes.

"I can't." I shook my head slowly. "I don't wish death upon him."

"You said he hit her."

"Ben, please. I don't like my brother, but I can't listen to you plan his downfall."

"At the end of the day, *you* are innocent. *He* is not. If anyone should be punished, it's not you."

Chris was a parasite to society whose appetite grew bigger day by day, chewing away other people's much-needed livelihoods. The higher he climbed in the political world, the more damage he would be able to unleash. If he walked away free from the incident with Alicia, he would soon be destroying the next woman's life and sequentially destroying millions of other people's lives simply by existing. But Ben's words incited a protectiveness within me. As much as I wanted to criticize every aspect of Chris, I couldn't allow an outsider to do the same.

"No one is a mind reader," Ben said.

"I'm aware."

"You're assuming he wishes the worst upon her. What if he doesn't? What if he feels guilty?"

"You're suggesting I go beg him to take the punishment in her place."

He shrugged. "It's the power of persuasion."

"It won't work. He has no sense of empathy or shame. Narcissists will never admit to anything that might harm themselves."

"You don't know that," he insisted.

His earlier slandering of Chris had annoyed me considerably, yet his defense of him irritated me even more. "I grew up with him. I know him well enough."

"I'm sure you know him better than I do, of course. But sometimes people who are directly involved in a situation may not be able to see it completely. It's like a mind block. From an outsider's perspective, it's likely that an abuser would feel regret for being abusive, especially to a family member, and especially in a life-or-death situation."

"He didn't seem regretful at all the last time I saw him."

"He also didn't come after you for hitting him, so that shows something. You don't necessarily have to beg him— you just have to talk to him."

I looked at the man sitting in front of me. I wasn't sure I recognized him fully.

I envisioned a future where Chris was sitting behind a tall metal gate, like a classic scene from the movies. He would be wearing an orange jumpsuit, and his hands would wrap around two metal bars less than shoulder-width apart. I would keep Alicia in my house, hopefully free of tears.

Chapter 17

"Would you like to stay for dinner?" Ben asked as he hunted down another piece of brownie. "I don't want to be an inconvenience."

"You're not! I already ordered food. Does your sister-in-law want to join us too? What's her name again?" He projected his screen for the second time, searching for *Christian Franklin spouse.* "Alicia," he whispered to himself as he scrolled down the page. "Wait, isn't her dad—I've worked for him before."

"Yes. Everyone in her family kind of died off, though," I explained. "Chris has most of their businesses now."

"It still says they're married."

"It might take a while for everything to update. They're pretty private people."

I stepped out of the room and phoned her. When I returned, Ben had gained a number of cake crumbs on his shirt and mustache alike.

"You know, sometimes I don't understand you," he

said.

"Sometimes I don't understand myself."

"Regardless, I admire you helping others. You rarely see anyone helping other people nowadays. So, how are things going with her?" Ben cocked his head to the left.

"Good . . .?"

"Don't worry, I got you." A smirk appeared. He sighed. "I haven't done anything remotely this interesting in forever."

An hour later, Alicia arrived. We stood to walk downstairs. When Ben stood, whatever he had consumed dropped from his shirt onto his loafers, eventually merging with the carpet. The soles of our shoes pressed them in.

A savory scent occupied the kitchen and living room. Two piles of takeout trays sat on the dining table nearby, covered by layers of aluminum foil. Alicia was with Caroline. They each had a glass of orange juice in their hands. It was the first time I'd seen Alicia wearing makeup since her arrival on the front porch of my house. She was wearing a light brown sweater and a pair of flared jeans. Her hair had a few artificial curls in it. When I walked close by, she smelled of a woody scent. She was laughing with Caroline and conversing like any other well-centered adult. In a way, I was proud of her.

"Alicia," I said her name with unreasonable awkwardness. "This is Ben. Ben is my mentor from work."

"Friends. Edward and I are friends." He laughed from his belly.

"The food's been delivered for a while," Caroline interjected softly.

Ben walked to the table and began uncovering each dish. "Thought we'd do something basic tonight," he said.

With silver tongs, he grabbed a piece of steak, suspending it in the air as if to show off how perfectly cooked it was. The crust was golden brown and decorated with coarse black pepper, rosemary, and sea salt. From the gaps in the tissue, areas of pinkness peeked out from the center of the cut. The juices, mixed with a slight amount of blood, flowed back down into the container as he transferred the meat onto a plate. The side dishes were simple: roasted golden potatoes, sautéed mushrooms, coleslaw, green bean casserole, corn salad, and a big portion of steamed carrots, each with a plastic green stem on top.

"Plating is an art," he said to himself with energy and passion. "It really enhances the dining experience."

Alicia looked at me; her gaze hid laughter.

"Anyone have any ideas for drinks? Alicia?" Ben turned to her with a wide grin. A small piece of mint from his afternoon dessert was stuck on a premolar.

"Should we do a red wine to pair with the steak?"

"Sorry, we don't have any red in the house—it gives Caroline a headache. Why don't we do a Chardonnay? I've read in a cookbook that it's one of the rare exceptions of white wine that can go well with red meat," he said suavely.

"Sure."

"Would you like something sweet or dry? Ah, we'll have you try both, and you can decide. Let me know which one you'd prefer."

He brought out two glasses. She tasted both and pointed toward the one with the paler glow.

"Excellent choice!" Ben picked up the bottle with squinty eyes, reading from it with a fake European accent: "The Domaine Louis Moreau Chablis Grand Cru Les Clos des Hospices." All four of us sat near the head of the lengthy table. "Why don't we toast to Edward for the next big chapter in his career?"

I didn't think beforehand about how candid Ben was going to be. It seemed like he had taken on the personal responsibility of making something out of Alicia and me. She glared at me. I lowered my head and took a sip of the drink, quietly hoping for him to begin stuffing his mouth again like earlier.

"This is such a good, sweet, and perfectly oaked French Chardonnay!" he exclaimed. "Alicia, you have very good taste in wine! And in people!"

"Even I've heard about it! Edward is very popular at work," Caroline chimed in.

The truthfulness of her testament sounded highly questionable. The couple had both become animated; their gestures were big, their voices raised. When they weren't actively speaking, a smile lingered on their faces.

I felt heat flush on my cheeks. I tilted the wineglass to my lips again, hiding my desperate expression. The so-called sweetness Ben tasted was nowhere to be found. Was it something he'd eaten earlier that had coated his tongue? I wanted to whisper to Alicia that Ben didn't know what he was talking about, but she already knew that.

"Did you know Edward is one of the youngest partners at the firm?"

"I didn't." Alicia shook her head slightly.

"That's why it makes me so sad to see him leave. I mean, he has so much potential. Look at him. He isn't just smart—he has rare talent and a great work ethic. Everyone loves him."

As Ben spoke, I felt Alicia kicking me hard with the tip of her shoe under the table. I tried to silently signal him to drop the topic, but this time, he conveniently buried his face in the plate in front of him.

"It's so hard to find self-sacrificing men these days," Caroline said.

"Definitely!" Ben finally emerged. He wiped his glistening hands on a piece of napkin. While everything being served was meant to be eaten with utensils, he couldn't stop picking up whatever chunks dropped on the table with his fingers and sending them into his mouth.

"Don't we wish for more people to be like him? This is how people should be."

"Nothing is more important than family."

"Thank you . . ." I said.

"You have no idea what a lucky girl you are," Ben said 'discreetly' to Alicia at a volume everyone else could hear. She pursed her lips in visible discomfort. Ben responded quickly, by patting her shoulders like a parent to a child. "I'm incredibly sorry for your situation." He finally lowered his voice. "Really, everything is unfortunate. But know that you've got someone reliable now. And don't give up either. You never know if the real criminal could be going to prison."

"Even I want to move out of the country someday," Caroline said. "Everything is better."

"Edward told me you met at equestrian school. Do you love horses?"

"I do," Alicia answered. I felt another, much harsher kick under the table, sending pain into my ankle.

"I'm sure I'm easy to replace at work. Plus, you guys can still visit," I said.

"If I can fly, I will. I'm not sure I'll fit!" Ben laughed. "Don't be too upset about what's being left behind. If we had kids, I wouldn't want to raise them here, especially girls. We'd probably pack up and leave before they reached into people's bedrooms. It's a little too late for that. Are you two planning on having kids?"

I choked on the food.

"At least we have clean air. And the earth is melting slower than before." Caroline shrugged.

"Now Edward has to be the one breathing polluted air filled with floating particles in Mexico," Alicia said sarcastically.

"It's worth it," I said.

"That's what I like to hear!" Caroline nearly screamed. "Ben tells me all the time about how upright his character is."

"Yes, yes. I can attest to that." Ben put his hand on top of Caroline's. He looked at Alicia and me from the other side of the table. Caroline didn't seem to mind the grease on his hand at all.

Alicia had no expression written on her face. I wished for her to kick me again. But she didn't.

Chapter 18

After a full round of coffee, dessert, port, and then more port, Ben insisted on walking Alicia to the car. With his alcohol-impaired mobility, I wasn't sure who was walking whom. He opened the passenger door of my SUV, watched her climb in, and buckled her seat belt despite her objections. He then shut the door like a gentleman who'd been alive one hundred years earlier. Thankfully, Alicia didn't report him for his discriminatory behavior.

I commanded her car to drive back on its own. When I turned, I was greeted by a tight hug. He spoke to me with teary eyes and a stuffed nose. I watched him leave. His shoulders were hunched, and his neck protruded forward. In the night wind, he shuffled slowly in the direction of his front door.

When I entered the car, a purse was thrown harshly at my face. I blocked it. Its contents spilled onto the seats.

"I'm sorry. I can explain." I picked up the items and restuffed them into her bag.

"What is *wrong* with you!" She turned away to lean against the window, her gaze fixed on house after identical house on the road. I saw her holding back tears.

"What's wrong?" I asked.

She told me to go fuck myself in Mexico alone. From that point on, she refused to speak to me, no matter how hard I pressed for an answer. I followed her steps as she stormed up the stairs and into her bedroom. She grabbed my pillow and threw it across the hallway. It miraculously landed on the makeshift bed that hadn't been put away yet. The tears in her eyes were now replaced by a burning anger.

She told me to go fuck myself again.

"Stop," I said. "This isn't helpful."

"Do you have any idea what you just did?"

"I'm sorry Ben was intrusive."

"I've *told* you to drop it, and you turn around and tell a random guy at work about something that is not only private but also *illegal?*"

I suppressed my instinct to match my volume to hers. "First of all, Ben is not a random guy. I trust him. I know how he feels about things. Second of all, I'm sorry I didn't get your permission beforehand, but you never wanted to be productive. And I needed someone to talk to."

"Did you ever think about how that's not what I want? You have no idea how hard crossing the border might be. I don't want to risk everything just to end up barely alive on my own in South America with zero support."

"I never said you were going alone. I specifically said I'm going with you."

"That's right, so you can make me sit through an entire dinner with people who can't stop praising you left and right. You made me look like a complete gold digger!"

"What?"

"You know what I mean—someone who's using someone else, taking advantage of them!"

"Isn't that what you're trying to do?" I asked her.

She didn't answer. She sat on the very edge of the bed, tilting her head to look at me.

"It's all right if that's what you're trying to do," I added. "I don't mind. They don't mind either. They're just old people who probably have extremely boring lives. They're not trying to make you feel bad."

"I don't need them to tell me to feel bad. I already feel bad!"

"However you choose to feel is not a crisis, and I've told you there's no need for it. What other options have you got? Chris will never in a million years give up his life for yours. Your only other option is to spend however long in prison and get executed. I know Mexico isn't the best place to be, but it's right next to the US and the easiest country to get to. And we're not staying there forever. I can easily get a work visa in the UK or anywhere else. It's not completely horrible."

"So you decided to drop your entire career and everything else? Friends? Family? And basically everything you own?"

"Not everything. We can get some money out," I explained calmly.

"That's not the point!" she screamed at the top of her

lungs. "You have a perfectly good life here, as you've said yourself. And you tell everyone on earth you're giving it all up just for me?"

"I only told one person. Two, including Caroline. And I didn't even tell her, Ben did."

"I didn't tell you to get involved in this. You shouldn't have."

"What are my alternatives? Do nothing? Watch you die? That's not an option. Because that would hurt me way more than giving up my career and whatever I didn't even earn myself."

"What is *wrong* with you? Why does it matter to you?"

"Because I'm a decent person. I'm sorry if you haven't been around very many of them."

"So if your wife didn't croak on the street, you'd still drop everything to smuggle me out?"

"That's not the case. She isn't here with us. She's dead. And you know what else isn't completely horrible?"

"What?"

"Her being dead! I'm glad she died—I'm so happy she died. Because I don't have to take her into consideration anymore."

"You are truly sick. *I'm* better off dead than being here with you." She rose from the bed and rushed to her closet, emerging with the same blue duffel bag that showed up with her on the first night.

"Stop." I grabbed her wrist firmly, preventing her from reentering the closet to retrieve other items. "It's late. You're not going anywhere."

As someone who was aware of our difference in

strength, she didn't try to escape my control.

"You wanted this to happen." She spoke in a near whisper.

It was as if I were naked in front of her, and she was entirely clothed. I was ashamed to have my most private thoughts read out loud. I had no rebuttal. With every bit of worry I felt for her, there was a droplet of excitement mixed with gratitude. The thought had flashed through my brain multiple times when I was conscious. And when I was near the edge of losing myself, it made me happy. I had experienced pleasure many times when I thought of her as helpless, optionless. Her body and mind were so scarred that they desperately needed me to heal them. I often pictured her submitting to me, sitting on her knees with her skin entirely exposed. Her back wouldn't be exactly straight; I would be able to see the crease on her stomach. I dreamed of patting the top of her head where her hairline met her forehead, offering my use and protection.

In the real world, I stayed silent. I couldn't explain my way out of what she said because I felt sick of hearing my own thoughts. Had she been judging me the entire time? Did her judgment really hold any value? Should it have the authority to hold any value at all in the first place?

"Speak up! Defend yourself!" Her small fists landed on my chest weakly. "Do you like this opportunity now? Tell me!"

"I'm glad there are options in front of us," I answered honestly.

"You're crazy. You need help." Her voice was filled

with disgust.

"I don't need help. And I'm not crazy. You can't police my inner thoughts. Those are for me alone. And I was doing just fine before you interrupted my life. Did I ever bother you when you were happily married? Did I overstep in any area whatsoever? Even when you showed up at my house, did I ever do anything unwanted toward you? I can think whatever I want."

"You're not a rapist—what a big accomplishment! Do you want a medal of honor?" She laughed out loud.

"You know, if you really hate me so much and think I'm so hideous, then why are you here?" I cocked my head, waiting for an answer I already knew.

"So you're telling me to go?"

"I'm asking why you came here in the first place. If I'm such a bad person, you'd probably want to stay away from me, right? You came here on your own in the middle of the night. You kicked me out of my room to sleep across the hallway from you with the door open. You stripped naked under the covers after your divorce hearing, knowing I was sitting on your bed. You randomly got jealous over a literal kid for no reason. If you really think I'm the worst person on earth, you would never have been here in the first place. You're here because you knew I was going to help you. You *wanted* me to help you. And you're being nothing but pretentious by fake-refusing it."

"Did you hear what you just said? You haven't even done anything, and you're already accusing me of using you. I don't need you holding this over my head for the rest of eternity. According to those two, you have a long line of people waiting to get with you. And you chose to do me this huge favor instead because you're self-sacrificing and so much better than the rest of us. You probably haven't even considered the consequences because you're so eager to stand on this moral high ground."

I could tell she was trying to process the situation logically, but logic couldn't be applied in all circumstances. The loss was always terrible. Unfortunately, a feasible alternative didn't exist.

"I don't want you to feel like you owe me for this. I'm not trying to fish for any sort of gratitude. I'm not Chris—my goal isn't to do something for you and use it against you afterward."

"Seriously? You sit at home trash-talking other people twenty-four hours a day, seven days a week, nonstop. And, at the same time, you completely violate my privacy and my basic autonomy so you can be viewed as a saint by others. If I continue to say no, will you tie me up and drag me across the border?"

I looked away. I had no trouble envisioning a scene of her ankles and wrists fastened together by zip ties. The plan she proposed herself sounded surprisingly reasonable. I'd probably choose a softer fabric to avoid cutting into her skin too much. In case she screamed, it was better to stuff something like a washcloth or dish towel into her mouth.

"If you really cared about me, you would have asked me first before blabbing to the entire world about how I'm a criminal and you're a savior. If you really cared about me, you would respect my choice. The only reason you think you have the right to decide for me is because you constantly belittle me, and you don't think I can decide for myself."

"If you are so well-centered and you're so independent and don't need any help, then why did you let him hit you? Why didn't you do something about it when *he* first violated your boundaries?"

She stopped responding. I'd made her cry.

I wasn't shocked by the words that flew out of my mouth. I was no better than those who sat idly, blaming victims for their unfortunate situations. Ultimately, I had fully intended to take advantage of her vulnerable state.

"I need to go," she murmured.

"Where are you going?"

She shook her head. "I don't know."

"I'm sorry."

I begged her to forgive me as she cried. What seemed like a decade of dead air passed before she collected herself. She nudged me toward the door until I was shoved outside the frame entirely. I tried to apologize again. She shut the door in my face.

Chapter 19

Her lock clicked as a form of personal statement. I had control over all of them inside the house; if I wanted to, I could walk in at any time. I considered returning to the bedroom and demanding her forgiveness, but doing so would only prove her view of my character correct.

I had no say in what she chose to do with her life, but if someone were to engage in self-harm, it would be too irrational to stick to a principle rather than intervening.

I should have maintained an apologetic tone throughout. I didn't need to argue with her. Again, I became worried about her leaving. She had no residence; I didn't know where she could go. At the same time, where she might go was none of my business. I thought about sleeping by her door and leaning against it. If she were to leave the house in the middle of the night, I would fall backward into the room and hopefully wake up.

I knocked on her door and told her I would be in my office.

When I woke up in the morning, her door was wide open. She was gone at an hour when she was usually fast asleep. She'd been quiet enough not to wake me in the middle of the night.

It was a horrifying sight. The bed was neatly made. She was notoriously lazy; she never cleaned up after herself, and I didn't mind it. For the past few days, I'd secretly enjoyed looking at the unmade bed, a reminder of where both of us had rested with our bodies pressed against each other at night.

I went through her closet. Most of her belongings remained, with the exception of her phone, purse, and coat. Panicking, I quickly got dressed and rushed to the garage. Her car was long gone.

I opened the door to my own car. Habitually, I turned on the commanding system. Before the screen lit up, I realized I had no idea where to go. She had taken too little for someone who was moving away. Yet if she'd left for a random trip outside the house, she had no reason to tidy the room. It was as though she'd intentionally cleaned up after herself so the rest of the world wouldn't need to witness her personal mess. Perhaps it embarrassed her.

I called her phone. As expected, it went to her voicemail. I wanted to harass her until she told me she was all right. That would be, once again, inappropriate. I texted her once on every platform I could think of. None of my messages were read.

I swore at the steering wheel. Whatever she had said in a moment of anger, all I needed to do was listen and apologize again and again until she could hear me. I wouldn't have cared if she wanted to use me as a physical punching bag to let off her steam. After all, I was in the wrong. I'd violated her rights. I'd allowed Ben and Caroline to embarrass her. I'd arrogantly believed I knew best and could decide for her. I deserved to be damned, the worst fate I could think of. I wanted a distraction, a physical sensation of pain to numb its mental counterpart. Humans had a natural survival instinct. If the discomfort was strong enough, I couldn't devote any of my attention to anything on a mental level.

I changed my mind on the way to her and Chris's apartment, the one I had been to before. The two months I'd been given initially suddenly sounded like heaven. The urge to scream, cry, or succumb to anxiety clawed at me. Time was a luxury I couldn't afford.

The car parked itself under the building. It was more than twenty stories tall. The windows were pitch black from the outside, and each reflected a blinding amount of sunlight. Without having consumed a single drop of water or bite of food since the night before, my mind was engulfed in a daze. If her goal was to end her life, she could have done so one way or another by now. There was no point in waiting. I didn't want to be the straw that broke the camel's back.

I stood by the entrance, where I was denied entry. I had been removed from the guest list. After about ten minutes or so, a security woman came out and shooed me away from the property. I spotted the nearest building covered with scaffolding. I walked toward it, hoping to find a hole or a weak spot so a piece of concrete or tool could fall on my head, too. The concept was far more appealing than the fear of not knowing what had happened to Alicia. My mind danced between the sight of her coming back to me smiling and the worst-case scenario.

At the intersection, I blended in with the swarm of pedestrians hurrying to and from their destinations. A man riding on a motorcycle chose to break through the crowd at an alarming speed, coming from the opposite direction. The dirty velcro on his plastic helmet flapped against the wind. A compact yet powerful speaker was clipped to the bike's handle, blasting music for the enjoyment of the entire city. The lyrics of the song were funny, a combination of "eh ugh ey-ey-fuck-shit-ey-ey fuck-ey shit." An electronic beat was added to the mix; each wave of sound made an attempt to pop the eardrums of the people nearby.

The small tower under construction was barely over ten stories tall. No workers were found on the scaffolding; it might have been time for their breakfast break. The sidewalk on the right side of the building was blocked by a group of homeless people. They slept on the ground, on top of thick jackets and cardboard boxes. The sight was jarring. I took a few strides to the other side of the building. I copied the homeless people I had observed in my daily life, slowly sitting and leaning my back against the wall. With a few scratching noises, my long jacket was successfully dirtied by gravelly particles. This was step one. I tilted my head and examined the metal bars of the scaffolding. There was a slight crack on the wall nearby. The chances were slim, but perhaps the entire piece of concrete could fall off and bury me, thus releasing me from my misery.

I took out my phone and called Alicia again. By some miracle, she might bother to pick up—or a violent person walking by would grow interested in it, snatch it away, run a knife into my chest a few times.

Near the end of the block was a green trash can. A drunk man swayed toward it. His hair was long and greasy. His pants hung around his kneecaps, exposing his private parts. The hair in his pubic region looked glued together by some solid that had perhaps once been liquid. With one hand on the trash can, he squatted and began relieving himself. After he was done, he didn't bother to wipe. He pulled up his oversized pants and tied a knot around his hips, humming a tune through closed lips. A foul smell traveled through the chill air and into my nostrils.

The people walking by refused to bat an eye, not at all bothered by the scene. The only difference in their behavior was how each of them took a hand to pinch their nose and sped up slightly as they moved on. The drunk man stood idly with one hand on his crotch, watching cars drive by. Suddenly, his body jerked. He quickly took one hand to the ground. Without bending his knees, he picked up the fecal matter piece by piece and threw it in the trash can. When he was done, he ran his blackened, sticky fingers along its metal rim, cleaning off the residue.

After the drunk man was gone, another more focused homeless man showed up. He dove his upper body into the trash can, searching through the human feces for some sustenance. A few seconds later, he came up with two bamboo skewers, each with a bite of corn-dog breading left intact. He ran his teeth through them with great enthusiasm.

As I watched the man lick away the leftover flavor from the skewers, my body told me to return to the car, where the environment catered to my liking. I no longer desired physical discomfort as a means of alleviating my anxiety. Nothing had fallen on my head. Daria had been spared from the ugliness of this world because she was too perfect and thus unfit for its dirty reality. As for me, who had hurt the only person I cared about, I was bound to endure continuous suffering.

I phoned Chris inside my car in sheer embarrassment. To my surprise, he didn't lose his temper, nor did he laugh at my misery.

"Go home," he said. "I'll take care of it."

It was the first time I had experienced loneliness despite living on my own for nearly a whole year. The house was dark. A newly emptied place was frightening. Her dishes were cluttered in the sink; they lined the counter and sprawled across the coffee table in front of the TV. I suddenly noticed her hair, the most intrusive force of all, scattered in every nook and crevice. She'd never occupied her room fully, yet for the short duration of her stay, she'd managed to invade the entire house instead.

For a brief moment, I thought about letting it all go. It was now the perfect opportunity for me to manually erase her presence. I wanted to throw out her things and go back to owning the tranquility I had never wished to break in the first place. But I couldn't possibly adjust myself. The air indoors smelled of her, from the artificial fragrance of her products to her natural scent. I couldn't forget it.

I went to her usual spot on the couch and looked around. I picked up the loose hair strands one by one. They were too fragile and too soft for my fingers. Unlike my own, or even Daria's, which was equal in length, I couldn't ignore hers. Due to its darker pigmentation, it refused to blend in with the surfaces it fell onto. I twisted it into a brown spider and threw it across the floor. Since no one was watching, I climbed the stairs to her room. I plummeted onto her side of the bed, held her pillow to my chest, and wrapped the sheets around my body. In a way, I felt like I was wearing her.

I woke up with a sudden jolt. The sky outside had already turned dark. The room light was on.

When I pushed myself off the bed, I heard the noise of heels clicking against the floor in my direction.

"You're going to bed this early?" She was staring at me.

I exhaled. Sweat rose on my forehead as my body relaxed. "Why didn't you answer my calls?"

She shrugged and stayed silent.

My attitude was not that of an apologetic person. I sounded like I was scolding her. Then again, I should have been scolding her for intentionally consuming me with worry when she could have easily answered me.

"I'm sorry," I said.

"I know."

"Are you okay?"

She nodded. "Yeah. I'm tired. I got a pizza downstairs in case you're hungry."

"You got a pizza?"

"I was just driving around. I had to use the bathroom at a pizza place, and I didn't like the environment, so I came back. Chris said you were worried." She took a step closer and planted her face into me. Instead of hugging me, she turned slightly, pressing her ear against my sternum. I held her. As I rested my chin on the crown of her head, I cried. "It was my fault too," she said quietly. "I shouldn't have said those horrible things about you. You were so nice to me. I know you're not evil. I always knew." She sensed my agitated breathing and looked up at me. "What's wrong?"

I brushed my lips over her forehead. "You scared me."

"I know. Chris told me. I know it took you a lot to talk to him again, especially after what you did. At first, I was really upset, and I was mad at you. And then . . ." she paused. "And then I wanted you to be worried because your calls kept on coming."

I laughed and held her tighter.

Chapter 20

S he hadn't opened the large box of pizza on her way back. Later that night, we found it inedible. There was a cockroach lying belly-up on a piece of overcooked pepperoni. Fortunately, it had already been dead for a long time.

The next morning, I woke up early. She slept peacefully, flipped over on her stomach and snoring lightly. The comforter was draped over her upper body. Her pant legs were rolled up above her knees, leaving her legs and feet exposed. I sighed at her sloppiness. I hovered over her and gently pulled the comforter over her legs without her stirring. I tucked the covers underneath her snugly, leaving her no chance of wriggling out of it. I then proceeded to do the same with the covers around her shoulders. I felt satisfied for having saved her from catching another cold.

The local flower shop sold handwoven picnic baskets. There, I picked up a nicely wrapped bouquet of fifteen roses, eight red and seven yellow. The woman who owned the shop made three different shapes of wicker baskets. I chose a medium-sized rectangular one with rounded edges.

It had a secure lid, which covered the checkered cloth sewn onto the brim.

I returned to the house, left the flowers on the kitchen island, and began working on sandwiches.

Frantic stomping noises came down the stairs from the second floor. I looked up from the counter. She was standing in front of me with her bare feet against the kitchen tile, panting. Some of her otherwise obedient hair was stuck to her face with sweat. The other strands bluntly stood on the crown of her head. Her cheeks were red. The top two buttons on her shirt were undone, resulting in an inappropriately low V-cut neckline that ran down her chest. She stared at me in acute irritation.

I checked the clock. "You're up early. I was gonna come get you at nine," I said.

"I almost overheated and died!"

I quickly wiped my hands. I turned around and walked toward the fridge to take out a chilled bottle of water and hand it to her. She gulped it down. I could hear her swallowing. The condensation formed a thick layer of moisture on the outside of the bottle. A large droplet rolled down her jawline and charged for her neck at an alarming speed. I saw her flinching in discomfort. It eventually disappeared into her cleavage.

"I bought you flowers." I pointed at the bouquet on the counter.

"Thank you." A smile appeared on her face after counting the number of roses. "Why don't we put it in a— I assume you don't have any vases in the house, right?"

I scratched the back of my head. "We can put it in a

pitcher or a glass? It's equally pretty that way."

The entrance of the zoo was no longer relevant after its closing. Three years ago, the last public facility containing animals in the country was shut down in San Antonio, Texas. The Bronx Zoo in New York had been closed much prior to that. I remembered visiting often with her and a few other childhood friends. We always got upset when the older car's GPS system didn't guide us to the main gate on Southern Boulevard. Today, the eye-catching sign with golden letters and blue animal patterns had been struck down. Still, the much newer car somehow knew to take us to the correct entrance, even though I never specified the parking spot when I made the command.

She carried the basket containing two sandwiches, two small cartons of orange juice, two Lunchables, and one cooling pack.

The pathway into the zoo itself was still clear, with only a few branches and twigs blocking the way. The small, once-manicured forest, which provided visitors with shade, had grown into a wild dance among different vegetation. More than half of the trees were starting to become barren. Gold-and-red leaves weaved themselves into a carpet covering the ground. When we walked forward, quiet yet crispy noises broke out underneath our feet.

We took a left and headed toward the children's petting zoo. When everything was still running, people could hear the exotic birds chirping from the three aviary enclosures nearby. It used to be too lively or crowded. Today, the silence was eerie.

"We're safe to be in here, right?" she asked.

"Yeah. Trust me," I said. I looked up at the deep blue sky. The sun was directly above our heads.

"I wanna see if the dinosaurs are still standing." She took a few quick steps forward, scanning beyond the concrete building covered by various plants.

"You mean the super fake animatronics that required additional tickets?"

"Some of them weren't that bad," she objected. "Look! The two T-Rexes!"

I followed the direction she was pointing toward. There were two big, fake, leather-looking dinosaurs hiding behind the leaves. The lack of maintenance over the years had dulled their colors to an unfitting pastel tone.

"Eddie, look!" She pulled on the sleeve of my jacket, alerting me to a new finding in the distance. "Someone put a whole iceberg lettuce in the mouth of the sauropod," she yelled. "It hasn't rotted yet."

"I wonder how they got it up there."

We advanced toward the seal's performance pool. The water had been drained, and the tiles were covered by dried mud. Some of the cracks in between each tile had widened, threatening to take down the structure of the entire pool. I remembered the way the seals swam back and forth at an alarming speed. Their bodies had looked like elongated ovals when their fins were tucked underneath them. When they reached the end of the pool, they flipped and turned with a fluidity impossible even for the best human swimmer.

She smiled. Once again, she grabbed the end of my sleeve and pulled me to the Grizzly Corner. She loved the harmless appearance of the bears. Despite their genetics, they were one of the most dangerous animals to encounter in the wild, which brought my thoughts to a brighter perspective: they were no longer a threat now.

I pretended to hide behind her for her amusement. We passed a number of herbivore enclosures completely barren of weeds or grass. The ground had a yellow sand-like texture. Some of the metal bars had been broken by force. Others were missing from the fence as a whole. I didn't dare to look any closer.

She spotted a dirt-covered picnic table. It wasn't the best place to sit down and eat a meal. In the bears' hills and caves, larger rocks had fallen due to the lack of maintenance and shattered into pieces.

As my own stomach tightened, she showed no fear in looking directly into the exhibit. Certain parts of the zoo were no longer to be looked at. They were neither a part of nature nor something regulated and made safe by humans.

"It's not the same anymore, isn't it?"

"Nothing is the same anymore." I sighed. "Let's just go."

She shook her head. I stood next to her. I saw her studying the bones.

Two skeletons of a large, doglike, predatory animal lay on the ground. Their skulls were pointy, and their spines were long. Each piece of bone was clearly distinguishable. Unlike the fossil pieces shown on TV, these skeletons were complete and, for some reason, well preserved. The larger one had a metal chain around a piece of neck bone, which connected to a tall in-ground pole. The smaller one roamed free yet was still confined inside the tall walls of the enclosure.

It was the way most predatory animals died, slow and torturous, with no way of fighting to save themselves since they were costly to maintain. For those that didn't get traded to other countries in time, there was no way to keep them alive under zero incoming revenue.

"It's not pretty," she said calmly.

I desperately wanted to protect her from the sight, yet she desperately wanted to see it for herself.

"It's understandable. No one was allowed to work here anymore. Who was supposed to feed them? Plus, no visitors, no budget to purchase meat."

She looked into the pit thoughtfully. "You know, they weren't closed for humanitarian reasons. They were closed for random reasons. When animals are useless and no longer profitable, they get starved. Same with people."

The question flew by in my head. She had wanted to see it of her own will. Yet when she was upset by the scene, I couldn't help but make it my sole responsibility to comfort her.

I dragged her away from it. With every reluctant step she took, she turned her head and went back to the enclosure.

When we were merely a few feet away, she stood her ground and suddenly broke into a series of sobs into the palms of her hands. "I'm useless."

"You are not," I said sternly.

"You hate it when I cry," she protested in a whisper against herself.

"I don't. I'd rather have you cry a thousand times per day with me than go through this by yourself."

"I don't know what to do."

"Take a break as long as you need to. It's going to be okay."

In the direction of the exit was a short flight of cobblestone stairs, which led to a semi-underground dent where the lions had lived behind tempered glass. Weeds and grass grew rampant, filling the entire viewing area. It was unoccupied except for a full set of lion bones lying right next to the glass. I wondered if, in the last few moments of its life, it had tried to claw its way out. The jaw of the skull was slightly parted, making the four keen-edged canines striking. I recognized the dental structure of lions. My mother had held an interest in them, while my father had hated them for their killing of the cubs and the banishment of young males. My mother had been a fan of Scar from *The Lion King*; my father had believed in Mufasa's reign and legacy. Simba couldn't possibly have been the dominant male of the pride. It would have been incestuous for him to mate within the pride he grew up in.

"Do you think they ate each other before they ran out of food?" she asked.

"It happens. The people could have done better. This was completely avoidable."

I remembered when equestrian labor first became illegal, thousands of horses throughout the country walked into a box to be electrocuted. At least they'd had a swift end to it, unlike the zoo animals who had slowly withered away in a confined space. If they had been let outside, many of them might have had a fighting chance. The working canines had a slightly luckier fate, as more people were willing to adopt them as pets. Horses were another matter.

We didn't go near the nature trek. The further we walked toward the Asia Gate, the more items we saw from other humans: soiled jackets, broken tents, and leftover wrappers of various snacks. The foliage rustled as if something was hiding inside. We retreated onto the path we'd initially come by.

Neither of us had any appetite left. The car set itself on the way back to the house with the basket still full of food.

She jumped suddenly when we took the ramp onto I-95. "I should have thrown my bloody ring in the seal pool!" She took a look at her left hand, still wearing the wedding band that no longer had any authority. The large pear-shaped glass was meticulously set on a platinum ring and decorated with numerous smaller diamonds around it. Together, the jewelry was blinding. "How long did you wear yours for?"

"Six months, I think? Six months afterward."

"Where is it now?"

"Jewelry box upstairs," I said. "If you're going to throw it away regardless, I'd rather you not do it at the zoo. I suggest the trash or toilet."

"Why?"

"Because you had happy memories there."

"They're traumatic memories now!" she protested. "Chris never liked going to the zoo with us anyway. He hated the regular kid stuff—the definition of abnormality, now that I think about it. Here." She offered her hand to me, gesturing for me to pull off the ring. "Throw it away wherever. Don't let me see it again."

I wriggled it off her finger. It was heavier than I thought it would be. I held it in my palm for a moment, soaking in its warmth before putting it in a small compartment of my backpack.

"I have something that might cheer you up at home," I said.

"What is it?"

"It's a surprise."

Back at the house, she stared at the cardboard box waiting for us on the front porch. It was almost half her height. The weight of it was surprisingly light. As I picked it up by the external handles, wood clattered inside.

"What is this?"

"Give me an hour max," I said in a hurry. "Go hang out in your room."

"I wanna put it together with you."

"I'll call for you when it's ready." I shooed her away.

"This better be good!" she yelled from the stairs.

At the very bottom of the box, I found a pamphlet of instructions printed in five different languages except for English. After an hour and a half, I presented her with a rectangular object in the living room.

I had covered it with a tablecloth. She approached it with caution, tilting her body in different directions, trying to get a peek of the surprise underneath the corners.

"Go ahead. Uncover it."

She picked up the blanket with two fingers. It was a chestnut-colored rocking horse with fake eyes, ears, and a short mane made of yarn. She gasped at the size of it. "It's so big! Where did you find this?"

"Well, I was able to get it in adult size through a rather questionable website." I laughed with crimson cheeks. "You said you wanted to go on a trail ride the other day. This is the closest thing to a real horse that I could find."

"You didn't have to!" She looked at me with puppy eyes. "Would I break it?"

"You don't trust my building skills?"

She hopped onto the horse, rocking back and forth. "This is too silly! I'm way too old for this," she said, catching her breath. "I think he does kind of look like Rashad. Their colors are similar."

"Well. I'm glad."

I nudged her off the horse and hopped on myself for a minute. She laughed nonsensically. She put her hands on the sides of her waist as tears of mirth appeared around her eyes. "Thank you."

"You know you can—"

"Still ride real horses in Mexico, right?" she finished the sentence for me.

"That's not what I was trying to say." I shook my head. "I was gonna say you can paint a saddle on him if you wanted to. Would you like wooden Rashad to be delivered to your room?"

"Later." She looked back at me. "Thank you for doing this."

"You're welcome."

Chapter 21

The premise of the claw machine was straightforward: the player targeted a prize within the machine by maneuvering a joystick. When the timer ran out, the claw would descend automatically, hopefully bringing up a prize on its way up.

Alicia harbored an ambitious aspiration of conquering it one day.

The mall nearby housed an arcade on the top floor. Throughout the majority of the day, she remained enthusiastic. We watched numerous tutorials on how to win prizes. The most commonly offered advice sounded counterintuitive: closing your eyes while aiming, then hoping and praying for something to come up. She called it nonsense and proceeded to brag about her first successful attempt at the machine, when she had managed to grab a stuffed animal in under five tries. However, the crucial difference was that it had been a nonprofit machine at a birthday party. If claw machines were easy to beat, they would have faced extinction long ago.

Fifteen minutes before the venue's opening, a long line had already formed outside the glass door. People of different ages waited eagerly for security to check their identification.

She shot me a worried look as we joined the back of the line behind two teenagers who wore their backpacks in front of their chests.

"I'll fight them off if they want to take your place at the machine," I whispered in her ear.

"It's not that," she said urgently. Her eyes lingered on the crowd in front of us. "Do you know anyone here? What if we run into someone you know? What if we run into someone I know?"

No one I knew was interested in a place this chaotic. The slight sense of unease brought by her words quickly dissipated. "We're not thieves. Why should we worry?"

I squeezed her hand hiding inside her coat pocket.

The line of people slowly oozed into the arcade when the door finally opened. We were greeted by loud music blasting from the ceiling speakers. The neon-colored machines formed a clear contrast with the low lighting and black, shiny tiles. We walked through rows of stationary motorcycles and race cars that made screeching sound effects capable of deafening someone. Rowdy children screamed and chased each other, running around in circles. We promptly stepped aside, afraid of accidentally running into them.

The list of items projected at the token kiosk had unreasonably high numbers. We studied the different packages. It was one hundred and fifty dollars for eight hundred tokens. The claw machines took one hundred and sixty tokens to play once. Five tries. I sighed.

"I assume you wanna play other games too. So why don't we do the eight hundred tokens ten times? That leaves us with basically fifty tries with the claw machine, or we can use it on other things too."

"I don't think they're *all* allowed to be scams. These have existed for decades—if no one ever got anything from them, they would have gone out of production a long time ago. Think about it. Why do people keep coming back for these?" she asked.

"Because people like to think they're luckier and more special than others?"

She shrugged at my honesty.

Apart from the two completely empty machines, the majority housed medium-to-large-sized plush animals that required two hands to hold. Her attention settled on a machine brimming with plush seals in pastel colors. The seals' bodies were elongated ovals, making even the slimmest part appear too bulky for the claws to grab. Chances were the already-weakened claws would slip right off once they made contact with the animal.

"This looks physically impossible," I said.

"I know. But they're the best-looking ones."

"Why don't we try these?"

There was another machine on our right. It had a thin layer of slightly smaller llamas scattered on the bottom. The online tutorials suggested that people should go for firm objects with lots of edges. The llamas' bodies were much more angular in comparison to the seals. In addition, they had a big rectangular head, a lengthy neck, and a square body. Their low number indicated that people had already taken some of them out of the machine. Unfortunately, they did have a funny expression on their face with black buttons for their eyes and a plastic X for their mouths.

"Edward," she said. "Those are beyond ugly. Their fur is uneven. And the color looks toxic."

They were neon blue and red. I agreed in silence. A different pricing sticker stood out on the machine. They cost only one hundred and fifty-nine tokens, which was one token less than their non-discounted counterparts.

"They cost less because they're ugly and no one wants them. Even if I caught one, I wouldn't be happy." She pulled me to a halt in front of a small mountain of robot plush toys. They were regularly priced. To my untrained eyes, they looked significantly more well-designed than the llamas. They were an old-fashioned concept of what a robot should look like: a big head with buttons for eyes, stubby antennas, and a small body with arms and legs.

"These look cute. As a compromise . . ." Her eyes began to light up slowly. "What do you think?"

"The size is good for the claw. The head has edges, and so does the body. I think it's worth giving it a try."

"But I'm asking if you think they look good."

"Of course. Anything you think looks good looks good to me."

It felt like an hour had passed. We were still standing in front of the machine, empty-handed. We tried every tip and trick we'd learned, in addition to inventing new ones on the spot. The machine had a timer of thirty seconds, which was more than enough to aim for an easy-to-grab angle. Unfortunately, the claw itself was extremely weak. Each time it made good contact with the robot, it immediately slipped and magically lost all strength once hanging in the air, dropping the robot back into the pile.

Alicia shifted her stance and covered her yawn with her palm. She commanded me to keep trying in her place, then wandered off to play other games. I was left alone. I moved the joystick randomly and then slammed the CATCH button. An arcade employee strolled by with headphones in his ears. He was humming a lighthearted tune. He witnessed the claw picking up a robot and promptly letting go of it in the air.

"Aw, what a miss!" he sighed with unparalleled energy.

"Do you have any tips for this machine?" I had the urge to ask him to open up the back of the machine so I could get one and pretend like I'd caught it while Alicia was away.

"Nah." The employee shook his head. "You just gotta work on your aim! Really work on it. If you keep trying, maybe next time you'll get something!" He gave me a finger bang and walked off, presumably to check on the other players. Before he approached a hoop-hopping game, he turned around and yelled at me again, "Really, work on it!"

Alicia came back with dismay written on her face.

"Did you not find anything fun?"

"The basketballs were all stuck in the hoops. The ones that were working had a line of kids waiting. The jump rope only lets you jump once for every swipe. Whack-a-mole was missing the hammer. I wanted to throw the rings, but the rings were all gone. I asked an employee, and they said they couldn't do anything about it. And air hockey takes two people to play. I did do the race car, but I didn't like it particularly. I just kept on hitting things on the road. You have any luck with the claw?"

I shrugged. "You wanna try one last time?" I asked, stepping away, allowing her to take over.

She closed her eyes and bopped her head a few times, feeling the beat of the background music. She pushed the joystick around with her eyes still shut, then tapped the button. The claw was off and was about to miss the robot right underneath, but as the grip weakly tightened on itself, the body of another robot was caught. As the claw raised, one of them was dropped in midair, but the other made it right on top of the dropbox.

She screamed as she witnessed her non-effort paying off.

"It worked! I caught one! I actually caught one!"

I watched her jump up and down like a little kid. I hadn't felt such happiness in a long time. She then demanded photos with the plush robot in her arms.

Even with two players, the air hockey table refused to turn on. We asked another employee to retrieve the basketball stuck in the hoops. He was reluctant. He told us he was going to retrieve the stick first. It took him nearly twenty minutes. When we finally had the ball in our hands, the rubber felt soft and spongy. The lack of air made it nearly impossible to shoot.

In the dining area, we sat at the high-top table. Our eyes scanned the people playing and sequentially giving up on the different games. While Alicia licked an overpriced ice cream cone, I sat the plush robot on the table, showing it off to the rest of the visitors. A few kids pointed at us, then nagged their parents quietly.

A young couple in their late teens argued in the food line. The topic was us. I saw the boy wearing a black First Robotics team hoodie. He was tall and skinny. The girl wore drastically long lashes and heavy eye makeup. A glittering powder covered the bridge of her nose.

"I'm sorry, but we already spent nearly a hundred dollars' worth of tokens. They're scams."

"If they're scams, then how did they get it?" the girl raised her voice, then covered her mouth in embarrassment.

Alicia ate half the cone and gave it up to me. One drop dripped over and stuck to the side of the cone.

When we looked for the exit, we saw the young man from earlier again. He stood in front of the claw machine, contemplating and drawing different patterns in the air with his fingers.

"Excuse me, people," he said timidly as he waved us down.

He looked to be in his late teens. Judging by the fact that he'd spoken to legal adults first, it was highly plausible that he was over eighteen years old. However, there was no way to be certain. One misstep could cause a slew of heavy consequences. He had big eyes and a sincere expression. If he had dressed more maturely, choosing to converse with him might have been an easier decision to make. The FRC T-shirt he wore over his long-sleeved undershirt exposed his high school studenthood, or he could have been a college mentor with a young face.

Alicia hesitated. She turned to look at me and then turned back to smile at the boy. "Uh . . ."

I scanned the boy from head to toe, unable to open my mouth.

"I turned eighteen last month." The boy frantically searched for his wallet in his sweatpants pocket. He brought out a state-issued driving license, which clearly stated his birthday.

"Oh! I'm sorry!" Alicia said.

"My preferred name is Richard. My preferred pronouns are *he*, *him*, and *his*. I'm a sixth-generation immigrant. I'm an ally and an advocate in multiple other underprivileged communities as well. Is it okay if I ask you people how you got the plush toy?"

"We tried for over an hour. It's mostly about luck. This is going to sound stupid, but have you tried closing your eyes and doing it?"

The boy's cheeks slowly turned red. "My friend and I are in robotics together. It's our last year. We lost in the Texas regional. She really wanted to go to the world competition. But we couldn't—our team was great, but our teammate was too slow. And . . . I saw the plush toy in the machine. It looks—"

"I know about FRC," I said. "Did you compete with team 9931, the Techno Penguins, by any chance?"

"Yeah. We did. They were our teammates who were too

slow."

I chuckled internally. "I used to mentor them until last year. I did nontech."

"Oh, I'm so sorry! Anyway, this plush toy kind of looks like our team's logo. My friend really wanted it, but we're running out of tokens." He looked at Alicia with pleading eyes. "You don't have to if you don't want to, but, um, I can give you the rest of our tokens if you can—"

"Take it." She pushed the robot in front of the boy. "Just say you got lucky with the machine."

The boy's face lit up instantly. We waved him goodbye as Alicia pulled me away.

Chapter 22

We were watching TV together on the couch. She wore a pair of fuzzy socks, brown leopard print.

The breakfast on the counter gradually grew cold as the morning turned into the afternoon. It was a combination of her favorites: blueberry pancakes with maple syrup, sunny-side up eggs, and a pitcher of grapefruit juice. The once-sizzling sausage links now sat, soggy and greasy, on an oversized plate. I wondered why excessive oil on hot foods made them more appetizing, yet as soon as the temperature cooled, the oil became thick and gag-inducing.

"Did you ever want kids?" she asked. She scooted upward slightly, putting her head on my shoulder.

"With Daria?"

"With anybody."

"I'd be responsible for all of the misery they could possibly encounter. I'm not sure if I could handle the guilt."

She turned away to look over the kitchen counter,

pointing at the food. "I'm hungry."

As she tiptoed away, my phone began ringing. It was hiding somewhere out of sight at the moment; the call was dropped, yet the caller was persistent. It began ringing for the second time right after. The volume was seemingly louder.

"Just ignore it."

"I can't. It's probably Meemaw. She's the only one who would call multiple times in a row."

I picked up the call and put it on speaker. Alicia went silent.

"Hey, Eddie!" Meemaw screamed. "Are you home? I'm about five minutes away! Just wanted to give you a heads up before I get there. Hope you haven't had dinner yet."

"Ugh. Yeah, I am—I'm in the middle of something, though. If I don't open the door for you immediately, can you wait a little bit in the car?"

"Oh, honey! You know I can't wait." Meemaw hung up the call.

Alicia's eyes widened. "You're going to let her in?"

"Fight or flight?" I asked her.

"Flight. Other people, I'm not sure. Meemaw? Definitely flight." She grabbed a paper towel and wiped her fingers. "My things—"

"Don't worry about it. Go into my office and lock the door. There are snacks in the mini fridge if you get dizzy. She always speeds."

I frantically looked for every item of hers—a jacket here and a hair tie there, some of her shoes and socks downstairs. I threw all of her clothes in the laundry room and shut the door.

The monitor had not yet alerted me, so I took a few seconds to text Alicia. I reminded her to stay completely quiet and assured her that I would come to find her as soon as Meemaw left. She came at me with a slew of questions. As I was typing up my explanations, I heard the sound of a loud car pulling up my driveway. I shoved my phone into my back pocket.

Meemaw closed the car door with a bang. I walked out of the house to greet her. Her medium-sized SUV from 2008 was parked in a surprisingly straight line. She'd only used one side of the slope, leaving ample room for another vehicle to pull out. She was standing outside the passenger door. Half of her body reached into the car's beat-up frame, her buttocks flung high in the air. With her jeans hanging extra low under her free-falling stomach, the top seam of her underwear waved to the rest of the world.

As usual, I looked away awkwardly. I waited to hug her until after her ordeal of getting things and herself out of the car was over.

I took the bags of food from her hands. They felt heavier than they looked, even for their abnormally large size.

She stomped her way inside and began looking around immediately. "Your house is still so sterile! What happened to my decoration ideas for you?"

She hadn't changed since I last saw her two months ago. Her hair was completely gray. Her powderless face was full of fine lines and wrinkles. However, her energy level remained unbelievably high for someone in their nineties.

According to her, she was a self-reliant woman. She lived alone in an apartment in the city and drove her way down south to visit old friends on a regular basis. Despite everyone's constant reminders for her to upgrade to a self-driving car, she could not let go of her Cadillac, which was older than me.

"I think you're getting skinny!" She squeezed my arm with force. Her bitten nails dug into my skin.

"I'm not." I shook my head.

"I just wanted to make sure you have something to eat and stay real safe. Look at you—you barely touched any of your breakfast, and did you skip lunch too? Skipping meals is not a good habit. Chris never listens to me, but you used to." She hovered over the breakfast, which was way too much for one person but was normal according to Meemaw's standards.

"I was called into an emergency meeting regarding a client."

"You have to eat on time! I got you some meat—" Her voice was halted by a loud crack from the floor.

I rushed over. She slowly lifted her right foot up. What used to be a pearl earring decorated with golden flowers was stuck under her cowgirl boot, crushed into many different pieces. A tiny amount of powder was scattered nearby.

I internally slapped myself for not having cleaned it up. The other earring was probably lying around elsewhere.

Meemaw bent over and picked it up before I could get there.

"Are you finally seeing someone, honey?" Her blue eyes

brightened. She was unable to hide the excitement in her voice.

"Actually, yeah," I answered.

"What is her name?"

"Scar."

"Scar . . .? Like the cartoon lion, or . . .?"

"It's just a forward-thinking name." I stared back at her and bit my bottom lip, suppressing a laugh.

"You mean she goes by Scar, right? It's not what's written on the birth certificate?"

"I don't think so," I said calmly.

"Oh, I'm so happy for you, honey! It's been way too long since Daria passed, bless her heart. Back in my days, men mourned for a week at most. You are such a loyal kid! So, how is this one? How old is she? Can she cook well? Does she have an ex-husband? Is she a single mom? I'm telling you, you have to stay away from those. They always bring you trouble. You are so much better than that."

"She's not a single mom," I said.

"How much money does she make? I'm telling you, you don't want to have any mooches in your life. Women today have no work ethic. Are you sure she's not trying to use you? If she ever shows any signs, you let me know, I'll box her off anytime . . ."

Meemaw continued to speak, laughing several times at her own jokes as I began moving the breakfast things off the table and into the sink. I was extra heavy-handed with the plates and bowls. The clunking noises drowned out her words.

She'd brought mac and cheese, mashed potatoes soaked

in gravy, fried chicken, meatloaf in red sauce, pasta, creamed corn, green bean casserole, and two whole pecan pies.

"I've been driving for a whole hour, honey. I hope you don't mind making an early dinner. The good thing about an early dinner is that you can always have a late-night snack if you get hungry." She dug her finger into the meatloaf, sapped up some sauce, and then licked her finger clean.

I thought it might be a better idea to put everything we wanted onto separate plates and heat them up individually, but Meemaw never cared about the temperature as much as the quantity. I needed to comply as much as I could endure in order to be rid of her. The best way to make her happy was to stuff my face. Her manners might have been impudent, but I knew her actions came from a good place. At the very least, she wished the best for me and Chris, in her own way.

She sat at the head of the table. I handed her a fork and knife and watched her dig into the mashed potatoes. According to her portion sizes, there would be no need to preserve the leftovers for more than a day. Everything would be finished before then.

I worked on the green bean casserole. At first, it was flavorful, but after the initial contact with my tongue, it tasted entirely of butter and salt. Her cooking had always been rich. The potent seasonings fought against each other to become the main character when they should have been the raw ingredient in the first place.

I ate as if I had gone back to the chow hall.

"So, honey, this new girlfriend of yours—do you have a picture to show me?" Meemaw said as she wiped her mouth against the back of her wrist.

Unless I wanted her to start wreaking havoc, making phone calls and breaking furniture, I couldn't show her a picture of Alicia. Knowing her, she was probably trying to find out "Scar's" ethnicity in a discreet way.

My father's side of the family was filled with true racists. Meemaw's behaviors and thought processes were not only publicly unacceptable, but they were also fundamentally filled with prejudice and tribalism that were intentionally malicious. She claimed she was too old for change. The claim had been effective since I was old enough to remember.

"It's still a new thing," I said.

"Well, what does she look like?" She raised her eyebrows.

"What do you mean, what does she look like? I'm sure you'll like her when I eventually bring her to meet you. I think she's really pretty." I chuckled at avoiding the topic that itched her heart.

"Um . . . does she look at all like Daria, bless her heart?"

"No."

"Well, uh, how is her hair?"

"Long."

"What color is it? Is it brown? Black? Blonde? Hazel? Curly or straight?"

"Oh, I think it's on the darker side of brown."

"And her eyes?" she followed up fervently.

173

"Brown," I said slowly. I could feel the desperation in her mind. Though she'd been born in a different era, she had learned to somewhat adhere to how other people acted in public—the key word being *in public*.

She swallowed hard, her lips pressed together in a tight line that moved in all sorts of directions. The dire question of race was about to jump out of her throat at any moment.

"Wh-what about her—"

"She's white."

"Is she mixed?"

"No."

"Oh, honey, I just want to see you with someone you're happy with. It really doesn't matter what they look like. You know, none of that superficial stuff matters. I've always hated people who are superficial. Beauty is all in the eye of the beholder. I was just trying to . . . get a better picture." She spoke quickly, and her tone became more relaxed with each word. "You know, unlike some folks who can only see color everywhere they go, I do not have a single racist bone in my body! I'm all for interracial relationships. As long as you have the same upbringing and principles, I'm fine with everything. But sometimes people of different backgrounds have very different upbringings—it's not exactly their fault, but for example, light-skinned folks tend to act a certain way, and dark-skinned folks tend to—"

"Meemaw," I cut her off. Her justifications in her deep Southern twang about how she was not racist only made her seem more racist in the end.

"I'm just saying, honey. Back in my day, and where I'm

from, people aren't so focused on this politically correct nonsense. We had observations, and we talked about it. Nothing I think in my head has an ounce of racism in it. For example, Black folks back in Alabama loved the idea of reliance—white folks didn't. Times can be equally hard on both groups, but we white folks worked and didn't want to rely on the government. And those Black folks, they loved to—"

"Meemaw, please, you have to stop!"

She shut her mouth but gave me a hateful look.

"We all know you grew up in a different time, but you know how time progresses and standards change? Maybe what you just said wasn't considered racist for the time period that you grew up in. But right now, it's different. You really can't say those things because they are . . . stereotypical in an inaccurate way. And it's just wrong."

"When you get to my age, you'll understand."

I kept quiet.

"You know, honey, I only want the best for you."

I plastered half a smile on my face and decided to let her be.

"Maybe I got a point on something. Did you see Chris?"

"What about Chris? I haven't seen him lately. I've been busy with work."

"Oh, honey, you ought to be careful. I dropped off some food for him the other day, and he's got a big black eye, random cuts on his face, and missing teeth! *I've* never even lost a single tooth before!"

I put on my best shocked expression. "Oh my God, is

he all right? What happened?"

"I don't know. He looks really bad, though. He said he fell," Meemaw said in her normal voice, then switched into a low whisper. "I think somebody beat him up."

"Really?"

"He kept on saying he fell. But it doesn't add up." She showed me photos of Chris, zooming in on each and every single one of his wounds. "Don't you think it's some sort of gang? And they threatened him not to talk about it?"

"I have no idea."

"I'm just telling you to be careful. Here isn't like Alabama. There are lots of groups of different people living together. You know which group runs the gangs, right?"

"I know you're just trying to tell us to be safe, but you have to stop this!"

"I'm saying this out of love! I only want the best for you." She hugged me tightly. "Speaking of, do you need more rounds? I'm happy to come by another time and get you more."

"I love you too." I hugged her back.

"Let's get some coffee and eat the pie."

"I'd love for you to stay for longer, but actually, I have another date tonight," I said, hoping for her to take the hint. It was nearly six.

"With a different girl?" Meemaw's eyes beamed. "Aw, what a smart boy you are! You gotta shop around for the right one."

She squeezed herself into the driver's seat of her SUV. Due to the length of her legs, she couldn't push the seat all the way back, so as she drove, the steering wheel was almost pressed completely against her protruding stomach. It was a safety hazard, not only to herself but to the cars and pedestrians around her. However, her driving skills were more than competent. She backed out of my driveway with only one hand on the steering wheel, then began dashing through the neighborhood roads at what must have been seventy miles per hour.

Chapter 23

The petals from the bouquet were starting to wilt slightly, darkening around the edges. The owner of the flower shop had put a special solution at the root of the stem, where the plant had been cut. However, dead flowers weren't meant to stay fresh-looking forever.

Alicia pulled them off one by one, throwing them into her bathwater. The yellow ones failed to make the cut and were left untouched. When they were still intact with the body of the plant, they had only a very faint smell. I had no idea how it became so strong once they were dropped into the bath.

She was leaning against the headrest with her eyes closed. I sat nearby. Her hair was let down and slightly unruly. The end strands were wet and were scattered around her chest.

"How come you like baths but not swimming pools?"

"Pools are cold, big, and intimidating. And you're forced to open your eyes against harsh chemicals. Bathtubs are warm and under control," she said with her eyes closed.

The same steam that was suffocating me gently glided past her face.

"The pool in the house is heated, if you wanna use it."

"I'll pass."

She rolled over onto her stomach, twisting her body at a strange angle. She created small waves using her arms. Her face was amused. "Why didn't you just tell Meemaw that you weren't home?"

"If I told her I wasn't home, she'd ask me to open the door for her remotely. And then she would take the opportunity to snoop around. If I'm there and actively watching her, I have more control over the situation."

"You let her walk all over you. We set boundaries with her. She was required to call at least three hours ahead before coming over and could only bring up to five dishes. And if we weren't home, she wasn't allowed to come inside, even if the housekeeper was there. You just have to be firm with her—she'll give in if you're adamant enough."

I swallowed my dismay at hearing her referring to her and Chris as *we*. "How do you even set boundaries with someone like her?" I asked wryly.

"You just gotta be tough."

"It doesn't work. She never listens."

"Make her. Give her real consequences, and she won't do anything you don't like again."

"Did you learn that from my mom?"

"Kind of." She blushed.

I told her I was sorry about her earring. Her father and Chris had both refused to buy her any accessories that weren't authentic. The only exception was the centerpiece of her old engagement ring, which had been passed down as a family heirloom from Meemaw. I couldn't remember whether it had been a promise ring given to her by a client who'd visited the brothel or if it had been something her parents owned. Regardless, being the only family heirloom, it had automatically gone to Chris. The imitation diamond had been called *paste* at the time; it was a type of leaded glass that was cut and polished to resemble the sparkle of a diamond. Later on, he added a great number of small real diamond pieces, which were much more expensive, around the fake stone.

"So if I'm Scar, who are you?"

"You can refer to me as Edward Parker Markson of New York, son of Parker Mark of Atmore."

We laughed together. When I was born, I didn't have the luxury of having my own identity. My birth mother had surrendered all of her rights. Chris and I had had a sister named Edi whom neither of us had met. Chris was born the year Edi died, and he should have been named after her. However, as he was wanted and I was not, he was allowed to develop into his own person. My mother had named me after our sister without bothering to give me a middle name. In her mind, and in my father's mind, I was beyond lucky to have a home, let alone a middle name, without even my father's first name as a placeholder. He had a Southern double name, Parker Mark. Ever since he left Alabama at eighteen, he'd only gone by Parker.

"Ever thought about how Meemaw is the reason why we can't eat hot pot in public?"

"What do you mean?"

"Because people like her are so unwilling to change, other people feel they have to be equally radical in order to combat them. At the end of the day, it only harms the vast majority of people who didn't really care either way."

"And the businesses are the ones taking the hit."

"If you have a business, don't you want the biggest consumer pool you could possibly get?"

"It's nothing you or I can change, though," I said. "We just have to comply with the rules. Only if there's a way to be away from the rules completely."

She splashed me from inside the tub. The distance was too far; a long stream of water rose from the back of her hand in a crisp roar and landed directly on the floor. There, it splattered down and lost all of its shape against the swirl of the tiles.

"You look pretty." I laughed.

"Since when did you develop an interest in hippos?"

"You are not a hippo. What are you talking about?"

"Compared to Daria, I am," she said casually.

"Compared to Daria, everyone is a hippo."

"Didn't Meemaw say how she was smaller than her when she was young?"

"Do you believe her?"

"No . . .? You wanna hear me make hippo noises? *Grunt, grunt.* Did you know that hippos can't swim? They just float in the water and paddle around using their little legs."

"Stop it. What's your ring size?"

"Six." She turned sideways to look at me. "Were you

unhappy?"

I spoke with honesty in mind. I told her about how I'd derived very little joy from the years I had been married.

When I first met Daria, I thought I had won the lottery. Her looks made the top line of models jealous. She was a natural blonde with big, innocent, blue eyes and a body most teenage girls starved themselves for. She rarely expressed any negative emotions, nor did she ever ask for help. I was aware of how it was impossible for someone to go through their entire life without feeling upset or needing support from other people. I chose not to put in the effort. It saved me time and energy.

As the years passed, her face became bland to look at. When all of her features were pieced together, she morphed into the pure definition of extreme beauty and lost her own identity.

There was an insurmountable distance between us. I wasn't sure which one of us had caused it in the first place. When I tried to reach out for her, she was floating in the air and refused to reveal her pain or weakness.

I was lectured by others on how I couldn't let go of such an opportunity. They had all dreamed of an errand runner, cheerleader, and arm candy in one package. Daria had no opinions of her own; with regard to the decisions in my life, she played the role of an eternal yes man. Pleasing me was the biggest aspiration of her life. I was compelled to be constantly happy. When I wasn't, I felt guilt gnawing at me. Internally, I was filled with exhaustion. I wanted to run from her, yet I lacked a valid reason. I knew she loved me with all of her might. If I had left, it would have been too cruel. I couldn't hurt her further than I already had.

Her career failed to make our conversations more interesting. As an attorney, she was far more successful than me. Her submission made very little sense to me. After she passed, I spent my free time replaying the video games I had enjoyed in the past and came to a revelation of where the dullness in our marriage stemmed from. When a game character had maxed out all skills and could slash through any enemy in a matter of seconds, the player began losing enjoyment. Since there was no challenge in the first place, I felt no joy or accomplishment.

"Am I a bad person?" I asked. "Am I ungrateful? Do I deserve punishment?"

"No," Alicia said. "Because you are aware."

"I tried."

"You don't have to explain. No one blames you."

She smiled at me. I watched her wash her hair in silence.

Chapter 24

A shooting took place a few days ago at a different mall nearby. We couldn't miss the opportunity; I rode in the back seat with Alicia. She made a reservation at the Saffron table, one of the rare fusion restaurants with the appropriate license to open to the general consumer. It specialized in French and Italian dishes.

Three o'clock in the afternoon was an odd hour for a meal, but it was the only available time slot at the restaurant, which was one of the most sought-after places in the mall. The parking lot was crowded. With the newly added security-screening process and extra police on-site, it was one of the safest times for people to go out in public. Due to the frequency of such events, the extra effort in mass shooting prevention usually went away within three to seven days.

The shooter had been a high school teacher with a clean criminal record and no mental health history. Something within the woman had snapped. She'd purchased an automatic weapon from her local grocery store, walked in, and blindly shot at everyone within close proximity. Five people were killed, and seven injured. As I had predicted before learning the details, the woman was not a resident of the area. Most of us could afford some form of coping mechanism without directly hurting others. She lived about three hours away in a different city. At first, she was mistaken for a robber, but people soon realized it wasn't the overpriced clothes she was after.

Alicia eyed the shoppers walking by our parked car. They happily chatted with each other. Some were holding hands. Others pushed strollers. They all looked grateful.

We cut through the stores on the first floor and walked straight to the restaurant. A long line of people stood outside, waiting to be seated. Most reservations required some form of additional wait time. Standing in the back of the line, I scanned each person's face, hoping they weren't someone I knew. The place was absurdly busy. Alicia reminded me it was owned by a social media influencer's cousin's stepbrother's neighbor's college roommate's best friend's coworker's niece.

The host at the stand wore a blazer with no shirt underneath. He was lean and muscular at the same time. His bare chest and hardened nipples showed periodically as he moved about, directing people to their tables. He held an old-fashioned tablet in his hands and a condom-like rubber protector wrapped around his tongue, which gave him a lisp when he spoke.

"Welcome, people!"

"We have a reservation under Edward. For two."

He raised the tablet near his mouth and began typing various letters using the tip of his tongue. From one step away, he looked like a dog attempting to drink water out of a bowl. He looked to be somewhat familiar with the keyboard settings and rarely needed to look down at the screen. The occasional mistakes he made were quickly fixed by the repeated licking of the Delete button.

"All right, you're all checked in. Please take a seat right here at this bench. The additional wait should only be about two to forty-five minutes."

We sat down obediently. The group of three after us was lucky; they were led to the main dining area right away. It was an older couple and their adult son. As they passed, a phone fell from the wife's pocket. I looked at the people around us. The host was walking forward; no one paid any attention to it. I stood quickly and chased after the group, returning the phone to the woman's hands as discreetly as possible. She thanked me in a hushed voice.

We were seated at a glass table no more than twenty inches wide. A single red rose stood in a tinted bud vase in the middle, occupying a big portion of the already cramped space. The two faux-leather backless seats looked and smelled brand new.

Alicia's mouth moved. Her voice was completely muffled by the blaring music coming from the speakers beneath the ceiling.

"What?" I yelled.

"Tongue!"

It was the only audible word I heard from her.

"I know!"

"That's the first time I saw someone doing that outside of a video!"

I looked around; there were no restaurant staff in sight. Every other table was busy yelling at each other.

"It's the strongest muscle in the body!"

"What?"

She couldn't hear the rest of what I said. Studies had found the tongue to be the strongest muscle within the human body; I'd learned about it during my weekly trainings at Montgomery. Since the study was first published, many institutions had realized the way keyboards and electronic devices were designed was inherently discriminatory. It was unfair that tools used for most important tasks were meant to be operated by the hands. The tongue deserved more usage and recognition. Last year, Montgomery Sterling had adopted a tongue appreciation week. Everyone working in the office licked projections, keyboards, and touch screens with their tongues instead of using their fingers. Our clients weren't at all upset, as they had gone through a similar experience during a different week. This year, the event had been canceled.

"It gets tiring," I said.

She giggled and covered her mouth with the back of her hand.

The venue was advertised as an upscale dining experience with unparalleled taste. Instead of the popular songs played at cheaper places, it blasted grand orchestral music. However, they weren't authentic classical compositions but symphonic versions of the most well-known songs used in short-form entertainment videos. The lighting was low and calming. All waitstaff wore variations of black suits and ties; the women wore a black lacy bra or a crop top. The only flaw was the tightness of the space. The tables were placed so close to each other that not only did the different conversations clash, but the different scents also fused together.

After the meal, Alicia ordered a dessert called *tiramisù al mascarpone con savoiardi inzuppati nel caffè e cacao in polvere*. The bill arrived as she took her second and last bite. As expected, we were both hungry afterward.

On the first floor of the mall was a boutique candle and cosmetics shop with a plaid, cream-colored façade. Three women dressed in cow onesies stood a few feet away from the wide-opened door. They were by no means blocking it, but they were enough to deter most people from even looking into the shop. The front of their costumes had two open holes, their uncovered breasts protruding through them. The one in the middle held a big cardboard sign: STOP EXPLOITING COWS FOR BEAUTY! CHOOSE PLANT-BASED ALTERNATIVES INSTEAD! All the letters were written in blood-colored paint. The two "cows" on the side each had a big baby bottle in hand, filled with milk resembling liquid but a lot less opaque and more powdery. Next to them were two other people dressed up like bees with glowing wings and antennas. They didn't have a sign, but it was enough for people to infer that they were protesting the company's usage of beeswax in their products. Trays of sticky-looking honeycomb chunks sat in their arms. One of them was so full that the golden semiliquid began pouring out from the edge and then drizzled onto the floor.

"It's a safe day, of course they'd show up," Alicia muttered under her breath.

A shop clerk walked outside wearing swim goggles and a plastic face cover around his head. He stood still for a moment, turned several times, and finally mustered enough courage to speak with the protesters. He had a mosquito-like voice.

The cows remained silent. The bees actively looked in another direction.

"Would you people like to learn about our new environmental commitments? I understand that maybe a lot of people haven't heard about it yet. But in fact, our company recently decided that by next year, more than 99.998 percent of our raw materials—"

Before he had a chance to finish reciting what sounded like a poorly written and ill-rehearsed script, the skinniest of the cows, standing on the right, took up the bottle in her hand and squirted a long stream of "milk" into his hair. The other two soon followed, attacking the crotch of his pants and his collar, neither of which had been protected by the face shield. The man naturally attempted to cover himself, but he was determined to keep on delivering the lines despite the fact that they had become indistinguishable blurs of noises. The bees acted right after, throwing two chunks of honeycombs at him. One landed on his chest but slipped off immediately, and the other made contact with his hair, unable to pass through the individual strands.

A few minutes later, the man retreated. Two other employees dragged him back into the store. Out of nowhere, a janitor walked in slowly, wheeling a portable bucket and a mop. He swayed the mop's stick back and forth but stopped meticulously at the line where the tiles changed for the store. What was inside was not his responsibility. The air smelled of an artificial lemon scent.

We turned around. A police officer was walking in our direction. Naturally, my eyes landed on him. To my surprise, he acknowledged me. He said my name.

His voice was firm yet exhausted.

I felt Alicia's body tense next to me. I squeezed her hand.

"Someone reported you," the officer said.

"For?"

"Unsolicited actions of a discriminatory nature. Approximately an hour ago, we received a report that you acted in a discriminatory way toward a person of advanced age. The cameras confirmed that you picked up the person's dropped item and returned it to them, signifying a belittling attitude that considered the person unable to perform the described activity themselves."

"So . . .?" Alicia spoke meekly.

"I need you to come with me. The victim of your actions asked to testify to their ability. So if they succeed, it won't be mandatory for you to spend the night."

"Spend the night?"

"If your action of hatred and belittlement is proven valid by the victim's inability to perform the said task, we would unfortunately have to detain you for the night."

We walked back to the restaurant. The presence of the police killed the opportunity to complain between ourselves. My brain turned at a godlike speed. I calculated how, in the worst-case scenario, I should approach surviving jail time.

The midday setup was turned into the evening venue. The number of people waiting for their chance to taste the most overly advertised meal of their lives increased exponentially. The line of customers extended all the way outside the double glass doors. Young women shivered in their winter bralettes and see-through tights, determined to capture a memorable photo.

A different, much more mildly behaved host worked the stand this time. For the efficiency of the evening hours, he typed with his fingertips instead.

The family from earlier stood in a line and pressed their bodies up against the wall. Each of them had their head lowered. Their faces were red.

Other innocent customers walked by the six of us, including the police officer. They eyed the scene with curiosity, but no one dared to speak amongst each other or point at the officer's shining uniform.

"So, earlier today you were recorded picking up a phone from the floor and handing it to this person. And your intentions, in that moment, were unclear. What made you decide to pick it up yourself, insulting the owner's ability to do the same?"

"I—I don't have an answer to that," I said.

"They had already assessed the situation," the old woman spoke up in a sharp, flustered voice, "and assumed

I was able to pick it up myself. They did so to save time, not to belittle my ability, which I will now demonstrate."

"All right." The officer took out a recording device similar to a phone. He turned the camera toward the woman.

"Do I begin now?" she asked.

"Yes."

The woman eyed the crowd, which was discreetly staring at her. She walked to the approximate place where she'd dropped her phone and lightly tossed it to the floor. It bounced for a few inches, then hit the ground facedown.

She was of an ample size. Smaller than Meemaw, yet she still held on to a large portion of her weight around her midsection. At first, she leaned forward, reaching for the phone with straight knees. Her fingers were nearly a foot away when she gave up on the first attempt. She looked down at the tips of her leather boots, unbuttoned her thick winter coat, and handed it to her husband; he held on to it with equal embarrassment on his face. For her second attempt, she came up with a different approach. Putting one hand on her hip, she bent her knees. Inches away from success, a quiet but distinct noise of fabric tearing came from her denim jeans. With an ever more focused expression, she reached down further, pressing her stomach tightly against her chest. She picked up the phone between her index and middle finger. After a short breather, she stood up straight in front of the camera.

"All right," the police said. "You have now successfully demonstrated your ability to retrieve the phone yourself. However, under the noise level of this environment—

which is, objectively speaking, slightly high—what is your justification for how you would have noticed the phone being dropped in the first place? How can you prove that this person acted out of convenience rather than attempting to give you special treatment due to your age, observance, and mobility level?"

"I heard it being dropped," the woman said. "I was just about to turn around, and this person acted before I did."

"So, is it now possible that they saw you turning around for it but insisted on handing the phone to you regardless?"

"No! It was just a thought. I didn't start the action."

"I saw her turning around, almost starting to reach for the phone, but it might not have been obvious to everyone." The son spoke quickly.

"What is your relationship with this person? The three of you were found together." The police eyed the woman.

"I am her child."

"Unfortunately, your testament cannot stand, as there is a potential conflict of interest at play."

"I am not her child." Alicia stepped forward and tentatively looked at the police. "And I witnessed the same event."

The police scanned her body from head to toe. He did not investigate further.

"All right." He paused. "That is acceptable and accepted."

We exited the restaurant. The family passed through the same doors. Their gaze was glued to the floor.

***

Near the exit of the building was a small cart selling cotton candy. Alicia stopped in front of it. The amount of floss was minimal for the overly long sticks that held them. They came in a large variety of pastel shades.

"Would you like one before we head out?" I asked.

She nodded.

As I searched for my phone to make the payment, a man came through the door. His face was oddly familiar, yet for a while, I couldn't recall his name. He was in his late fifties or early sixties. There were two small girls next to him, approximately a couple of years apart. He was taller than me. His posture was upright for his age, except for the way his neck leaned slightly forward, making it seem disproportionately long.

The man looked back at me tentatively.

"Your mom," Alicia muttered.

"What? That's not my mom."

"Boyfriend!" she yelled at me in a whisper, frantic, as if she were about to cry.

To the man, seeing me and Alicia looked like a pleasant surprise. My mother had started dating him the same year my father died; I had only seen him twice before, as he never made an effort to get to know us. When we spoke with each other, he attempted to act like an open book. He was well-versed in trivial topics yet remained secretive every time his work was brought up. He was a professor at a university. When I'd asked for the school's name, he'd evaded the question. I supposed he was ashamed to face us due to how soon their relationship began. In truth, he did not need to ask for our permission. We respected our mother's privacy and choices.

"Tristan," Alicia said as she hugged him cordially.

The little girls stared at us as I shook hands with him.

"This is Marie, and this is Taylor."

"May I have permission to interact with these persons under the age of eighteen under your current guardianship?" I asked.

"Oh yes, yes. Of course."

The younger-looking girl waved at me with a smile while holding onto her big sister's hand. I waved back at her. Both girls wore their school uniforms on a Sunday. Their bulletproof vests peeked out from under the seams of their sweater vests.

"So, what are you guys up to today?" Tristan asked.

"Chris and Alicia wanted to help me pick out some home decor."

"Good! Good!" He nodded mindlessly, not paying much attention to my explanation. "I'm watching the kids for the weekend. Thought I'd take them out for some fun. Is there any area of the mall that we should avoid today?"

"Oh, there's just a small group of animal rights protesters in front of Earth's Candles. I think that's it," Alicia said.

"Where is Chris?"

"He got hit by protesters with honeycombs. He's in the bathroom."

"Public places can be pretty crazy sometimes."

We looked at each other for a brief moment, unsure of what to say next. Tristan spoke quickly before an inevitable silence erupted. "Well, I think I'm gonna take the girls to the carousel now and walk around for a while."

We politely said our goodbyes.

Chapter 25

M y friend Ian returned from the Texas Robotics Regional. Like every other year, our team had failed to make the finals.

He showed up with bags of groceries in his hands.

Alicia stood in front of the oven. She wore a half apron over her clothes. She waved at him. Lowering his head, he smiled for a very brief second.

"Your house is still basically all white," he said.

I made no objection. I freed the bags from him and found more than a dozen different ingredients; some were even exotic. "This is a lot."

Ian put his hands behind his head and leaned backward slightly on the couch. "The last supper. Do you even realize how many things are needed to make hot pot? Granted, I'm the only one who can enter the grocery stores here. But you guys can't just treat me with nothing."

"You can have water," I said.

"I can pour you a glass of water," Alicia called out.

"And what are you going to do for me?" Ian looked at

me.

"He was in his office for the whole day. He said he had work. I don't know what," she said.

"Just give it to me quick and fast. Which one of you has cancer?" He stared straight into the TV projection. It was playing a forbidden cartoon from the last century. A squirrel was beating the head of another squirrel using a flat iron skillet. The victim's body compressed into a small ball and then quickly bounced back to its original shape. It sounded like a spring folding, then unfolding right after.

"No one has cancer."

"Who has a brain tumor, then?"

"No one has a brain tumor."

"Then who murdered Chris?"

"No one murdered Chris."

I explained the miscarriage before he walked out due to the redundancy of the conversation. Facing his reaction was a chore. I didn't want to ride through the same emotions I had already been through once myself. I couldn't bear to look.

"I'm assuming Chris is not doing anything about it, which fits his personality. Unless—"

"It's not me."

"Thought so." Ian shrugged. "This is worse than cancer."

I gestured for Alicia to stay quiet. She cocked her head and looked at me for an explanation of the silence. Ian's eyes were glued to the cartoon playing on the TV. The two squirrels were now happily making raspberry pies together. He didn't blink. He was biting on his upper lip and upper lip only. It looked funny.

"How many more days do you have left?" he asked.

"Less than two months," I answered.

"Be safe getting out. The problem is that you can't really wait till the last minute. Let me know what I can do."

"What are you talking about?" Alicia asked.

"Ian likes to problem solve," I said to her, then turned back toward Ian. "Here is where Alicia and I disagree. She wants to go to prison and get her death sentence. She thinks it's the right thing to do."

"Are you stupid?" He shot her a sharp glare.

Taken aback by the sudden bluntness, she covered her mouth and said nothing.

"It doesn't matter," Ian muttered. His gaze landed on her, quickly shifted away, then met her eyes with clarity. His voice dramatically softened. "It's just that—don't, like, you know, ruin Edward's life again. And your own, of course."

"She didn't ruin me," I said.

"Maybe not intentionally, but you are inherently stupid."

"I'm not inherently stupid."

"Yes, you are."

A portable stove sat in the middle of the dining table. Ian had been in charge of bringing the cans of gas. Alicia and I put the empty pot onto the dormant stove.

The two large cartons held a small mountain of lamb and beef that was slightly frozen. I was told to take those out first and leave them on the table to thaw. I then followed Ian's instructions to put each set of other ingredients on individual plates. There were servings of sliced mushrooms; various leafy, green vegetables; lotus roots; sweet potato; quail eggs; glass noodles; shrimp paste; cuttlefish balls; miniature octopuses; crab sticks; small squids; and a bowl of golden-skinned fish tofu.

Ian took a short trip to his car and came back with a smile plastered on his face. It had questionable authenticity. He dug out a few bottles of unopened sauces: a lighter and a darker soy sauce, a sesame sauce that resembled peanut butter, and a bright red chili oil.

"You'd burn your hands with forks." He ripped the packaging of three pairs of beige-colored chopsticks and began washing them in the sink as if he were in his own home. "Go ahead and start the fire. It might take a while for it to boil. And get a bowl to mix your own sauces."

When the seasoning of the broths dissolved, one turned out to be red and oily, while the other was milky white. Steam rose into the air. The room suddenly smelled warm and strangely inviting.

"The pot was a gift. Isn't the dual setting neat?"

"It's called a 'lovebird's pot.'" Ian laughed.

"It was a present from my coworker's parents. They insisted on taking a photo with me. I think they are a part of Rosa's cult."

"Hail Rosa!" Ian called out. "It's the mandarin duck pot. There's nothing to it. It's basically just a pot that holds two different broths. Search for 'mandarin ducks playing in water.'"

Alicia looked up from her phone and gagged.

"It may be unpleasant to you, but to some people, it's more appetizing," Ian said. "So, uh, it's been a while, right?"

"We haven't seen each other in, like, what? Seven years?" Alicia said.

"Six or seven." He ate quietly for a while, then looked up and set his chopsticks down vertically along his bowl. "You two better act fast. If you end up dying in prison, he's going to off himself too."

"That might be an exaggeration," she muttered.

"It's not."

"How was the Texas regional?" I asked.

"Overall, we did pretty good."

"Oh, really? I thought 9931 was too slow and tanked the first pick robot."

"You had the time to watch the competition?"

"I didn't. We ran into a robotics kid at an arcade. It came up during the conversation. He said our robot prevented them from going to the world comp."

Ian sighed. "We didn't break down that much. The driver student's mom showed up during our last round and started yelling at him out of nowhere. He had a panic attack. She's a devoted disciple of Rosa."

"Rosa is one of the evilest people alive," I said.

"Edward!" Alicia elbowed me. We sat on the same side of the table. Because I was left-handed and she was the opposite, she could only sit on my right.

"Are you going to report me for calling a woman evil?" I asked.

"I might!" Ian joked. "But you are right—my aunt got into Rosa's work, and now my little cousin is clinically depressed."

"I'm sorry to hear that." Alicia inhaled. "I'm just happy we grew up before she became famous. How do the disciples do the salute again?"

Ian moved a few feet away from the table and then knelt. "Hail Rosa!" he said as he raised both of his arms straight above his head. He then dropped his forehead against the floor three times. He stood.

"Is that it?" Alicia asked.

"Hail Rosa!" Ian knelt again. He dropped his forehead against the floor three more times. He stood and then immediately knelt. "Hail Rosa!" Ian spoke louder. He banged his forehead three more times and stood, looking at the toes of his feet. His expression was the sternest I had ever witnessed from him. After a moment of solemn silence, he returned to his normal self. "Like that. You're supposed to do that every time you see her in person." He laughed. "Regardless of how much you cared about your wife, her murderer walked away free because of Rosa."

My face flushed. "I cared about her plenty."

"Are you inviting me to the next wedding?"

I couldn't recall much about the small ceremony we'd had. Daria had wanted something grand but as usual, she'd complied with whatever I said. Most of my associations regarding weddings came from Alicia's. They weren't positive. However, I had been mentally stronger at the time, so things had naturally been more tolerable.

I'd survived the ceremony, the speeches, and the garter. The honor of the best man was given to Chris's friend. I stood with the other groomsmen and remained silent. The older guests had already left as the casual part of the dance party began. They were either getting tired or feeling like they couldn't stand the loud music and flashing lights. I, too, wanted a room to myself. The DJ primarily worked with upbeat songs that were only somewhat vulgar. I thought Daria might have wanted to dance, but I soon discovered that she thought I was the one who was reluctant to leave.

I was secretly hoping to be rid of her for some time. Ideally, she would get too tipsy, so she'd go back to our hotel room first. However, I knew there was no way for me to outdrink her. She grew up drinking vodka like water. If I was lucky, someone would run into her and spill some drink on her dress, so she'd need to go back and change.

"There's a few people I wanna talk to." I spoke with difficulty. She didn't know anyone there besides me.

"Oh, no problem!" She took the hint immediately and went away. I assured her that I would find her again soon.

I poured liquor into a water cup. I didn't want to be seen as someone who drank excessively. It wouldn't make Chris look good. We were on friendly terms at the time.

Ian was there. He didn't drink much, being someone who strictly followed the age limit even though no one enforced the rules. He eventually caught me in the corner of the venue when most people had left. I was hiding behind a decorative tree. I'd refilled my cup a handful of times. I estimated I'd drunk about four water cups of hard liquor in addition to the cocktails from earlier in the day. The alcohol had affected me faster than I anticipated. When I realized I had spent too long sitting alone, I was past the "little bit" I'd promised Daria. I dreaded how I was forced to go back to someone I didn't care about. I dozed off, accompanied by short and sporadic dream sequences. I saw a small hotel room with a single bed covered by red sheets, different from the one where I was staying in the real world.

Ian had shaken my eyes open. I didn't want to get up when he attempted to help me, so he threw a cup of cold water in my face. The ice had long melted. I coughed and watched a large droplet fall from the tip of my nose and onto my shirt.

"You need to go back to your room," he said.

"Why?"

"Because."

"No." I spoke with my head down.

Ian began dragging me across the empty dance floor into a hallway and an elevator. The lights had already dimmed themselves. The journey was blurry and quiet. We didn't run into anyone who wasn't wearing a hotel maid uniform. I became more conscious when I saw the door handle to my room. Ian was still supporting most of my weight. I grabbed his arm.

"Can I stay in your room instead?" I asked.

"No," he said firmly.

"I'll stay in your room, and you can go to mine."

"No. You need to . . ." He kept on talking. I didn't catch the rest of his long speech.

I'd felt sorry for manipulating Daria, yet I was angry at her as if she had been the sole cause of my misery. Regardless, I couldn't face her. And then, I was thrown into the glory of my hotel room. The blonde stood in front of the door. She looked worried. I heard her speaking with Ian before he left. I didn't want to throw up on the room's carpet when I felt nausea making waves inside my stomach. I walked to the attached bathroom and dropped on the tiles near the toilet.

The next morning, I woke up on the couch with little recollection of how I got there. My head rested against a cushion. I felt ashamed. Yet, reading from her expression, she was more than happy. My guilt about abandoning her worsened.

Now, despite being the same age as me, Ian looked like he had not aged one bit since back then. Aren't you two doing another one in Europe?" he asked.

Alicia looked at me with clear eyes; she refused to answer.

Ian picked up a small octopus. Its eight tentacles stuck to each other flaccidly. There was a layer of mucus covering the body, making the skin look smooth and slippery. Instead of using his chopsticks normally, he stabbed the pocket under the head. Upon making contact with the boiling broth, its tentacles curled up immediately. After a short while, the mucus was boiled away. Ian picked up its now purpled body. He bit off the head with his front teeth, then ate the rest slowly, dunking it in sesame oil.

I couldn't comprehend his savagery. Octopuses were too intelligent to be categorized as food. Although the animal was long dead, his behavior made it seem like he'd murdered it for a second time.

"Isn't it necessary for you two to be married if you want to get the same work sponsorship? So when Edward finds a job, he can take you over with him?" Ian said.

"Have you been doing research on this?"

"Someone from my work got out a year ago. They're living in Germany now."

"What did they do?" Alicia asked.

"He threatened to hurt an ER doctor."

"Can I talk to him?" I said eagerly.

"Of course. There are actually a lot of resources for people who are looking to get out. You just have to talk to the right people."

"Ian, you don't have to—you could get in trouble," she said.

"First of all, no one should be punished for an arbitrary crime. Second of all, they don't care."

"What do you mean?"

"They can't put everyone in jail," I interjected. "It's more show than action."

"I guess you won't be able to see the Techno Penguins," Ian said to me. "Should I tell them to take you off the mentors list?"

"I'm sure they already replaced me. I'm nontech. It's not that important."

"What does nontech do?" Alicia asked.

"A lot of things. Mostly fundraisers, hosting student events, grant writing . . ."

"And what do you do?"

"I teach grant writing. Most of the grants the kids wrote were never sent out because chances are that 95 percent will get rejected. All of the grants that actually got us money came from the mentors. It's a way to make the kids feel like they did something valuable without touching the robot."

"Edward's really good at grant writing. He can write two grants in sixty minutes!" Ian said loudly.

"Chris taught me. He can write three. If your goal is purely quantity, then quality doesn't matter. It was to show the mentors and the other kids how hard you work. You just follow a template and change out some words here and there according to the prompt."

"Chris never told you about robotics?" Ian raised an eyebrow.

Alicia shook her head.

Chapter 26

After dinner, I let Ian into my office and closed the door on Alicia. I didn't want her overly involved in the planning process; she might have protested if we ran into the slightest obstacle. She had not said yes, nor did she choose to complain about it.

A guest room had already been cleaned and prepared for Ian, yet he insisted on leaving in the middle of the night, claiming a fear of spirits. I found it comical. It must have been due to his lack of understanding of Daria's character. She didn't have enough vigor in her to successfully harm other people. The most drastic action she would take was crying underneath the covers. It was unfortunate. I wished she was less self-sacrificing and more assertive. But if she had been that way, she would have left me a long time ago, rightfully so.

"The smallest room in this house is bigger than my parents' big bedroom," Ian said. He never planned on moving out of his parents' home. Even though he made well above the average income of the state, he couldn't afford his own place.

The man who had escaped was named Mitch. He had once worked on a project with Ian, but they were by no means friends. About ten minutes into our conversation, he had to leave and called for his wife to take over. Jen insisted that we speak using voice-changing software. We sounded like three raccoons on helium. I saw Ian's lips flipping upward but he suppressed his laughter quickly.

It was easy to get in touch with a coyote. There were code words on the internet that people could look for, or they could visit old sites of women's shelters. Sometimes, the middlemen would leave contact numbers on the debris of the buildings. Since we were already in contact with each other, Jen offered the number of an agency. Due to the sheer amount of people, especially women, leaving US territories, smuggling criminals was now a booming small business. There were different steps to the process. The coyotes transported clients from border to border. The agents negotiated pricing and collected fees. There was also a group of people who took care of the preparations and the organizing of the moves. They were called the "executives." I wanted to request the same people who'd helped Mitch and Jen. Unfortunately, clients could not choose their group. The crew either worked on a rotating schedule, or the assignments were random. Jen said she didn't know the metrics that marked a good coyote.

"Whatever they ask you to do," she said, "just remember their goal is to get people to their destinations."

I wanted to pin down the small hesitation in her voice, but it was all that she was willing to say: coyotes were adamant about their control of the journey. It was important to listen to them at all times and temporarily give up individual will. The conditions were harsh, but it wasn't unbearable, even for people still recovering from medical incidents.

"You have to trust them," she said, "no matter how untrustworthy they seem."

I took a long nap in the morning. When I woke up, I found Alicia in the sunroom. She stood to greet me, holding her phone by her side.

"Ethan died," she said.

My eyes widened. "Rosa's son?"

"Ethan Almend. Your dad's friend."

"I thought his sentencing was lighter than that," I responded reflectively, trying to recall the exact number of years he was due to serve.

"It was from prison wounds."

"When is the funeral?" I asked. "Are we or Chris—or my mom—going?"

"His wife said she wanted it to be close to family only. She didn't want to make a scene."

The man had done robotics with my father when they were both in high school. While my father had lost interest in it, Ethan never had. Robotics became his lifelong career. Eventually, he made himself well-known. He didn't comply with federal regulations and decided to run an underground STEM scholarship fund for low-income students. About a year into it, someone reported him for public and private belittlement in the form of financial assistance. The person remained anonymous. Ethan was sentenced to a few years in prison. He was seventy-one years old. Since he wasn't allowed to be discriminated against or treated differently from others, his wheelchair was confiscated. He performed daily mandatory labor and received unofficial beatings like everyone else.

"Ian and I got in touch with a middleman last night," I said to Alicia.

"Where are we going to live in Mexico?" she asked.

"A refugee center."

"What's the name?"

"I don't know."

"Where exactly is the exit point? Where is the entry point?"

"They couldn't tell me."

"How long are we staying there for?"

"I have no idea."

"I'd rather die instead of feeling like I owe you for the rest of my life."

Briefly, I felt stunned. I was close to success, yet she chose to be the one working against me. I soon found the only plausible answer to her ill-constructed logic. Chris had, in the past, made her feel a similar way. I couldn't let myself be blamed for something I didn't do.

"Do you actually wanna die?" I asked her.

She didn't respond. Grabbing her wrist firmly, I dragged her across the sunroom, through the hallways, and into the main bedroom. I felt her swinging her arm behind me, attempting to break free. She winced, begged, and kicked me. And then she used her other hand to try to pry my fingers open. Once inside the closet, I pointed at the black gun case hiding on the top shelf.

"You are not gonna die jumping out of the window from three floors," I said. "You should probably shoot yourself leaning over the balcony."

I had only wanted to scare her, yet she had a tendency to take things literally. There was genuine fear in her eyes. Her face and cheeks turned bright red as she cried. She began mumbling incoherent phrases as she shook her head violently, refusing to take a single step closer to me.

"If you don't know how, I'll teach you. But I'm not doing it," I said.

She crouched to the floor. Her responses were muffled by whines and sobs. I dragged her up by her elbow. She let out a high-pitched scream at the top of her lungs. I ignored her. I threw her over my shoulder, using one arm to clamp down on her legs.

"I wanna talk! I wanna talk!" she cried.

I took her back to our bedroom on the second floor. When I slammed her body down onto the mattress, she bounced slightly. Her face was covered by a strand of hair. I brushed it out of the way for her to see me clearly. I pulled her legs apart and leaned over against her. She squeezed her eyes shut, turning her head left and right to avoid my gentle lips. Eventually, her resistance pained me. I rolled off her in defeat.

It was puzzling when she climbed over me after I had mocked and debased her. She slowly straddled my hips, bent down, then kissed me on the mouth. I tried to speak over the motions. She parted her lips and bit down on mine. Her teeth were sharp. I tasted blood as she let out a series of small moans. Her tongue was agile and far too warm. When it glided over the incisions she had just made, it burned.

For whatever reason, we did not progress to having intercourse that day. When she withdrew from me, I felt an unprecedented emptiness wash over me. It was an illogical thought, yet I was certain I had lost the only chance of ever being with her.

I undressed myself and held her in bed. The idea of doing so made me feel closer to her. Naturally, she looked at me. Without making comments, she curled up next to me, obedient like a dog or a cat. I stroked her back as I considered apologizing, even though I knew it wouldn't have sufficed.

"Will you please tell me that I'm better than dying and Chris?" I asked softly.

"Yes."

I thought through the most convincing phrases of devotion and dedication I could think of: how I'd never loved anyone else but her, or how I couldn't bear to go on in life myself without her. As truthful as they were, I found them excessive.

"Even if you don't love me," I said, "and you possibly never will, I want to be in a place where, even if we part ways one day, we'll both be safe."

"Even if I don't love you?"

"That's all right." I nodded.

Chapter 27

I asked if she wanted to come with me to pack up my office. We stood in the dual-sided closet in the main bedroom. Daria's side was empty. There was no incentive to put anything there to fill the space. Alicia opened the glass drawer where the ties were arranged. Someone else's work, not mine. I dressed myself with care.

"Don't eat at the office. I'll cook dinner," she said.

She walked up to me, unrolled a deep red tie, and swung it around my neck. It was as if she had already measured where exactly the two ends should fall on my body. Her fingers moved with precision, twisting and pulling with a smoothness that came from habit rather than love. My chest tightened. Her movements were sweet, almost nonchalant. She'd done this many times before. I couldn't change the fact that it hadn't been with me. She patted my chest, signaling for me to turn around. Her touch was heavier than it should have been, as though she was trying to slap me. I glanced at the overly complicated knot sitting under my collar. It was one of those knots people wore on occasions when they wanted to be a show-off.

I assured her I loved it. Then I kissed her goodbye in front of the car like a normal person on a normal day.

On my way into the office, I saw a simple banner welcoming a group of law-firm trekkers from California State University Short Beach, which was not a school the firm usually recruited from. The students were accompanied by another partner named Edward. The young people listened attentively and quietly chewed on the hors d'oeuvres. Every ten seconds or so, their heads bopped up and down in unison, regardless of what the speaker had said.

I asked around about the purpose of their visit. Someone told me that starting next year, the firm would be hiring summer associates from the top 2 percent of students outside of the T-14 range. The obvious compromise was that these hires would be paid half of the market's salary and stripped of all bonuses. I asked if anyone would sign up for this, and the person told me that it was not so much about the money but the honor of working for the firm instead. It was also a charity act; one, to give the students who didn't make it into a T-14 law school for whatever reason a second chance at their career, and two, to add funds to the equity partners' personal bank accounts. It was a double win.

The cardboard boxes had been waiting for me in the same position for days. Being nearly empty, the room seemed exceptionally big. It had not been mine for long. I comforted myself that someone else would put the space to good use.

After loading the boxes into my car, I turned back toward the dining area. I asked the food and drinks workers for a small box to pack some snacks for Alicia. Turned out that whoever put in the order decided that a non-T-14 school deserved unappealing snacks only. There was a generic tub of cream cheese left at the welcoming station, along with some crumbled oyster crackers. Next to them was a tray of assorted fruits, mostly made of a small mountain of unevenly chopped cantaloupe with a handful of blueberries thrown on top. A few grapes lay next to it; most of them contained a large crack where the stem had been pulled out. The cantaloupes had been exposed to oxygen for too long; their edges began to turn transparent. Sugary juices leaked onto the tray. In the air, two gnats circled the fruits, refusing to land anytime soon.

I turned my head toward the window and waited for sentimental feelings to hit me. They never did. The view of the building across the street looked the same; it felt like every other day at work. It was not the ending I had envisioned.

My phone vibrated persistently from the inside of my pants pocket. I glanced down and saw my mother's name blasted across the screen. She rarely called before sending a text. I didn't know what to say to her, but picked up the phone regardless.

"Where are you?" she asked.

"Is everything okay?" I bent forward momentarily; my gaze landed on the tips of my shoes. There was relief in my lower back.

"Can you come over?"

"Tomorrow?"

"Today."

"I'll come over for dinner tomorrow."

I'd put on my best pretense. I knew I sounded relaxed, yet her tone grew more demanding with each word she spoke. She was likely to have found out about Chris, Alicia, or both. But clinging onto the possibility that she hadn't felt like great comfort.

"I'm not inviting you to eat food," my mother said.

Chapter 28

My mother was not gullible like Meemaw. Unlike her boyfriend, she possessed a caring attitude. Even if I tried my best, I didn't stand a chance of avoiding her judgment.

She lived in the old home Chris and I grew up in. There were four bedrooms and a few other ones to spare. She showed no fear of living alone. It had been redecorated and refurnished many times since we'd gotten our own homes. Now, it was fashionable enough to be featured in aesthetic videos circulating around the internet. The walls and furniture were white or a cream color lighter than coffee. A few paintings of abstract-looking vegetables hung around the kitchen. However, the most prominent decorations were scenes and flowers sculpted onto the plain columns. To make the space even more open, she had removed the walls sectioning off each area on the first floor. When I spoke, my words jumped back at me clearly.

My mother did not bother to stand when she saw me. She crossed her legs on the couch, a woven blanket draped loosely over her knees. She was in a pair of loose-fitted white pants and a deep blue shirt. Her perfume smelled like jasmine. She had always been thinner than most women her age and appeared borderline unhealthy. She took pride in looking younger than her real age while avoiding surgery and most injection formulas. Her rituals were complicated, and her choices of food and drinks were particular. She could go on and on, explaining the benefits of each ingredient and then proceeding to never consume more than a few bites of each. She routinely practiced yoga and meditated to the point of becoming slightly spiritual.

When I was young, I thought she had been bored or that every woman simply lived like her. When I grew a little older, I thought she was attempting to stay youthful to keep my father within the marriage. Perhaps she was suppressing the competition filled with much younger women, like my biological mother. However, in more recent years, I'd learned that she had been the unfaithful one, far more so than my father. She was a romantic person at heart. It wasn't for my father. My father was not romance-inducing, neither in his behaviors nor in his appearance. The day before he passed, I saw him begging from his hospital bed for my mother to spare "only a fraction of her love" for him.

I picked the armchair across from the couch and sat in it, leaving a slight distance between us. She stared at me aggressively.

"Are you going to offer me anything to drink?" I asked.

She cleared her throat. "There's water in the fridge."

"Okay."

"God, I don't even know where to start."

"I don't either." I tried to focus on anything else in the room that wasn't my mother. There was a stuffed celery plush on the dining table next to a stuffed eggplant. They each had big, puffy eyes and other facial features. They were too childish, hopeful, and utterly out of place. She had rearranged the Andean cube puzzle we played with as kids into the shape of a bird and hovered a glass shell over it. It was now on top of the fireplace. "Would it make you more comfortable if I just go?"

"I had to hunt Chris down. He wouldn't see me or talk to me. He said he wasn't being careful and he fell. But . . . I just want to say that I don't blame you for that. He had three implants and one extraction. So, four in total."

"I'm not proud of that. I'm sorry."

"You don't need to apologize to me." She smiled. Her voice was amicable yet distant.

"I'm sorry you had to find out this way." I didn't know what to say next. My loyalty to Alicia must have seemed like a form of betrayal to my mother. I wasn't good at saying goodbye. I wouldn't know how to comfort her when she began to voice concerns over how we may never see each other again. I never wanted to leave her, but I knew she would survive, even if she were stripped of everyone who cared for her.

"Edward?"

"Yes?"

"I understand where you are coming from. But please don't. I'm being very serious—don't do it. Don't go down that route. I know Chris is not a good person, but please don't, not to that extent."

I frowned. "What do you think I'm going to do?"

"I don't condone his behaviors. But it's not that he did something deserving of *that* punishment. Yes, he should face consequences. But . . . if you do something to get him to that point, you may not regret it now, but what if you do later? How will you feel?"

I became upset at her true motives. She hadn't called me over to express concern about my safety. She wasn't worried about cutting ties with me. And for some reason, she didn't think I was going to consider the more difficult option for myself.

"What do you want me to do?" I asked.

"Just stay out of it."

"You stay out of it."

"Why would you involve yourself in a situation that doesn't and shouldn't involve you?" She spoke in her own way of quiet rage. Growing up, she'd rarely raised her voice at us. Whenever she felt severely upset, she slowed down her speech and squeezed words through clenched teeth.

"So you want Alicia dead," I said.

"That's not what I'm saying." She lowered her head, trying to collect herself. "What I am saying is that you shouldn't frame Chris for something he didn't do."

She sounded like a protective female bear looking out for her cub's safety and willing to go to hideous measures to keep it safe. I felt disgusted. "How do you know he's not to blame?"

"I don't know. No one knows. And you can't just be listening to her. Because what if she isn't telling you the full truth? Because what if she's using you as a way out? She could tell you anything." Her face dramatically softened. She was now playing mother bear for me too. But I wasn't in need of her protection.

"Then so be it."

"Do you understand how people in dire situations do things that are out of character and completely horrible?"

"Are you defending Chris, or are you talking about something else?"

"I'm not defending Chris," she said. "What I'm saying is that Alicia could be using you for personal gain."

"Because you think I'm stupid? Or is it because you're the type of person yourself who lies to other people and uses them when needed? Even if she is using me, then that's my own problem. You don't need to involve yourself in a situation that doesn't involve you."

Her mouth gaped. She inhaled slightly, produced half of an inaudible, monosyllabic word, then gave up. Her eyes grew red. She knew she was not winning.

I stood from the chair and began making my way toward the door. I was aware of the disrespect, but I couldn't continue with the conversation. I told her I'd come back another time, once we were both a little more collected. Then she chased after me, blocking the exit with her body. Her face became twisted, no longer poised or beautiful. "I'm concerned about you!" she yelled.

It sounded like she thought she was being as sincere as possible. But she couldn't mend the pretentiousness overflowing from her words.

"I'll be fine. You don't need to worry about me."

"Then what are you going to do?"

"You don't really care about what I do, Mom." I sighed.

"Tell me what you are going to do."

I wanted to tell her it was none of her business. Out of the very little patience I had left in me, I swallowed my words. Instead, I asked her what she wanted to hear from me. She avoided my eyes. Her cheeks flushed, and her lips trembled. After a long pause, she squeezed out Chris's name.

"Promise me you won't hurt Chris. Please. I beg you."

It was hard to remain calm when the other party was completely enraged and insane. I could have complied with her and told her I hadn't been planning on framing Chris for the miscarriage in the first place. However, her complete disregard for me and her baseless slandering of Alicia made me want to do anything to discourage her. If I were to comply, it would mean she was right to think so little of me. Perhaps the thought of Chris dying put her in such deep distress that she was finally capable of expressing her unmasked thoughts. No matter how much she pretended like she'd treated us equally in the past, in her mind, Chris and I were never the same. I was naïve.

"Do you even care about me?" I laughed.

"Of course I care about you!" Tears welled up in her eyes as she screamed, "Please, Edward. Just—I need you to promise me you're not going to hurt Chris."

"Do you really think I'm going to do that?"

"Are you?"

"I'm not obliged to tell you anything."

"Please, Edward, don't."

"So you're just assuming that's what I'm going to do?"

"I don't know! I don't know *what* you're going to do!"

I asked myself what it would have taken to make her day a little better. Before I let myself cry in front of her, I backed down. "I'm not going to do anything to Chris."

"Thank you." She nodded repeatedly. "I know he was in the wrong. He deserves consequences—"

I glanced over at her. She quickly gave up her act.

With my newly gained freedom, I suddenly didn't want to leave anymore. I leaned my back against the wall. "So Chris's well-being matters more than mine? Right?"

She seemed caught off guard. She shook her head using the smallest range of motion possible.

"For obvious reasons, you know," I continued.

"I've been a fair parent!" my mother exclaimed.

This was factually accurate. The genetic stranger standing in front of me had indeed been "fair," and for the little amount of time she'd spent with Chris and me, she'd treated us with near equality.

"Did I tell Chris to press charges on you? I don't want you to get fired, and I don't want Chris to die. That's all I'm asking for. Is that wrong?"

"Hmm. Why was I sent to private school in high school and middle school?"

"What?" She threw her hands in the air. "How is that relevant?"

"I'm asking you, why was I sent to private school?"

"Because you failed the entrance exam?"

"How come Chris could get in but not me?"

"Because he passed the exams?" My mother's

expression grew bewildered.

"You know how to get kids into high schools. It's not that hard. You just hire them the right help."

"Chris did not cheat, nor did we pay for his way in."

"When you saw how I wasn't performing at the same level as him, why didn't I get extra help?"

"It—it was your dad," she stuttered. "He wanted to give you the same opportunities."

I sounded entitled, even to myself. I had blamed my parents from nearly twenty years ago for a failure of my own accord, which had been by no means detrimental to my future success. However, I knew I had been right. My mother was a reasonable referee, yet not an unbiased parent.

"You can't expect anything else from me." She looked at me, her eyes weary. "I've given you a very privileged life which you otherwise wouldn't have had. I housed you, fed you, and made sure you had everything Chris had. I'm not asking you to be grateful, but you have to realize that there are others who would kill to be in your position."

A part of me wanted to tell her how I'd never planned on framing Chris before her intervention, how I was just leaving Montgomery Sterling to pack up my office to make sure the only person making a sacrifice in the situation was myself. Pride forbade me from letting her have her way. I tried again not to let myself cry; I didn't want to let her know that she still had the power to hurt me.

Chapter 29

I wanted my mother to chase me down the elevator and tell me that she'd used the wrong words or that she'd been overwhelmed by too many emotions and couldn't express herself clearly. But when my car left the parking garage, she was still nowhere to be seen.

I wasn't sure if I had gained any new information. My being second priority to Chris was no secret or surprise. Yet when such a fact was blatantly presented to me, I felt extremely bothered. I was too old to have parental problems. If it were necessary, or if I had simply wanted to, I could cut my mother out of my life in one motion. Yet if I had really done so, I would have been completely rootless, as if someone had taken a hammer and knocked down the very foundation on which my entire personhood was built.

Sometimes I imagined an alien invasion where they put all humans into a rating system in order to exterminate the lackluster ones. The metrics were complicated: looks, fitness, education level, intelligence, their influence on the rest of the world, et cetera. I wondered where I would fall, or if I would survive to the end. I knew Chris would. There was no disputing that.

When I came back to the house, the kitchen smelled like rotted tomatoes mixed with different spices. Alicia walked down the stairs wearing a long nightgown. It was a white satin dress with a lace pattern embroidered in front of the chest area and a high slit on the side for walking. Her hair was freshly combed and draped over one shoulder.

"Are you eating dinner or are you going to bed?" I asked.

"Both." She looked taken aback when I didn't compliment her appearance.

"What's wrong?"

I cleared my throat to speak. Yet I didn't feel like ripping the bandage off a freshly healed wound, so I told her what I could in the most concise manner possible.

She had the exact reaction I had expected. She acted like anyone else would upon hearing the news. She covered her mouth, widened her eyes, and looked at me with concern and uncertainty.

"It's nothing I don't already know," I explained.

"Did she find out from her boyfriend?"

"No."

She sat next to me. I realized the dress was more sheer than I had first observed.

"What do you want from me?" I asked.

She scooted further away from me and then refused to engage. I demanded she speak to me; whatever it was, I wanted it to be over with.

"I wanna go see my dad before we go."

"Sure. I don't see why not."

"Is it okay if Chris comes with me? He always goes with me; my dad will wonder why he didn't come."

I wasn't sure if her father was cognizant enough. A simple lie or excuse could have sufficed. I answered yes regardless.

"You know Chris was scared of you, right?" she said.

"I'm the least scary person I know."

"He's had a hard life, in a way," she added. "He didn't like how you grew an interest in all of his hobbies, aspired to attend his dream school and follow his career path."

"I wanted to be like him because I looked up to him."

How could he have possibly understood that if I hadn't aspired to be like him, I would have stayed away from everything he did? I had zero malice in my thoughts and actions. Factually and logically, I never stood a chance at changing him.

"When we see him, will you talk to him?" she asked.

"What about? Beg him to turn himself in?"

"Will you tell him you're sorry?"

"Does my saying sorry to something irreversible suddenly change him into a different person?"

"I don't think you really know him," she said in an educational tone.

I blinked. I didn't like to be confronted by the reality that Alicia and Chris had known each other on a deeper level. They'd likely had a bond of a normal marriage for a certain period of time. I never had the chance to form one with my wife.

Chapter 30

A benefit of being a bastard child in my situation was having two mothers. A few days later, I sat in a plastic folding chair inside my biological mother's living room. Her two-seater couch was occupied by a mountain of unfolded laundry. Jeremy, her older son, was kneeling on a bag of pasta.

Since I'd received her contact information at eighteen, I rarely connected with her. My father had paid off her student debts, and she had moved on to another man, married him, and had two other children.

Reaching out to Bethany had been easy. I made a phone call and asked if she wanted to get together for my upcoming birthday. She was elated, almost desperate, yet didn't want to push our relationship beyond its capabilities. When I suggested that I drive down to her house, she couldn't stop asking what I liked for my meals: savory or sweet, crunchy or soft, satisfying or healthy. Before I even brought up the excuse, she blurted out how she knew I was busy and far away. Therefore, it never had to be the exact date.

She lived in a small town in Pennsylvania with her husband. On my drive there, I asked myself why I had avoided her. In theory, we should have been able to connect like peers. She was much younger than most of my colleagues.

The ranch-style house was small and poorly maintained. A wooden coffee table and two plastic chairs sat abandoned in the front yard. They had endured ample amounts of rain, sun, and snow. While the plastic was discolored, the wooden table was bent in the middle. Underneath the polish, the fillings had turned to an off-black color. In contrast, a brand-new stone statue stood perfectly by the muddied front door. It was shaped like an oversized rolling pin. Before I had the chance to look into the unique piece of decor, high-pitched screaming punctured the exterior walls. It sounded like multiple voices mumbling incoherent, long speeches and weeping at the same time.

Bethany welcomed me inside with poorly disguised rage written on her face. Blonde hair grew from her scalp, untamed; it stopped at her shoulders and puffed out toward the sides. In her left hand, she held a rolling pin that looked similar to the sculpture outside the door.

"Come inside, come inside," she said. "The food will be ready soon. I'm just doing something at the moment."

I looked through the door. A boy about the age of a middle schooler had his head buried in a textbook at the table. He was writing something furiously on a piece of paper, using a wooden pencil sharpened to an ungrippable length. When I walked in, the floor squeaked. The boy kept his head down, ignoring me on purpose.

Jeremy, his older brother, was kneeling by the couch. He was about sixteen years old at most, with light brown hair and a pair of green eyes that were too big for his skinny frame and long face. His sweatpants were rolled up to his thighs, exposing his kneecaps, which were decorated with multiple marblelike bruises.

Bethany went into the kitchen area; an aluminum pot was boiling on the stove. A considerable amount of steam rose from it. She retrieved a bag of spaghetti noodles from the pantry, walked to Jeremy, and ordered him to stand up. She tore the bag open and poured the noodles onto the floor.

"Get down again," she said through gritted teeth.

Jeremy quietly obeyed with hands at his sides. The noodle strands crackled when he put his weight on them. I saw him suck in a shallow breath. He lowered his head and bit both of his lips, then remained silent.

When their mother turned to set the table, the younger boy looked at me with worry in his eyes. I chased after her.

"I'm sorry." She spoke to me with exceptional gentleness, unlike how she was toward the boys. "It's just that something happened today. I know I shouldn't do this in front of you. But their dad is running late with work. And I just needed to do it."

"Do what?" I asked.

"I needed to enforce punishments."

"Because . . .?" I didn't wait for an answer. I ran to Jeremy, grabbed his elbow, and told him to stand.

"No." He shook his head firmly.

"Do not stand up! You useless piece of dog shit!" Bethany shouted at the top of her lungs. She charged at Jeremy with the rolling pin in hand and swung it full force toward his legs. She put in so much strength that her own body nearly lost balance from the strike. I blocked her before the rolling pin made contact. Jeremy remained still as the younger boy stood and gasped.

"You can't stop her!" he warned me in his prepubescent voice.

"Are you going to hit me too?" I asked Bethany.

"No, no. Of course not."

I let go of her arm. She gave me a long, blank look that was impossible to decipher. She turned around, dropped the weapon to the floor, and began weeping uncontrollably.

I helped Jeremy up. Harsh indents covered his knees. A few of the spaghetti strands dug into the surface of his skin. Thin trails of blood ran down from the newly formed cuts.

"You don't understand," Bethany whispered. "How could you possibly understand?"

I asked myself what was the worst thing a teen might have done to enrage a parent to this degree of madness. Perhaps he'd committed theft, gang violence, or accidentally gotten a girl pregnant. I tried to get an answer out of her repeatedly. She responded with desperate, heart-wrenching howls. The boy couldn't have taken someone's life; if he had, he would be in police custody and not at home. I sat her on a chair nearby and took a seat myself.

Jeremy voluntarily knelt on the pasta strands again. "I deserve it."

"What happened?" I asked.

"I didn't make baseball captain."

"Not even co-captain," Bethany added.

"But—but—" I stuttered. "There are forty kids on a team. Not everyone can be the captain. It doesn't make sense."

"How is he gonna go to college now? Where will he find a job if he doesn't at least get into Berkeley? If he doesn't get in, we'll both die! DIE! I've given him everything! And he can't even become a baseball captain to repay me! Do you realize how hard I've tried?"

I had no idea why I chose to comfort a child abuser. Out of reflex, I couldn't stand her crying anymore. When she breathed, snot bubbles burst near her nostrils. I looked around for a box of tissues and failed.

"I'm sure there are other schools . . . and with college applications . . . you never know about these things. He could still get in."

"You don't understand the competition. If he doesn't get into at least Berkeley, he'll never find a job."

"I do understand the competition. I'm sure it's not the end of the world if you don't get into a certain school."

"You do NOT!" she shouted. Gradually, the anger on her face dissipated. She moved closer to me, reaching out as if she were leaning in to give me a hug. When I showed signs of hesitation, she retracted her arms and pressed them closely to her own body. She then looked at me, dropped her voice to a whisper, and smiled eerily. "I'm happy for you, Edward."

Soon, she walked to Jeremy, who was still kneeling on the floor, and pressed her lips to his forehead.

"I'll try harder next time," Jeremy said as tears streamed down both of their faces.

Bethany then walked over to the younger boy to caress his cheek with the tips of her fingers.

"Did you know Edward went to a really good school? Isn't he accomplished?" she said. "Ask him for advice."

Chapter 31

Alicia spent nearly an hour dressing herself. She thought I didn't pay attention to her indecisiveness in the closet. In truth, I chose to walk off to give her privacy. She yelled out a few poorly made-up excuses in my direction, such as how X item was in the laundry basket or the Y pants were bad at concealing her ankle monitor. She had never once exposed it unless it was purposeful. Whoever she was dressing to impress, it wasn't me.

She twisted her body back and forth in front of the mirror, ending up in a short sweater that stopped at the small of her waist. The jeans had a colorful pattern running down the back. It was the type of design intended to show off one's buttocks.

The facility her father was in looked to be a hybrid between a hospital and a luxury hotel. At least, that was the impression the lobby gave me. It was a big open space with a tall, curved ceiling. The walls were red. A few red leather couches were placed on top of a big embroidered rug.

There was an espresso machine in the middle of the wide coffee table. It wasn't exactly elderly-friendly, as it required an extensive motion to reach forward in order to retrieve a cup of coffee.

I didn't know what the inside of the facility looked like, but I was certain that this wasn't like the common nursing homes that abused their residents. Alicia said the next step would be to go to a real hospital. But some patients, especially those with Alzheimer's like her father, could potentially stay here for a long time.

I sat in a corner of a couch. The uniformed worker at the front desk turned her head toward me, likely wondering why I had not checked in with her yet. She sent a robot with a projection screen rolling toward my feet, which played an upbeat instrumental tune during its short journey. It had pink bunny ears taped at the top of its head. It asked me what it could help me with today. I tapped on *No, thank you; I don't need any services at the moment.* It then asked me for a tip. After I paid the lowest amount, it projected a thank you message, sent a receipt to my phone, and then rolled back to the front desk.

Chris arrived early. Alicia went straight to the elevator as soon as we saw him. She put her old glass ring back on to pretend like everything was still as usual in her life. I couldn't stop her, so I let her slip it onto her finger freely. She said she was going to give it back to Chris so he could give it to whomever he wanted to next. I silently mourned for the next woman.

In about an hour, I saw them walking out together. Neither seemed upset. They kept a slight distance between each other, with Chris a few steps behind her. The sight of them in each other's proximity made me realize how extremely well suited they were, even to my unkind eyes. I was forced to submit to their compatibility, something that could only be achieved through endless time and interactions together. They were a natural pair, despite their ill-fated marriage. I had witnessed them next to each other countless times. When I was younger, it stung me greatly. Gradually, the irritation stopped until today, when I wanted to pull her away and say that there was no reason for them to be in the same building anymore, as the visit was over.

I stood to greet them. Alicia took a side step away from Chris.

"I'll take one of the cars back," she said quietly. "Bye, Chris."

"Bye."

Her heels made a series of steady clunks. Chris turned his head in her direction until she made her way out of the lobby through two sets of automatic sliding doors. He looked even thinner than our last encounter. The areas near his eyes were a shade of blueish green. I wasn't sure if it was from a lack of rest or from the facial trauma. The bruising and cuts on his face had healed tremendously. However, they were far from disappearing. The gaps caused by the missing teeth were gone, even when he opened his mouth to speak. He spoke rather normally. But the time of the facial trauma occurring was too recent to put in implants. They had to be covered by flippers.

He turned back toward me.

"Can I talk to you?" I asked.

"Yeah." He looked around the lobby. "My car?"

Chris drove a black sedan, which was nowhere near as ostentatious as his residence. It hid itself well among the other cars in the crowded parking lot.

He opened the door to the driver's side and climbed in. I held a preconceived notion that the passenger seat was going to be pulled up to accommodate someone of a shorter stature, likely a woman. To my surprise, it was set to give the same amount of legroom as the driver's seat.

He had owned the car for a handful of years, yet the interior was more sterile than a hospital. There were no personal items stored in it, nor did it smell like anything other than the cold air outside. I turned on the heating under my seat.

Chris rested his hands on the steering wheel. I could count the number of tubelike tendons protruding against his paper-white complexion. His knuckles looked enlarged, and the sharp bones were barely concealed by a thin layer of skin. Long blue veins ran down the palms of his hands and then disappeared into the sleeves of his jacket.

"Are you going to work afterward?" he asked.

"I'm unemployed."

He looked at me and sighed.

"I'm sorry," I said.

He took a moment to respond, then smiled at me with his lips pressed together.

My jaw dropped at his lack of combativeness. I had not anticipated this level of self-awareness. It was a miracle that a simple apology from my end was able to bring out the goodness in Chris, at least on a superficial level. "Are you in a hurry? Can I talk to you about something?"

"Of course. I can cancel as many things as I need to."

"I'm sorry about the other day. It was uncalled for," I said, repeating myself.

"You know tooth damage is permanent, right? Implants have to be replaced every ten years. I've only had one cavity my entire life. Now I'm in and out of the dentist's office all the time."

"Meemaw came over and gave some inappropriate guesses on how you were hurt."

"Ha. Meemaw." Chris raised his voice slightly. "If it makes you feel better, I had to get stitches in my mouth as well as dig out the leftover roots that were still in the jawbone. I hope it makes you less upset."

I felt bad for deriving pleasure from someone else's misery, yet I was very much doing so.

"I don't know what would be enough of a punishment for me," Chris added. "Probably falling into a pit of anteaters or something like that."

"I don't know what you mean by anteaters. She said the same thing once before."

"It's . . . an inside joke," he explained. It sounded provocative, yet it was probably just an innocent and honest answer.

I didn't know if there was anything else left for me to say. My scalp tingled. If the conversation wasn't progressing to something important, he would quickly find a reason to kick me out and command the car to drive away. He was known to be busy.

"Will you take care of her for me?" Chris asked. "Cut

the 'for me' part if it makes you uncomfortable," he added generously.

"I—" Based on the sincerity on his face, it didn't look like he was lying.

"Tell her I love her," he said.

"What . . .?" I nearly threw up at his lack of shame and his ineffective attempt at salvaging his broken image.

I told him if he wanted Alicia to know anything, he should have said it to her himself.

"Just do me a favor. I know you don't like me much," he continued. "I was still going to take care of the situation. But then she went to you, so I figured I shouldn't complicate things."

"What were you going to do?"

"There're ways to get around it."

"How?"

"There are ways. You'd be surprised how many things can be done differently if you speak to the right people. If it all goes well, then she won't need to serve for more than sixteen months. And once she gets out, I'll step out of her life."

I was stunned. "You just said you love her, but you want to put her in prison for sixteen months? How do you justify that? Do you think she's fit for prison life?"

"It's not ideal." He semi-laughed at me. "How many times do I need to tell you that I'm not a perfect person?"

"At least you're honest. Because who would sacrifice themselves when they can sacrifice other people?"

"Hey," he whispered, almost coddling me in my loss of temper. He looked weak and desperately in need of some food. I noticed the hollowness in his cheeks and gray hair emerging against the dark ones. A grayish film hovered over his brown irises. It wasn't how people with naturally gray eyes looked. His were murky and contained a great lack of focus, to the point where I questioned his sight. "If you are going to hire a coyote—assuming you will— whatever they tell you to do, know that they have good intentions."

"What do you know that I don't?"

"Nothing." Chris shook his head. It was the sloppiest lie I had ever heard from him. It was a refusal to answer my question, not a disguise or evasion. I couldn't have gotten any more information out of him, even if I had physically tried to pry his mouth open.

"Is there anything else you want to say to me?"

He looked straight through the windshield. "No."

Chapter 32

Chris killed himself that day.

At approximately five o'clock in the afternoon, which was when he made his way home, he took out a handgun, loaded it on the spot, and shot himself through the temple. He carried out the sequence of actions with fluidity. It was well executed yet extremely spontaneous at the same time. There wasn't a will or a message left. He never even bothered to close the door when he entered the apartment. He had scheduled to have dinner with a friend that night. When it was half an hour past the set time and his phone wasn't being answered, the friend became worried.

I received the message late at night. Alicia was asleep. I slowly slid myself out of bed to answer the call in another room and successfully managed not to wake her. I threw on some clothes and ran to the garage. About a mile into the drive to my mother's, I made the car turn back. I snuck into the house and moved every electronic device I could think of to the back seat of my car: phones, watches, glasses, computers, et cetera. I couldn't leave her with methods of being notified about what had happened. I needed to be there when she received the news.

My mother's boyfriend blocked me at the door. He was wearing a set of pajamas with a robe on top. He looked like he had not slept in years. "She doesn't want to see you," he said.

I tried to go around him. He moved with me and grabbed me firmly.

"She said you are the last person she needs right now," he explained. He was calm but not at all apologetic or sympathetic toward me.

"This has nothing to do with you."

I hated how this random man was now projecting authority over me, controlling whom my mother could see or not see. He tried to talk to me about how I had other options—to come back at another time or to ask for a search of Chris's belongings; maybe he had left a hidden will or letter.

His effort at barring me at the entrance was persistent. As I argued with him, my mother came out from the hallway. She wore matching clothes with Tristan. I felt like an intruder. She cursed at me, demanded I get out, and screamed about how she hated me. I told her to calm down when she began throwing whatever object she had access to in my direction: a bottle of vitamin C, a box of tissues, and a tube of disinfecting wipes. Tristan held both her arms together. She kicked and grunted like a mad dog. She managed to take a few steps forward to claw at me with her sharp nails. I watched her until Tristan lifted her feet off the ground.

On the drive back to my house, I thought about how Alicia would react in the morning. Would she direct her grief at me and behave like my mother? I tried to come up with a script of what to say to her when she woke up. There was no way to deliver a piece of bad news gently; no matter how many words of cushioning I was going to use, I had to state the facts.

She didn't give me the opportunity to watch her being taken apart by hysteria. When I went inside, the lights were on. She sat on the floor, leaning her upper body against the drawers built into the counter. A long stream of blood ran down from her left wrist. It remained a fine line for quite a distance. Near the end, it gathered itself into a puddle. She must have found out on her own. As I ran to her, I saw the puddle spreading wider.

I didn't like the sight of blood. But I didn't have the right to decide what I liked and didn't like, just like how I didn't have the right to react to Chris's death the way I organically wanted to. I was furious at her for doing whatever she wanted without considering the consequences her actions had on others. And I was forced to take on the role of the sane person who cleaned up after her mental instability.

The smallest of my cutting knives lay inches away from her body. I grabbed the closest kitchen towel within sight. It was clean. I tied it around her bleeding wrist securely and pressed on it as hard as I could. She looked at me with hateful eyes and punched me weakly, telling me to leave her alone. I held her down.

I was frightened by how much blood the towel absorbed within seconds. Redness traced each horizontal and vertical line of cotton thread, weaving its way through the crosshatched patterns that held the piece of fabric together. It was like putting a piece of tissue against the tip of a fountain pen. When I used one for writing, I did so to check the flow and to clear out potential small blockages. Each time, I saw the small black or blue dot crawl into a sizable stain, following the internal pattern of the tissue, which looked like the spreading roots of a fast-growing plant. Or human capillaries. I knew a pen could hold plenty of ink, and a new bottle could always be purchased. Still, I was always anxious about pressing the tissue against the pen tip for too long, thus draining it entirely.

After her short burst of exertion, her body went limp. I patted her face, shook her shoulders, then begged her to tell me how much she hated me.

Taking her to the hospital would be theoretically faster. If I were to call for an ambulance, she could receive attention as soon as the paramedics arrived. When I let go of the pressure on her wrist, even for a brief second, blood immediately began oozing out uncontrollably. With one free hand, I reached for my phone and dialed 9-1-1.

A robotic female voice answered after the first beep:

Thank you for calling 911 emergency services, brought to you by the American Center of Emergency Safety. Powered by the Mary Stilwell Foundation of Electricity, who invented the incandescent light bulb in 1879. Your call is very important to us. If you know the extension of the entity you are trying to reach, you can dial it at any time. Please listen closely as the menu has changed. For emergencies involving weapons or an active shooter, please press 1. For emergencies regarding threats of attack or dangerous personnel, please press 2. For emergencies regarding wild animals, please press 3. For emergencies regarding break-ins or theft, please press 4. For emergencies regarding transportation safety, including but not limited to rear-end collisions, head-on collisions, sideswipe accidents, speeding, or single-vehicle accidents, please press 5. For emergencies regarding all manually operated vehicles, regardless of the type of collision, please press 6. To request ambulance services, please press Star to connect with a customer representative.

I pressed Star.

Thank you for contacting the emergency medical transportation department. Your emergency is very important to us. If you do not have a medical emergency, please press Pound to return to the main menu. If you are requesting a transportation vehicle, please stay on the line; a customer representative will be with you shortly. In the meantime, to learn more about our other services, please visit our website at www.asapsafety.org. That is W-W-W dot A-S-A-P-S-A-F-E-T-Y dot O-R-G. Due to a high volume of callers, all of our customer representatives are assisting other callers on the line. Your current estimated wait time to speak with a customer representative is one hundred and twenty minutes. In the meantime, feel free to leave a voicemail message by pressing 0. Otherwise, please stay on the line and wait to speak to a customer representative shortly.

I moved Alicia to the back seat of my own car. I regretted that I hadn't done my research before calling the national emergency number. The automated voice began repeating the same message. With a stained thumb, I tapped the hang-up button. After a few tries, I noticed that the color of the supposedly red button had dulled. To prevent callers from hanging up, the system had dismantled its function.

The car drove on. I held Alicia's wrist with one hand as I tried to get the 9-1-1 voice to shut up. I pressed Pound to return to the main menu, and then I pressed to hang up again. The screen refreshed itself, and the voice continued; this time, all buttons were dimmed.

Thank you for contacting 9-1-1 emergency services, brought to you by the American Center of Emergency Safety. Powered by the Mary Stilwell Foundation of Electricity, who invented the incandescent light bulb in 1879. Your satisfaction with our services is very important to us. Would you like to participate in a quick survey at the end of the call? Please state yes or no.

"No."

No problem. Is there anything else we can help you with today? Please state yes or no.

"No."

All right. Thank you for choosing 9-1-1 emergency services. If you need any further assistance in the future, please know you can depend on us at any time. To hear about our environmental protection policy, please state "environmental policy inquiry." To hear about our pledge to end socioeconomic discrimination once and for all, please state the "antidiscrimination" policy. Would you like to add a tip for today's services? How much tip would you like to add today? Your options are two hundred and nine dollars, one hundred and sixty-nine dollars, and one hundred twenty-nine dollars. Please state the desired amount.

I threw my phone toward the front of the car. After landing on the windshield, it bounced back and ended up in the passenger seat. Like it had been advertised by the seller, it was *undamaged, uncracked, and unstoppable*. The voice grew louder and louder, eventually becoming a reminder of how much time I had wasted on the drive. At one point, I couldn't endure it any longer. I reached for it and stated, "One hundred and twenty-nine dollars."

Would you like to enter a specific payment method? Please note that we accept credit card payments with a 53 percent transactional fee. Electronic checks are preferred with a one-time guaranteed transactional fee of fifty-nine dollars and ninety-nine cents. Please say "specific payment" method. Otherwise, we will be happy to send a bill directly to the address linked with your phone number. Please say, "Send my bill to a different address" to send your bill to a different address. Otherwise, please expect your invoice to be delivered in the next five to seven business days.

Thank you for choosing 9-1-1 emergency services, brought to you by the American Center of Emergency Safety, powered by the Mary Stilwell Foundation of Electricity, who invented the incandescent light bulb in 1879. We hope to service you again soon.

When I entered the emergency room, I was certain my lack of knowledge had killed her. How could I have wasted such precious time trusting the ambulance over myself? My clothes were covered in red fingerprints and smudges that were either hers or my own. I told the medical staff that, if she needed a transfusion, we were a match, and they could draw as much blood as they needed from me. After they wheeled her away on a stretcher, a different doctor came to speak with me.

"You don't need to worry. We ordered a pregnancy test ASAP. We'll be able to intervene as soon as the test comes back negative." She smiled at me reassuringly.

"She's not pregnant. Can you please do the test afterward?"

"Customer, you have to understand that we can't legally help people with uteruses until we confirm a negative pregnancy test."

"But she's not pregnant."

"It's for liability reasons."

"She's passed out. How are you going to do a test?"

"We ordered a blood test."

"You're drawing more blood?"

Annoyance quickly rose on the doctor's face.

I knew they were going to take too long at that point, or simply forget to help her. I didn't know why I was so heavily compelled to argue with medical staff at that moment. It wasn't her fault. She was simply following standard protocol. However, in the immediate moment, she was the person with the highest level of authority, who was refusing to spare an ounce of kindness. We went back and forth until the alarm rang throughout the entire building, accompanied by flashing yellow lights. Someone had been identified as an active shooter. I lost the attention of the crowd.

Chapter 33

Like most shootings, the shooter had only shot himself. After he fell from the wound, he was wheeled into an operating room.

Because Alicia and I had the same last name, at first, the hospital staff mistook me for her husband. A younger version of me would have felt overjoyed by it. I clarified immediately and told them I wasn't her husband, and that her husband had killed himself less than twenty-four hours ago. They looked at me like I was crazy and quickly walked away.

The doctors said I was entirely overreacting, and Alicia was never in any critical condition to begin with. They said the fainting was a result of low blood sugar and not the loss of blood in its volume. They blamed it on her eating habits and an unbalanced diet. She was generously given a room out of caution and was expected to be discharged in the next few days.

From the hospital bed, I couldn't tell how "fine" she was. Although she had regained consciousness, she was weak, lethargic, rarely ate more than a few bites, and didn't speak more than a few words at once. The doctors and nurses eventually grew tired of my asking if she was truly safe, or if they could give her more attention or pain management. They began ignoring me.

I called Ian. He brought me and Alicia both some clothes and other miscellaneous items. He sat with me in the room for a long time on the initial day. We both kept silent—not to avoid disturbing her, as she had her eyes open and was actively looking at us, but to avoid the pain of having to bring up the incident. There was nothing to say.

At night, she was given medication to make her drowsy. Even when she slept, I felt incapable of doing the same. I was given a brown faux-leather chair. The bottom extended for the user to put their feet up, but the back was stiff and remained at a ninety-degree angle. When I closed my eyes, I thought of Chris. Not about his smugness or the terrible deeds he had done—instead, I recalled us playing together as kids and his surprise visit to my first FRC competition as a driver student. I attempted to think of unpleasant memories of when we had our disagreements or the occasions when he spoke to me with condescending conciseness. When I waited for sadness to settle over me, it never did.

Ian took our old clothes back to wash. I no longer looked like a murderer, yet I felt like one entirely. I never took into consideration the signs of distress: Chris asking me to tell her how he loved her would've only been disgusting if he had chosen to stay out of the situation to save himself. As a form of last wishes, they were perfectly reasonable to the degree that I could even argue that he was sincerely sorry. If I had called Alicia as soon as I started driving back and told her what he had told me, she would have recognized the problem immediately. I knew she would have.

I pushed the chair closer to her bed and watched her sleep. When I was tired enough, I began having hallucinations of Chris entering the room. He walked straight to her bed nonchalantly and spoke to her as if she were aware. My presence was ignored by both of them. Their dismissiveness comforted me in a familiar way.

When I shook myself awake due to an inability to rest, I cursed Chris. As a murderer, I had failed horribly. His death solved no existing problems and, in contrast, created even more. He must have done it to spite us. If he were regretful, he would have left a message. While most people hoped for their deaths to serve some form of meaning, Chris made himself a burden for others. I couldn't think of any other behavior more spineless and self-centered.

I contacted the police again and requested a thorough search of everything Chris owned, including his notepads on all of his public and personal devices. Before they returned an answer, I fantasized about Alicia's murder charges being dropped. If Chris had taken responsibility for it, I planned on forgiving him instantly.

On the day she was to be discharged from the hospital, the police informed me they had found nothing in Chris's belongings that contained what I was looking for. They had read through his handwritten journal line by line and word by word, including the entries from years ago. There was nothing substantial. I became even more enraged by his lack of basic human decency. If he had truly wanted his hypothetical pain to end, why not help out someone else he'd hurt in the first place? It was the simplest act of kindness with zero consequences; he wouldn't need to live to see himself being condemned. He didn't need to experience the shame attached to his confession. I tried to ask myself what he had gained from committing the act in his way. If he had wished for freedom or relief, how could he possibly have gained it through not solving the problem that he'd created? And if he wanted to remain malicious, he should have lived to show every person he had hurt that he was able to move on with his life in complete happiness.

Alicia looked better but was far from being "in excellent health," as labeled by the hospital staff. A tint of color returned to her face. Her hair grew greasy and formed thicker strands, especially near her forehead. I couldn't identify if the extreme mellowness in her movement came from a lack of strength or a depressive mindset. The doctors promised she would be "jumping up and down" within the next few days.

Since wheelchairs were no longer used at medical facilities, I carried her out in my arms.

I knew she wasn't going to give me the luxury of cooperation once we got home. She had only behaved perfectly in the hospital because she knew she couldn't have gotten away with their suicide prevention protocols. I could tell how she was planning on stirring up trouble again by the defiant look she gave me on our ride back.

A few hours later, she threw her dinner at my face. I

told her it was going to take a while until she could starve herself to death. I was too sleep-deprived to continue my previous coddling of her. The only way to keep her safe was to physically limit her freedom. I took several exercise bands from the gym and tied her feet and her right arm to the bedposts. I made sure the knots were too tight and too complicated for her to unfasten with her injured hand.

With her immobilized, I lay beside her and slept. I woke up to her calling out my name. Outside, the sky had turned to the darkest shade of blue before the night's total takeover. A few bright stars hung near the corner of our window. They were premature.

"I need to go to the bathroom," she said.

I untied her and walked her in. To my surprise, she didn't fuss.

When we passed the counter, she tilted her head down and looked at it intensely. She plunged her body forward, directing her head at the tip of the faucet. It was stupidity at its finest. I caught her body with her head less than a full inch away from making contact with the metal. I told her she was not going to the bathroom anymore.

With neither of us in our right minds, I threw her over my shoulder and slammed her back onto the bed. Ignoring the reddened circles around her ankles and wrist, I tied them back to the bedposts, including the bandaged arm this time. She struggled against me and attempted to push me off her. I could have been more considerate; due to how she was fighting, she could have potentially burst open her wound or ripped off the bandaging. However, if I were to calm her down by letting her have her way, she would have ended herself long ago.

When she finally stopped tugging against the restraints, her voice became calm. I told her to shut up. I needed to keep to my word. Her lack of consideration annoyed me. I had not had my time to grieve yet. Regardless of my true feelings, it should have been a happy occasion for her and a gut-wrenching one for me. Chris had never harmed me. Our roles should have been reversed.

I watched her plead, using her best ability to reason. She twisted her body left and right, then pretended like she was sorry for causing trouble.

How hard could it be to change some bedsheets? There were plenty of extras stored in the closet. I could temporarily untie her feet, wipe her off with a towel, then simply strip the sheets and mattress cover and put on a set of new ones. Crazy people did not deserve freedom. It would have caused some pain, but in theory and in principle, I was correct. She needed to start behaving like a rational person in order to be treated like one. Her so-called pain was not an excuse to make me a disposable servant.

She struggled for longer than I thought before she peed herself. When I went over to check on her, she refused to look at my face. She made a series of guttural noises. Two white stripes were left on her face, in the place where tears glided against her skin. She winced when I began removing the sheets from the bottom of the bed. She tilted her head backward, pressing it forcefully into the pillow. Her chest heaved up and down in the most violent way I had ever witnessed. I could see her ribs protruding underneath the fabric of her shirt. With each shortened breath that lasted for a fraction of a second, she gasped sharply, like she was struggling to acquire oxygen.

Despite what had been absorbed by the sheets, the anti-moisture mattress protector managed to collect the urine into a small puddle. Since her shirt was long, I needed to peel off her clothing entirely. The other option was letting her lie in filth.

I fought against an erection. I must have been a hideous person to the highest degree to derive pleasure from another person's pain. Yet, I wondered to myself, why were the noises of discomfort so similar to the ones people made when aroused? In sex, the short-term intrusion or irritation was usually followed by a longer duration of euphoria. In this case, I had no happiness to offer her afterward.

I couldn't imagine the amount of humiliation she was feeling at the moment. Had I elicited pain in her just to assert power over her and show her that she had none, even over herself? Had I purposefully done this to her because I knew she couldn't fight back?

No words of comfort could roll off my tongue in a half-sincere way. If it had been something medically necessary, I would have been able to comfort her, as well as myself, due to the moral high ground of helping someone. Instead, I was facing a mistake that I'd created out of ignorance and stubbornness. My intention to keep her safe had turned into additional harm that was completely artificial and avoidable. By standing firm behind my so-called principle, I'd created an impossible situation to navigate.

When working on a computer, there was a reliable button to undo the last command. With one click, the previous mistake was erased, and I was given the opportunity to change the past. In life, not only was I forced to live on with the mistake, but I was also forced to continue its trajectory. At that moment, with my hands on her naked body, I wanted to turn back time so I could watch our lives together as an outsider who had no right to walk away.

"Why would you do this to me?" she asked when I finished freeing her from the bedposts. She held her arms out as if asking for a hug. Since the drive to the hospital, I had carried her body many times, but I had only held her out of necessity rather than intimacy.

I leaned over and put my forehead against hers. The strands near her face were wet to my fingertips.

"I'm sorry, I'm sorry," I repeated. "I know you don't wanna see me right now, but I'm not going anywhere this time. I shouldn't have left you alone."

I sat on the bed next to her. She propped up her body with her good arm. I pulled her into me and patted the back of her head. Slowly, she wasn't shaking anymore. "I miss him," she said.

It felt like hours until she tired herself out. The guilt hanging over my head dimmed itself temporarily. I walked her into the bathroom and helped her into the tub. I lathered her legs with soap and rinsed her off with the showerhead. I then filled the tub with warm water. She sat in it, leaving the bandaged arm outside the rim. I leaned her back until the line of water crept up near her eyebrows. I rubbed shampoo into her hair, then her conditioner.

Chapter 34

We ate junk food together late at night.

"Steak," she said.

"The meats are in the freezer. Is there anything else you'd like?"

"I'm not sure."

"I don't know either."

"Can we order pizza?"

I agreed. She carried our pillows in her arms, and I carried her down the stairs. The couch in the main living room doubled as a bed. We ordered a large pizza. It came with a liter of lemon-flavored soda and a box of glazed chicken wings. The dipping sauces never arrived. Luckily, the chicken was fully cooked. With Alicia under medication, we did not drink.

A glowing layer of red oil floated on the surface of the pizza and gathered itself in the indents of the pepperoni slices. The cheese was cold and hardened after the delivery. After heating, it became too far melted to stay in its original shape.

She covered her legs with a blanket. A cushion was behind the small of her back. She sat cross-legged.

"Do you want to see a movie?"

"I want to see an animated one," she said.

"Let me see . . . live-action *Finding Marlin 8*?"

"No."

"Live action *A Bug's Life: Into the Future, Part IV* ?"

"No."

We watched the first movie that showed up on the recommendations page. A twenty-minute-and-thirty-second unskippable ad came through in eight-minute increments. She scolded me for not paying for the ad-free version of the streaming application. I told her it was about principle. Then she scolded me for the inconsistent ad blocker I'd installed.

It was the only meal I had the opportunity to eat the entire day. When the first few bites entered my system, I felt a sudden wave of lightheadedness. In a daze, I recalled the way my family had once eaten together. My legs had dangled due to the height of the chair; I had worn a pair of red Crocs. I couldn't have been older than five or six. My mother was an unwilling participant.

My father had hovered over the table. He had a very particular relationship with food; he consumed meals in large quantities with a cherishing attitude toward every shred of lettuce and every crumb of bread. This attitude was inherited by Chris, though its effect looked completely different. They'd both mastered the artistry of dissecting chicken wings to clean the bones to the highest degree possible. After eating the easily accessible parts, they broke the flat wings in half through the connected cartilage, either with their fingers or by biting into it. Then they would suck on the thin bones vertically until they were completely free of any meat, tendons, or even the purple blood vessels. Chris said it was similar to digging up his own fossil pieces. Therefore, it was scientific and mentally stimulating. He would piece the cleaned bones back together in the wing's original shape on a napkin. Granted, he was not much older than me.

My father, on the other hand, possessed a strong hatred for food waste. He grew up starving and frequently skipped meals. It was a prolonged experience Chris and I could not replicate. I was puzzled by their behavior. I saw no purpose in my father's unnecessary appreciation, nor in Chris's methodical approach.

Thinking of them, I stared into the box of chicken wings sitting on the coffee table and cried. It startled Alicia. I realized, in that moment, that I still loved Chris. Even though I had no reason to, nor did he deserve it.

Alicia held me as I sobbed. In a way, it felt ceremonial. When I was calm again, her head bopped back and forth. It was late. She closed her eyes for a brief moment and spoke in a whiny voice. "What if I just go to bed without flossing today?"

"Absolutely not."

"Just once?"

"No."

"I'm surprised your mom didn't turn you into a dentist."

"I had a phase where I wanted to fill teeth for a living.

My dad said he wouldn't pay for dental school. I don't know why."

"Did you? How is your mom doing, by the way?"

"She's fine. I saw her boyfriend there with her."

She hummed and shifted the way she sat. I didn't want to leave the scene of the two of us sitting in front of a TV at midnight. It gave me delusions of peace. But I couldn't stop reality from settling itself in between us.

"I'm sorry," I said again.

"What for?"

"When I talked to him, he wanted me to tell you he loved you. I thought he was being disingenuous, so I didn't take it seriously. If I had told you about it, things might have been different."

To my surprise, she did not have a reaction to my words at all. "Do you think he's happy now? He has to be, right? Because who would do something that doesn't make themselves happy?"

A hypothesis occurred to me without warning: if Chris had confessed his crimes and solved the problem at the cost of his life, he would have been granted redemption. An easy choice had sat in front of him. However, what if he never wanted redemption in the first place? I could have remembered him as a loving brother. His deeds would have been erased from all of our minds. What if he had wanted forgiveness but didn't feel like he deserved it? What if he had hated himself so much that he couldn't let himself be redeemed?

"I think if Chris was here, he wouldn't have liked what you did to yourself," I said.

She nodded softly. "Everything hurts."

I took her bandaged arm and placed it on my lap. "When I tried to call for an ambulance, it gave me a wait time of over a hundred minutes just to speak to a dispatcher. And then I got mad at myself because I didn't do the research beforehand. I'm suddenly becoming worried. Not just for you, but for myself too."

"What do you need to worry about? Has anything ever concerned you?"

"Everything. And it's not because of you. How can I be happy when everyone around me is angry and upset? How can I be successful when everyone else is failing? Even if I can reap the most benefits by staying here, how long would that last? Don't blame yourself for what is temporary. I can never blame you. And if, one day, you are so sick of me and want to get rid of me, I want us to be in a place where everyone will be safe in the end. Is that all right with you?"

She turned toward me. With the light coming from behind her body, I couldn't read her expression clearly. Slowly, she leaned her head on my shoulder. I wished that she would not blame me for what I had done to her. I couldn't forgive myself at all for my behavior. Yet although I felt bad for her, deep down, I knew that there was nothing she could do about it, and there was no one else for her to run to.

Chapter 35

A couple of weeks later, I got a call from Ben. He told me that Henry, the junior associate, couldn't go to work due to an urgent housing issue. He had previously contacted two of his friends to assist him in moving to his new apartment. Unfortunately, neither of them were able to show up.

"What housing issue?" I asked.

"I don't remember exactly what it was—it was something about his landlord. He just has to move today. I signed you up for it as soon as he told me. I thought you might have been free," Ben said enthusiastically, as if he were granting me an irresistible favor.

"I am free." I looked at the half-packed boxes in the closet, waiting to be picked up by Ian and shipped later.

"If there's time after you guys are done, would you like to have dinner?"

"Of course."

Alicia was sleeping. She was breathing peacefully with her eyes gently closed. She hugged a body pillow snugly;

one of her legs made its way on top of it, making her look like a koala hanging onto a tree trunk.

I was happy to see no sign of pain in her sleep. Something within her had changed recently, but I couldn't pinpoint the reason behind it. She wasn't cheerful, but she rarely shed tears. I had become the one to cry more often since Chris's passing.

On our way to Henry's apartment, we sat together in the back seat of my car while her sedan drove itself behind mine. She'd put on a pair of light blue overalls and found some leather working boots for herself. As she slipped them on, the length and width of her feet had dramatically increased. She covered the crown of her head with a red scarf. The brown curls in her hair draped around her shoulders.

After we injected ourselves into the traffic streams of the city, we passed by a drive-through Dunkin'. A long line of cars stalled in front of us to pick up their preordered items. Once we entered the lane, there was no way to back out. People stuck their heads out of the windows every minute or so, despite the chilling weather. Only one of the windows was serving customers. When I was younger, the entire street would have been bombarded with honking noises. Lucky for the few workers in the store, all honks in vehicles had been mandatorily removed.

Alicia received the wrong donut and a cup of hot macchiato that wasn't much taller than the width of her palm. The top of the lid was stained, and its rim had collected a thin strip of spilled coffee. She took the drink in her hand and looked at me with widened eyes. I pressed my lips tightly together, attempting not to laugh at her reaction. Suspicious of its weight, she pried open the lid carefully without getting her hands wet.

"Someone drank out of it!" she exclaimed.

I turned my body toward the window and chuckled.

She held the cup close to my face. The brownish liquid, which smelled nothing like coffee, was filled about halfway to the top. It swayed freely back and forth with very little risk of pouring over, even in a moving car.

"No one drank out of it." I pointed at the minuscule amount of bubbles clutching the walls of the cup. "They had to leave room for the foam. I told you to get an extra large, didn't I?"

She tilted her head back and swallowed the drink in a singular, determined gulp. And then she looked at me as a burst of laughter escaped her. Her eyes sparkled like it was the funniest thing she had ever experienced. She had a high-pitched laugh, almost cartoonishly evil. When she inhaled, she involuntarily made an oinking noise. It sounded like a pig, but I'd never told her that; I was afraid she would have thought I disliked it and then stopped laughing in front of me.

Our cars stopped in front of a small building covered in deep red bricks. The street was crowded and filled with small, similarly designed buildings. Henry did not own a vehicle, as he took the subway daily to commute to work. By taking both my and Alicia's cars, we should be able to finish the move in one trip.

The apartment complex Henry lived in was about five stories tall and seemed to be too old to equip elevators.

There were two steps of concrete stairs leading into the rusty entrance of the building. A big corner of the top step had fallen off and broken into different pieces on the ground. One big trash bag was leaning against the front door, leaking gray garbage juice. I wasn't expecting a penthouse or a suburban mansion, but I couldn't help but double-check the address on my phone.

I shrugged at Alicia and walked into the building with skepticism. She took my hand and followed closely. The black, dusty stairwell scared her. I made up a story in my mind of how Henry spent most of his paycheck on weed, alcohol, and a slew of other drugs, so he was forced to live in a building like this. Maybe there was a much more disoriented side of him that I had not witnessed. He could have been a big partygoer or someone who donated endlessly to streamers on the internet. I then recalled how reserved he was at the firm's karaoke functions. He seemed like a responsible person and was even put off by disco lights.

The hallways smelled of fried egg mixed with a lemon-scented cleaning solution. The stairs underneath us creaked in different spots as we climbed up.

I comforted her, "At least he's not on the very top floor."

"He's getting an upgrade, right?" she whispered. The door we passed by was blasting a boxing match loudly, accompanied by a male and female voice screaming at each other at the top of their lungs. Besides the curse words, the only word I heard clearly was *crab*.

Henry waited for us in front of his apartment on the

fourth floor. This level of the building smelled of a different type of rancidness. It was no longer fried eggs. It was sewage.

Presumably, all of his belongings had been piled up in the hallway. The carpet they sat on was a mixed shade of green and gray. It was falling apart. There was one big black suitcase and extra-large cardboard boxes. Two laundry bags with strings were stuffed to the max and tied on the top.

The young lawyer was wearing a yellow raincoat stained at the sleeves, a pair of black rubber boots, and gloves. He was a sizable man in all directions, considerably taller than even Chris. The oversized protective gear was making him look like a walking tent.

"Edward! Thank you so much for coming!" He smiled at us. His skin was dampened with sweat. Several red curls stuck to his large forehead. The gloves covering his hands were visibly wet from a mostly clear liquid.

"This is Alicia," I said.

"Hello!" Henry waved at her. "I'm Henry. *He, him, his.* It's very nice to meet you. I would shake hands, but . . . you know."

"Is there anything inside we need to move besides these?" I asked, glancing at what was in front of us.

"Yes. I just have two more bags inside."

"I'll go get them."

He stopped me from following his steps into the apartment. "It's kind of offensive in there." He returned to us quickly with two large white trash bags in each hand. "These two are trash. And these can go in the car."

He pointed me toward the trash chute. The door was

sealed shut by layers of duct tape; its handle was rusted and barely hanging on. A very large, presumably sturdy trash bag was tied to and held up by it. Bags of other trash had filled it nearly to the brim. I squeezed one of the bags in and left the other leaning against the wall. A thick, whitish, creamy liquid leaked out from the bottom and onto the carpet. To temporarily address the spillage, someone had put a thin layer of plastic film over it, trapping it into a sealed puddle. It must have been there for a number of days. A green-colored mold spread itself in circles in various spots underneath the film. The stench was overwhelming, and there was a mix of rotten food, sewage, and an unidentifiable odor similar to the disinfecting sprays used in public restrooms.

"I already got everything out," Henry said. "If you people can start moving some to the car, that would be great. I don't mean to rush you. But the dorm I'm moving into only gives me a forty-five-minute moving window with guests."

"You're moving into a dorm?"

"It's a long story. But I'm thankful for it."

Alicia tilted her body, attempting to see into the apartment through its opened door. "Is everything okay . . . ?"

"The toilet was kind of spitting water. That's why I have to get out today," Henry explained.

"Have you talked to Montgomery about it? Why don't you ask if Travels can put you in a hotel for a while? If it's a plumbing issue, they have to fix it fast, right?"

"Oh, the landlord is going to take months to fix it. The

dorm will let me live there until June, and I can look for a new place in the meantime."

"But plumbing is an urgent issue. Shouldn't they fix it immediately before the entire building floods?" Alicia sounded stunned.

"There's a policy that no amenities will be fixed unless more than ten units are affected. They came to put a bucket under the toilet and taped the lid and body together. It'll be fine for a while," Henry said, his voice surprisingly relaxed. Although it was his apartment that was collecting water mixed with fecal matter, he seemed less bothered than Alicia and me combined.

He did not own any of the furniture in the studio apartment. Luckily, the dorm at SDU provided all the necessities. It was slightly concerning how a grown man was going to be living in a college dorm next to a group of undergraduate kids. He had asked for a graduate hall but was denied by the administration. It turned out that SDU had partnered up with law firms in the New York City area to provide affordable housing for junior associates under twenty-six years old.

I wondered if I was so out of touch with reality that I had never heard about this housing option for young associates. No one had ever brought up the topic of personal finance at work. As a group of people, we were far more interested in other companies' numbers than our own, yet even the post-tax salary of a first-year associate should have been enough to provide a comfortable lifestyle. The situation Henry faced was absurdly unsanitary. I had the urge to take out my phone to take pictures and send them to Ben and everyone else at the firm.

Henry quickly peeled off his rain gear and left it in the apartment. He stacked two of the large boxes on top of each other and picked them up easily, leaving me with the lighter boxes.

Alicia grabbed the straps on one of the laundry bags. She was only able to minimally lift it off the ground. She put her hands on her hips, trying to use her thigh to help move the bag along by kicking it forward. After taking five or six quick steps, she gave up and began dragging it against the dirty hallway carpet.

"Sorry! It's a little heavy for some individuals." Henry rushed over to her. "Without trying to undermine your strength and capabilities, of course, everyone has their on-and-off days. If you don't mind, you don't have to carry that thing, if that's okay with you."

He shifted the weight of the two boxes to one hand, lowering his chin to stabilize them at the top. He took the laundry bag from Alicia effortlessly with his free hand and led the way back to the entrance.

On the street, a young man about twenty years old and in baggy clothes was standing on the hood of Alicia's sedan. His pants were so low that they managed to reveal the entire shape of his buttocks, which were tightly wrapped by his dark blue underwear. He held a sturdy red brick in one hand, which was the exact same shade as the building.

Alicia gasped.

"Hey!" Henry shouted loudly while stomping his foot.

The young man turned toward him, still on top of the

car.

"Clay! I know these people, these aren't it! Get off!" Henry hollered.

"Ugh. Seriously?"

"Seriously."

Clay was annoyed. He slipped off the hood, giving up on smashing its window. He tossed the brick onto the curb and put his hands into the pockets of his hoodie. He stopped himself and turned around before walking through the apartment entrance. "If you need anything, call me."

"Thanks." Henry smiled back at him amicably. "You too, man!"

"Bet."

"I'm really sorry," Henry apologized awkwardly. "His parents are on the same floor as me. You people's cars are just a little different. The dorm's parking lot is safer, though."

I looked at our cars. They looked like normal cars. Alicia exchanged a glare with me, her eyes occupied by terror. Having visited my father's childhood home, I had a slightly more thorough understanding of the environment than her. The sight wasn't pretty.

The SDU dorm was a seemingly normal building about twenty stories tall. The windows looked small and endless from the outside. The lobby was modern and mildly sterile, similar to a hospital's. Henry used his ID card to scan all three of us through the metal gate. The gloomy-looking security guard did not bother to raise her gaze from her phone screen.

The room was only big enough to be a single. Based on not having a vomiting toilet alone, the room was a substantial upgrade. The unit consisted of a narrow hallway with a tiny gas stove, a main area, and a bathroom. Funny enough, the bathroom was nearly as big as the main room. In theory, the usable spaces in this studio apartment were very much acceptable. In reality, no one wanted to live in the bathroom.

The previous tenant had taken a black crayon and slashed it against the walls; from afar, the black streaks looked like cracks from a lack of maintenance. They hadn't just been an impressionistic artist but a poster enthusiast as well. There were countless blue sticky spots in the shape of rectangles. On certain parts of the wall, pieces of paint had been ripped off, presumably during the removal of the posters.

The floor was made of some sort of light-colored stone with a natural pattern. Dust and microscopic garbage pieces were scattered evenly throughout the entire unit. The amount of dirt doubled where the floor met the bottom of the walls. Perhaps someone had swept the unit before Henry moved in, but instead of dumping the dustpan in the trash can, they had pushed the filth into the corners.

The wooden door leading to the bathroom had suffered significant years of abuse. The corners were starting to rot or go missing. It contained a large number of black and brown marks, specifically on the bottom half. A big hole was right above the door handle on the side that was facing the main room, the possible result of a kick or downward punch.

Inside the spacious bathroom, the tiles were small and gray. The gaps in between each tile were stained various colors: yellow, brown, black, and red. There were two square metal towel hooks next to the shower, both of them completely covered in bronze rust. The bottom of the shower curtain was discolored, most likely by a red hair dye.

The school had been generous enough to provide a single twin-sized bed with the standard blue mattress, a small desk, and a dresser. It was a mean assessment, but the bed did not seem like it could comfortably support the width of Henry's body.

"All right! Looks like a good place to me!" he said with energy.

"Yeah." Alicia plastered a smile across her face. "Do you wanna also maybe call someone for some cleaning?"

"They've already cleaned to the best of the school's ability." Henry pointed at the trash can nearby. It was empty and covered by a clear plastic bag, hinting that the cleaning crew had recently been inside.

I could no longer contain my urge to overstep. "Henry, I don't mean to be rude, but doesn't the firm pay market?"

"Oh, it does! I'm very happy with it!"

"But—but this—"

"Student loans." Henry turned to haul the big black suitcase onto the bare bed. "I wanted to pay it off before the interest goes up next year."

"What's the rate?" Alicia asked.

"Two hundred and two hundred and nineteen for

some. It's been stressing a lot of people out for a while."

"Edward's dad paid for everything. He doesn't understand student loans," Alicia volunteered.

Halfway through her sentence, Henry twisted his body sharply in my direction. He was bent forward at the hips, crouching over the half-zipped suitcase. His fingers stalled as he took out what was crammed inside. His eyes found mine immediately. They glistened under a ray of the late morning sun that seeped through the window blinds.

The way he looked at me was calm yet penetrative without warning. Subconsciously, I shifted my gaze to another corner of the room.

When I looked back, he was scratching his head and laughing lightheartedly. "Oh yeah! Of course. Everyone comes from different backgrounds, you know. Difference is power!"

I laughed with him, not knowing what to say.

"The office helped me a ton with this, though. If they didn't use their contacts, SDU would normally charge seven thousand or more for this setup."

"I'm sorry. I'm old," I said.

Chapter 36

Ben and Caroline met us at Luigi's Authentic Italian Noodle Bar in Midtown.

I felt sorry for Henry, having to shower in the dorm's bathroom before coming.

"Hoping your housing issue is okay?" Ben asked loudly, matching his volume to every other customer's.

"Oh yes! I can't thank Edward and Alicia enough. They really made the whole move so much easier." Henry rubbed his palms against his pants.

"How do you like your new place?" Caroline asked. She didn't attempt to read the menu, unlike her husband, who carefully studied it under his reading glasses.

"Oh, it's awesome. So much better than before," Henry answered immediately.

Alicia choked on her iced tap water. She coughed and then covered her mouth with her napkin.

I understood why Henry was being enthusiastic about the dorm. Any negative comment about the place would have made him sound ungrateful. However, I wished

Henry knew that all of us were understanding of the situation and genuinely wanted to help him to the best of our abilities. He wasn't at an interview. We weren't there to judge his character.

Ben finally lifted his head out of the menu. He put his glasses into a leather case as he spoke. "I'm very intrigued by the chef's tasting courses. What do you guys think?"

The rosé was buy-one-get-one-free tonight. It wasn't my drink of choice, but it was what Alicia preferred. We soon learned that the restaurant's definition of buy-one-get-one-free meant dividing one glass into two separate servings. They never bothered to switch to a smaller glass; the amount of liquid sitting at the very bottom was comical.

The chef's tasting menu could only be ordered if all members of the party agreed to get it, according to the restaurant's policy. It consisted of one appetizer, soup, salad, main dish, and dessert. Supposedly, the serving size depended on the number of people at the table, since all dishes were meant to be shared.

When the waiter brought out the appetizer, Ben's mouth gaped. He made sure to stop him and ask for the appetizers for the rest of the group. The waiter dryly told him that what was placed in front of us was for all of us. All that was served was five thinly sliced, two-inch-long cantaloupe pieces with a small square of unfolded prosciutto placed on top. The sparse amount of food was laid on a long ceramic plate with a gentle curve. The garnishing was placed like artwork with drops of balsamic vinegar, basil leaves, coarse black pepper on the meat, and one singular blackberry.

"This is unacceptable," Ben said.

"Maybe the rest of the dishes are bigger. Let's just wait and see," Caroline shut him down.

The soup of the day was able to temporarily restore our faith in the service, as it was served in five separate bowls. They weren't big, but they were sufficient to show that it was not one serving divided up between five people. Unfortunately, the salad and the main dish reverted back to the style of the appetizer. The main dish was pasta with clams cooked in garlic and butter. Each plate had a single small clam placed in the center of the swirl of noodles. The amount of pasta itself was atrocious, enough to be devoured in one big bite or two small ones.

I was completely lost in what was the purpose of ordering the tasting menu five times when all we received was one serving of each dish at best.

"I can't—" Ben wiped his mouth. "What is this? Scam pasta?"

He began making calculations. Each of the tasting menus cost three hundred and five dollars. What we were served was essentially one dish from each category. If the table had ordered each dish separately, the total amount would have been less than half of what we were asked to pay.

"Back me up, everyone," Ben said swiftly before calling over the waiter with sheer confidence.

Henry looked at me helplessly. I knew too well how he wanted to please Ben. Yet very few people would have felt comfortable acting like a terrible customer at a restaurant and risking being recorded and put onto the internet.

"Can we see your manager, please?" Ben was diplomatic.

"Is it something that *I* can help you with?" The waiter gave him a judgmental look.

"We have a dispute regarding the pricing."

The waiter walked away in dismay. Ten minutes later, a man with brown hair in his mid-thirties showed up. He was wearing a slightly different variation of the waiter's uniform.

"Is there a problem?" the manager said with a cool tone; it sounded closer to a threat than an enquiry.

Ben began explaining the price difference he'd found. The manager stared at him as he spoke.

"But, customer, your math was incorrect. I can guarantee the portion size matches our chain's policy for five people."

"No," Ben objected, "I've seen the food brought out as a standalone dish at the other tables. They looked exactly the same as the one we got. And that was meant for one person. We have five people." He raised his hand, displaying the fact that he had five fingers on his palm and the fact that he could count to five.

"Customer, if you had not chosen the tasting menu, you would have ordered four more of the main dishes and soup and salad, so it would actually cost more for the entire table. Therefore, our pricing and portion sizes are, in fact, correct. But since you are unhappy with our service, we are willing to take the first round of drinks off the as compensation for your subjective dissatisfaction."

I wasn't sure if anyone was able to follow his logic. Even if Ben's calculations had been wrong, which they weren't, it was never a good idea to argue with a paying customer. The manager could have solved the issue of the table being still hungry by simply bringing out another dish. The drinks we had ordered cost more than one new dish alone.

"It's not about taking the drinks off," Ben contested. "It's about your portion sizes not matching our party size. We are each spending three hundred and five dollars; we shouldn't just be getting one serving of each course. We should be getting five servings."

The manager shrugged and left us without saying another word. Within a minute, the lifeless waiter brought out the dessert, along with the tablet with the bill. The dessert was five completely frozen cannolis.

Henry forced a smile onto his face and reached into his pocket, fishing for his wallet.

"I got it." Ben halted him. "I'll mark it as a work dinner and let the office cover this."

As soon as he was finishing making his payment, uncivil noises broke out at the waiters' station. The workers raised their voices among each other, seizing everyone's attention. Ben smiled in a wicked way, being the only person who was able to ignore the chaos nearby.

"Stop that table!" Two waiters rushed toward us.

"They tipped 50 percent!" someone shouted in the distance.

"Fuck them!"

"Customer." One of the waiters blocked Ben's way. "I

need you to adjust your tip. Otherwise, your entire party will be banned from all of our locations in the future."

Ben shrugged. "Ban us. We don't care."

Almost every person in the room had their head turned toward the direction of the quarreling. I wished the ground could open up and swallow us whole.

Caroline took a few steps away from her husband, leaving Ben alone in a standoff with several restaurant staff. I could infer that it wasn't the first time he had done something similar.

"It's okay," she whispered apologetically. "You guys can go. I'll go wait for him in the car."

"No. The restaurant is wrong!" Henry said loudly. He had chosen to gain a partner's favor over avoiding public embarrassment.

We stood in a half circle behind Ben as he argued. The amount of staff engaged in the matter quickly doubled. Even the chefs came out.

"Customer, it is unacceptable to tip such a low amount at a restaurant like us. I am kindly asking you to please adjust your tip amount to a reasonable number for our staff," the manager said, containing his anger poorly. He was doing the famous slow breath-calming exercises when he wasn't speaking.

"The mandatory gratuity charge by law is 50 percent of the subtotal. I paid 50 percent," Ben said firmly. "And I have no gratitude toward your service tonight."

"Yes." The manager nodded heavily. "However"—he lowered his voice—"your given options were 75, 80, and 95 percent. It is not *socially* nor *morally* permissible to tip below the 75 percent mark."

"Well, it is not socially nor morally permissible to *scam* people with your tasting menu either!"

Faint discussions broke out at the tables nearby.

"That's enough," the manager said in a harsh tone. "I am now kindly asking you to leave our restaurant now."

Ben rolled his eyes at the staff that had piled up behind the manager.

The manager accompanied us to the front door, along with three other waiters. To make matters worse, the sky, which had been mildly drizzling when we arrived, was now pouring freezing rain. The parking lot was five minutes away. We stopped under the overhang of the building, waiting for the cars to pull up.

"Excuse me. Please leave our property completely."

"Can't you see that it's raining?" Alicia turned toward the manager. "Our cars will be here in a minute."

"Our property includes our overhang." He looked at her out of the corner of his eyes.

A blond waiter bolted at us from inside the entrance. Without warning, he shoved Caroline out of the overhang and into the rain. She tripped over several steps but eventually caught her balance.

"Seriously? Out of everyone here, you chose to push her?" Henry asked.

"Are you saying that just because she's a woman, she shouldn't be treated equally?"

"You haven't pushed anyone else—how is that treating people equally?"

"Oh, I can push you too!" The waiter charged at

Henry. He bumped into his broad body with all of his might. Henry stood his ground, unaffected by the minimal physical assault.

The waiter growled at him in rage and humiliation. He turned toward Ben, who was helping Caroline stand up. He ran over and shoved him from the side. Ben toppled over without a fight. His body landed sideways on the hard, wet concrete, his temple only inches away from a broken piece of sidewalk. He sat up with one hand on his head, covering a streak of blood running down his face.

The restaurant staff didn't bother to react. They went inside the building and closed the door behind them with a hiss.

We sat in the emergency room for hours. The bleeding on Ben's head had long stopped. The nurses took his vitals and told us to wait in the lobby to be called in. They gave him a white gauze to temporarily cover his wound and a blue throw-up bag in case he had a concussion and was going to vomit.

The front desk staff was in the middle of a heated game of Monopoly. Someone had built three houses on Boardwalk, and the rest were terrified of landing on it, even though the color set only made up two spots on the entire map and were naturally hard to land on due to their being after Go to Jail.

No one had been called into the back for a long while.

"Seriously," Ben said, "you guys should go. I can wait here by myself."

Chapter 37

The middleman gave me a date to meet up in California. Unfortunately, Mexico was not next to the East Coast. The border itself had become a wide-open area a handful of years ago. When I was growing up, there were still migrants from other countries, mostly South Americans, traveling on foot into the US. Now, it was mostly Americans driving out of the country and heading into South America.

I read about security regulations on domestic flights. It was perfectly fine to fly with an ankle monitor of Alicia's type. Perhaps it was due to the sheer number of criminals like her that there was great difficulty in containing them.

I had not been on a commercial flight in years. The rules had changed. TSA made everyone take off their clothes in the security line. People and their clothing were required to go through two separate scanners in order to stop people from sneaking objects into their pockets. Carry-on items were not allowed onto planes, with the exception of an ID and one small electronic device.

Airlines imposed steep fees for checked bags. Airport shops set their own sky-high prices on whatever they sold. There weren't enough lawmakers proposing a change to such outrageous occurrences. First, most people in those positions chartered their own flights without the limits of public security. Second, airlines were private companies.

It took decades for them to learn that people would fly no matter how horrible the experience was because of the need to travel. Therefore, the newer the plane, the worse the condition. In the beginning, first-class tickets skyrocketed in price, and then they were canceled altogether. The aisles of the planes slowly transitioned from being in the middle to the sides of the plane's body to fit as many passengers on board as it could possibly carry. To move around the cabin or get to the bathroom, people crab-walked on either side of the plane.

Since I purchased four tickets all at once, I was automatically enrolled in Epsilon Airline's Platinum Bronze Triple Star One Badge membership program. The high ceiling inside the airport provided an excellent environment for people's loud chatter to echo when standing in the bag-check lines. Scanning through the herds of people, we found a significantly shorter line that was only accessible to Epsilon Airline's Platinum Bronze to Platinum Diamond Triple Star One to Three Badge members.

The only humane aspect of the security line arrangement was that both the partial nudity and full nudity areas were blocked off and covered by a thick black draping to protect the privacy of the travelers. Minors were exempt from the full stripping requirement; they were escorted to a different area of the checkpoint, away from their parents.

"I'll cover my eyes to the best of my ability," I said, "but honestly speaking, I don't think anyone cares. People are just trying to move as fast as they can. Don't be scared if they yell at you."

Alicia pinched a corner near the opening of the black draping and squeezed herself into the TSA area. I followed closely behind her. A man in his late seventies was slowly taking his shirt off. His movements were stuck at his shoulders; it seemed like with his arms crossed in front of his chest, he couldn't lift them over his head.

I grabbed two trays, one for my coat and boots, the other for the rest of my lighter clothing. Alicia untied her shoes and unbuttoned her jacket before her tray could hit the first roller.

The old man was finally able to remove his shirt and undershirt after nearly a full minute of struggling. His hairy back was exposed, filled with white hair, saggy skin, and many areas of hyperpigmentation. He was still stalling at the same spot, now attempting to bend to remove his shoes. The people in front of him had already moved past the scanner and into the pat-down area.

Alicia looked at the gap the man had created and then looked at me, unsure of whether to cut in front or wait in the order of the original line.

A TSA officer in a blue uniform noticed the gap and began vocalizing before I could think of what to do. "Hey! You!" The officer put her hand on the short baton hanging on her belt. She was looking in the man's direction but did not specify which individual person she was alerting.

We were startled. Travelers began to quickly drop the items they were holding onto and put their hands above their heads.

"You!" the officer shouted even louder. "Traveler with short, white hair and light tanned skin, you are holding up the line! Move faster!"

"I—I'm trying," the old man answered fraily. His hands were still awkwardly hanging in the air.

"MOVE FASTER!" the officer bellowed.

The old man's body was shaking uncontrollably. His unstable fingers found the fly of his trousers, unzipping it slowly.

"You!" the officer barked again, still in the same vague direction. She would have been more effective if she walked closer to whoever she was talking to. But apparently, she was trying to conserve her energy for further yelling. "Traveler with medium-length brown hair!"

Alicia stopped taking off her socks and raised her hands in the air again.

"Move past the slow person in front of you! Everyone else, move—MOVE! FASTER!"

Alicia ran toward the scanner. I cut in front of the old man and placed myself right behind her, sensing it was what the officer wanted. A slew of people soon followed. The awkwardness of undressing among total strangers was lessened by the urgent yelling of the TSA officers. Based on their level of energy, it was clear how passionate they were toward their job.

When I gathered my clothes after the additional pat-down, I looked back at the line. The old man was still not completely undressed. I saw a different officer dragging him forward by the small amount of hair still present on the top of his head. He was in visible pain.

The main cabin of the plane was loud. There was no longer an arrangement with individual seats. What greeted us was a long row of hard benches. The seat belts were the only markers providing any form of structure. Alicia and I purchased four seat belts. The collective length of the bench did not meet the space needed for the nine seat belts provided. The divider had likely been removed so the smaller people could take up less room and let the bigger people push into their space.

People chatted with each other; some were even smiling and seemingly excited about the flight. Everyone shuffled sideways through the aisles, regardless of their body size. They looked like fast-moving crabs on the beach. A national boycott had not happened yet. When every service provider in the industry treated their customers like cattle, people had no choice but to give in and even treasure the minimally less horrible ones.

"This is way more space than AeroStar's planes," I heard a man say to his wife.

Soon, every inch of space was filled. The cabin reeked of human odor as everyone was sweating from the forced proximity. There was a pocket on the back of every bench. It contained two paper vomit bags in case people felt sick. They did not look sturdy enough to hold any form of liquid until the end of the flight.

A baby's cry broke out in a nearby row after we were in

the air. They sounded exhausted and helpless. A parent
bounced them and muttered an indistinguishable phrase
repeatedly. The smell of feces rose in the air. The parent
stood; it was a short man. He was in the middle of the
bench a few rows in front of us. He held the baby in one
hand while trying to navigate his way to the aisle where the
bathroom was. No one stood to make room for him, but
he squeezed himself out somehow.

Chapter 38

I wiped off the saltlike particles that formed on my forehead from sweat during the flight. I only saw a handful of people throwing up; they all contained themselves fine. People's ability to endure suffering had a much greater magnitude than I had imagined. Alicia and I survived the plane ride like everyone else. However, I was puzzled by the airline's greed. What if an accident happened and an evacuation was called for? How could people crab-walk out of the plane in a timely manner, given how tight the space was?

An unmanned taxi drove us to a short-term rental property near the south of Los Angeles. The duration of the stay was only two nights. A bus driven by the coyotes was supposed to stop by on the third day and pick us up.

Ian's friends, who had migrated previously, had told me how the coyotes were against self-driven cars. It wasn't that they were old-school, but cars with computers installed were easier to track down if the government wanted to.

The rental property had been picked out by the coyotes

and sat near the edge of an ultra-urban neighborhood. It was an exceedingly small house with only one bedroom and bathroom available to use. The rest of the area was blocked off by two giant plastic boards with a lock in the middle. They looked like they could be removed easily.

The bedroom contained no furniture other than a full-sized bed. The sheets and comforter had been rolled messily into a ball. There was only one pillow. Evidently, someone had slept in it not too long ago.

"Business must be pretty busy," Alicia said.

"When do you think they'll go public?"

"Soon." She laughed.

"I know the bathroom here is disgusting, but we're not going to see a real shower for a while."

"Why do you think people keep on saying to listen to the coyotes?"

"I don't know." I shook my head. "I think people who are in the coyote business are all a little crazy. Hardened, or whatever. I don't think digging under their mindset is worth it."

The bathroom had a shallow, dirty bathtub with a rusted showerhead attached to the wall. The standalone sink was missing a corner. I turned on the faucet and let the sink run; luckily, the water was clear.

Alicia raised the toilet lid, screamed, and slammed it down immediately. She took a few steps backward, looking like she was about to cry.

I was expecting a dirty toilet bowl. What greeted me was a grayish-looking snake. It had folded itself over several times in the middle of the bowl. I could see its smooth, scaly body coiling comfortably in the water. Some parts of its body were darker than others.

"It's just a snake," I comforted her to the best of my ability.

She shoved a broom into my hands, and I held it at arm's length.

Calling animal control was not an option. I gently prodded the snake from a safe distance, hoping to guide it outside. The snake, however, showed no inclination to leave. I reached for a thick towel on the racks and draped it over the toilet bowl.

"Can you go find something like a basket?" I asked.

She scurried out of the bathroom. A few minutes later, she came back with a plastic storage container, holding the lid in her other hand. I put it next to the toilet. Using the towel as a barrier, I picked up the snake with my hand. Though it wasn't moving, I felt like I was holding on to a big wriggling worm in the center of my palm. Slowly and painfully, I forced it into the container and closed the lid.

Two days later, the coyotes arrived on time. We spotted a medium-sized bus with white stripes driving down the neighborhood road slowly; it was a model from at least ten years ago, with a set of new, sturdy tires. We were ready on the curb.

A juvenile-looking man stepped out of the bus and blocked us from looking into the vehicle. He had a head full of red curls, similar to Henry's, and was almost as tall as he was. However, this young man was spindly skinny, even under his intentionally baggy clothes.

"Go back into the house," he said.

Despite his adolescent facial features, he commanded us with full authority. His eyes briefly landed on Alicia, and he kept silent until we were led back into the house.

"What is this?" He frowned when he saw the plastic container with the lid on top and the snake still inside.

It was unidentifiable whether it was alive or not. We had thought about letting it free but were worried about how it could become a new safety hazard for others in the neighborhood. Killing it would have been too brutal and too unkind. Since the lid wasn't airtight, I hinged my hope on the coyotes' thriving business. Maybe the next group of migrants would know what to do.

"It was in the toilet. We were worried it might come back or harm the neighbors if we released it," I said.

"So you stuffed it in a box? You guys are cold-blooded." He moved the container out onto the front lawn, quickly unhooked the lid, and dumped the snake onto the half-green, half-wilted grass. It slithered away with speed. "These aren't poisonous, even if they bite. By the way, we need another $100K from you. Cash."

"I already paid for everything," I said.

"That's not my problem." The young man raised his right arm as if he were reading the time from his watch, but he had no watch.

"We can go to the bank for cash," I said, "but we don't have the money right now."

Alicia gave me a death stare and shook her head nervously.

"I guess not." The man turned around, beginning to make his way to the front door.

"Wait!" she called out. "May I know your name?"

He turned around and sighed loudly, inserting both his hands in his sweatpants pockets. "Max."

"Max," she repeated. She wriggled the straps of her backpack off her body and sat it on the dusty floor. Her hand reached into the main compartment and she extended her arm all the way inside. A rectangular strip of glowing gold appeared in her palm.

"Max. Thank you for helping us with the snake. Can you give us a few minutes to talk?"

Max smiled at her in approval. He fondled the gold with his long, pale fingers, throwing it up in the air, then catching it with one hand. I wanted to stop him when he bit into it with his front teeth. He walked into the bathroom and closed the door behind him. "Hope you come up with the rest."

A noise of piss trickling into the toilet penetrated the thin walls.

"Where did you—"

"I put some in your backpack too," she said sternly.

"Why didn't you tell me?"

"I thought we needed tips. No currency beats real gold. Did you know that knights back in the day used tips to guarantee safe passage?" She fished out a handful of gold strips from her backpack. I mirrored her actions. "How much money did you pay them exactly?" she asked.

"$450K."

"Damn it, Edward! Not everyone has that much money to spare! And not everyone has a $100K on the spot. You have to think about why they asked for that amount."

"I'm sorry."

"It's whatever," she muttered. "They're probably just trying to squeeze out as much as they can by percentage."

The toilet flushed. The sink did not run. Max walked out of the bathroom, whistling.

Alicia grabbed all the gold as soon as the door swung open. "Here. This is all we have."

I wasn't sure if it matched the amount requested, but Max seemed pleased. He stuffed them into his pockets and then glanced at Alicia's hands. "Give me your phones."

We turned in our phones, which had already been wiped.

Chapter 39

The bus was strategically filled from back to front. Some people were lucky enough to sit in a real seat, while others sat on the floor, presumably per the request of the coyotes.

Max jumped into a comfortable spot next to the driver, whose upbeat punk music leaked from his earbuds.

A few people tilted their heads to look at us as we walked through; others looked down at their hands. No one spoke. The majority of the travelers were women, all wearing dark-colored winter jackets. Some leaned against their stuffed backpacks, and others held them in front of their chests.

The windows were heavily tinted both from the outside and the inside. With a very limited view of the bus from the floor, I had no idea where we were driving. We made a stop in a parking lot. The driver stepped off and came back with a cheesesteak sandwich; its smell traveled all the way to the very last row of seats. Max did the same after the driver came back. He ordered everyone not to move. My eyes searched for a bathroom. A narrow door with the toilet sign was hidden in the corner, obscured by people's heads.

For the next seven hours or so, we stopped in front of various houses, through suburban neighborhoods, freeways, and occasionally dirt roads with bumps. The man next to me was carsick. He covered his mouth and dashed toward the bathroom multiple times. He eventually switched seats with someone who sat right in front of the entrance. The ventilation wasn't great, but it was far better than the airplane ride into the state. A couple of the big windows had openings at the top about two to three inches wide. When the bus sped up, a breeze of cold air kept us sane.

Max was kind enough to pass everyone a sub sandwich with a single slice of turkey, along with a bottle of water. From the perspective of customer service, he easily outperformed every single regulated airline in America. Some people chowed down on their sandwich like they had not seen food in days, while others slowly ate from their own backpacks. The bread was as hard as a rock from being inside a cooler for too long. On the bright side, it had very little chance of being spoiled.

By the time the sky grew orange, the bus was filled to nearly 120 percent of its capacity. A man wearing a black jacket entered at some point and took over the driver's spot while the old driver sat next to redheaded Max.

For the rest of the houses, one of the coyotes got off to collect the personnel like Max. The amount of time they spent speaking with the newcomers varied. Some took less than a minute, others up to twenty or even half an hour. For a few other groups, the travelers waited in front of the bus and got on without a question from Max and the rest.

It was clear they hadn't chosen the closest entry point possible. From the few freeway signs I saw, we were moving east. Ian's coworkers had guaranteed that the coyotes were going to drop everyone off at a refugee center. I knew we had not pushed for the border yet, as they wouldn't risk transporting multiple ankle monitors at the same time.

Through the chattering among the coyotes, I learned the first driver's name was Beau, a middle-aged man with tan skin and a sturdy build. He was looking forward to eating lamb chops and tomato lentil soup once his business trip was over. The small group of men acted lightheartedly, joking around in English and Spanish, then laughing together loudly. It all made sense; the smuggling of criminals had become a developed chain, and therefore the people running it were quite good at it. Max was the only one who possessed a juvenile look, but from his body language and the way he expressed himself verbally, he was not an underling. He was in charge, despite every other person being at least ten years older than him in appearance. Perhaps it was his family's business.

Well into the night, we stopped at another parking lot. Max stood. "You're staying in here for the night."

My legs were stiff. My back ached from an entire day of folding myself on the floor. I looked around; everyone else's expression remained blank. No whining, no word of objection.

Max continued, as if he had read people's minds, "You can't leave, but you can move around."

"Can we speak now?" someone asked quietly behind me.

"Yes."

Contained conversations stacked on top of each other. People mostly talked within the group they were traveling with. Some had come in big groups of six or seven members, while a few others were completely alone. As if under a collective calling, everyone stood at the same time to stretch their bodies.

Max took a peek at the windshield. He turned back to us. "Everyone with a tracker, come outside and form a line."

Three men and a sizable number of women began standing, both in front of and behind Alicia and me. She didn't look at me and quietly merged herself with the group. I followed behind her.

She was agitated. "What do you think they're doing?"

"They're probably cutting the ankle monitors," I whispered in her ear.

The outside temperature was freezing in comparison to the interior of the bus, which was warmed by the herd of human flesh. It was a distinct feature of Californian weather: scorching hot during the day and icy cold at night.

People stood in two long lines about ten feet away from the body of the bus. In the distance, I saw the headlights of a similar-looking bus slowly moving toward the parking lot. There were two people waiting to take care of the situation; Beau squatted on the ground, holding a miniature chainsaw in one hand. An Asian man wearing glasses stood beside him with a black cloth bag that had been halfway filled up with cut monitors.

Beau tilted his head up to look at Alicia. He put a finger through the band of her anklet.

"I already set it to the loosest notch," she said.

He picked up a small piece of metal board from the ground and slipped it underneath the band as a barrier. It was about the same width as a deck of poker cards but was nearly a whole foot long. She looked away, her hoodie blocking her expression. From the way she extended her leg, I could tell she was trembling. Within the blink of an eye, he raised his arm. The Asian man picked up the broken monitor without words.

"Where is yours?" he asked.

"I'm with her," I said.

"He said only the people with monitors were coming out." Beau looked at me up and down; his gaze stalled briefly at the zipper of my jacket. He spoke again before I apologized. "You get a free pass this time. Get back in there."

I trailed behind Alicia and back onto the bus. Our original spots were now occupied by other exhausted people in need of more space. I grabbed our backpacks and found two new spaces closer to the driver's seat. This time, both of us got to sit in a real seat with a backrest.

By the time I woke up, we were on the move again. It was 6:30 in the morning. The visible piece of sky was white from the top of the window. Alicia sat quietly next to me.

Her eyes were wide open.

"I should have brought a book," she said. "I need entertainment."

It wasn't entertainment she needed but a form of distraction. Boredom wasn't scary, but not knowing where we were was eminently more frightening.

"Books take up space. We don't have a lot of that."

"Books can be useful as a survival tool."

"How?"

"Toilet paper." She grinned. "Tear off a page whenever you need to. Some authors intentionally print their books on rolls of toilet paper."

I nodded in agreement.

"Can you tell me a joke?" she asked.

"Hmm. Okay." I cleared my throat. "It's going to be an interactive one. Are you ready?"

"Yes."

"There are a hundred bricks on a plane, and one falls off. How many are left on the plane?"

"I don't know. It's not very funny so far."

"You have to cooperate."

"Ninety-nine?"

"That's right. Remember that. How many steps does it take to fit an elephant in the fridge?"

"One, kill the elephant. Two, dissect it into pieces. Three, put the pieces in the fridge."

"Wow. That's one way to do it. It is actually three steps, so you are right. But you were supposed to open the door, put the elephant in, and close the door. So, following that logic, how many steps does it take to fit a giraffe in the fridge?"

"Three!"

"No, it's four. You open the door, take the elephant out, put the giraffe in, and close the door. Every animal went to the lion's birthday party, but one wasn't there—which one was it?" I asked again.

"The hyena!"

"Nope! It's the giraffe, cause it's in the fridge."

She lowered her head to hide the laughter escaping her lips.

"Okay, we are almost there. An old lady—let's say Meemaw—is crossing a river where a lot of crocodiles call home, but she somehow survives. Why?"

"Because Meemaw survives anything and everything."

"Yes, but no. It's because the crocodiles all went to the lion's birthday party."

She wasn't visibly amused. But a few other heads turned toward me. I couldn't tell if they were disturbed by our whispering or if they were genuinely curious.

"One last question," I continued. "Unfortunately, the old lady wasn't actually Meemaw. She died shortly after crossing the river. Why?"

"The brick!" a man's voice erupted somewhere near us. "The brick from the plane fell on her head!"

"That is absolutely correct!" I raised my voice to match his.

Chapter 40

Around noon, Max hurried everyone off by the door and counted the number of people with each wave of his hand.

It was not the stereotypical desert of my imagination. The ground beneath my boots felt like white dirt mixed with gravel. Even though the scenery was endless, there were no clear location marks like distinct succulent plants. What did grow were small and well hidden under rocks of various sizes. The sun hung in the middle of the sky, casting a hazy glow over the landscape. The air around me was dry but strangely freeing. In comparison to the East Coast, the temperature was unbelievably warm for the season. I guessed that it was a national park. We were waiting to be picked up by vehicles that could cross the terrain more easily. There was a smaller personnel transport truck waiting in sight. However, it had nowhere near the capacity to take everyone on board.

I began to understand the size of the crowd once we were out in an open space. The coyotes had managed to squeeze close to one hundred people onto the bus. No one articulated their thoughts, but I could feel the fear spreading from one person to another. The coyotes didn't specifically instruct us to keep quiet, yet everyone matched the behavior of those around them, keeping silent.

The way he grouped people looked like a selection process. Max found a piece of rock nearby; it was barely big enough for him to sit on. He took out a bottle of water from his jacket pocket, twisted off the cap, and then threw it onto the ground. The wind quickly blew it away. He tilted the bottle back and gulped down the water. Despite occasionally glancing down at his feet or throwing a few pebbles into the distance, his eyes were fixed on the travelers. I could see his brain turning relentlessly. What was happening in front of me was unclear. Beau, or another coyote, was picking out people from the front of the crowd and physically pulling them into a separate, smaller group. Finally, I heard a few short conversations breaking out among the people. The exact words spoken were muffled; it felt like a dispute.

Luckily, we weren't near the front of the group. At the same time, being left in the wild to wait for the new trucks became a more urgent concern. I didn't know when the next car was going to come, or if there would be one in the first place. I worried that the coyotes were only taking thirty people with them in the existing truck and leaving the rest of us in the desert alone. What would happen then? They had already taken everyone's payment. And since we were all committing an illegal deed, there were no rules or regulations forcing them to take us across the border. Even if we all became piles of cold bodies, nothing punitive could be done to them. It made too much sense not to bother helping us.

I soothed Alicia to the best of my ability. Her eyes were filled with redness and rimmed with dark circles due to the lack of rest. I wanted to tell her how everything was going to be all right and that we were almost in Mexico. The plane tickets to London had already been bought, and within a month, we were going to be on our way. It was going to be a normal airplane, without Epsilon's bench seats.

Unfortunately, I couldn't bring myself to open my mouth.

The coyote moved quickly. He soon picked out a group of around thirty people and walked them toward the smaller truck. He didn't get on himself. I exhaled involuntarily. If the coyotes were willing to stay, then the worst-case scenario was they'd wait here until the truck dropped off a group and made its way back.

Alicia and I were now standing near the front of the group, waiting to be selected next.

Max stood from the rock, whistling a lighthearted tune, and walked toward the crowd while his coworker took his old seat. He pointed at a few women and told them to stand nearby. He then looked at me with piercing eyes. I stepped out of his way, trying to dodge the hostility. But he chased me down until I was standing face to face with him.

"You." Max's voice was low.

"Can she come with me?"

"She can come with my group later." For some reason, he then decided to smile at me, genuinely and amicably.

"We want to be together," I said.

"Come on, man." He patted me on the shoulder. "It's all the same. You go with Beau right now. He's nicer. We are all going to same place anyway."

"Please."

"Can I come instead?" a middle-aged woman spoke up nearby.

Max rolled his eyes at me, then took a pointer finger to the woman.

The sky first grew cloudy, then darkened slightly as the hours went by. Reassuringly, the bus that took us to the wild was still there. Everyone went back inside. The last group to leave had the longest time to wait. Perhaps they had only two trucks running, so to pick up a third group, the first one had to make its way back.

Now that the bus was no longer overloading its capacity, the conditions inside felt very comfortable. Max and the other coyote, nameless to me, remained in the exact same spots. I held Alicia's hand and walked closer to the back.

"I wanna go ask him something," she said.

"What? No." I pulled her down immediately. "Why?"

"I'm just going to talk to him." She brushed my hand off her body.

She came back to me a few minutes later with a smirk on her face. A thin bar of chocolate was hiding inside her long sleeve. She dug it out and handed it over to me. It was a generic brand. I tore it open, broke off a small piece following the grid, and gave the rest back to her.

"He said we'll be here for another hour. And he said he likes California better than Arizona."

"I had no idea he was that approachable," I whispered.

"He is."

"Did you buy this from him?"

"No. He just gave it to me."

"He looks at you weird." I sighed.

"He's just a kid. I don't think he's that bad."

Another truck came back to us in the afternoon. There were no more selections to be made. Max hugged the nameless coyote goodbye and did a complicated fist bump routine with him.

"Don't forget your things," he called out. "If you do, they'll be ours."

The back of the truck was tall and had no deployable ladder. Its exterior was made of sturdy steel covered by yellow paint. The tires had a distinct pattern of lines. It was similar to the military personnel carriers in terms of size, but in appearance it resembled an enlarged safari tourist truck. Two long rows of benches faced each other. There wasn't a top to shield people from the sun or the rain, with the exception of the front of the vehicle, which was designated for the coyotes only.

There was a singular step welded onto the platform near the height of the tires. Max grabbed onto the railings and flipped his body into the back of the truck easily.

"You two. Help everybody up," he said, standing with crossed arms.

As I pulled everyone up, I assessed the group we were

traveling with. Within the thirty of us, six or seven were men. The rest were women between the ages of twenty and forty. There was also a family of three easily set apart from the others by bringing the only minor on board. The parents were in their late forties and wore glasses. Their daughter was about eight or nine years old. Her parents called her Clove. The child behaved perfectly.

We were locked behind the metal gate like a herd of cattle. Max walked over to the front and once again began blasting music with the driver. An upbeat rhythm punctured the thin divider. A few minutes later, the smell of marijuana followed.

Looking at the landscape could not resolve any boredom. Everything was too vast and too similar throughout. The family of three sat diagonally across from me and Alicia. The girl had asked for "the toy" multiple times before her father fished out a palm-sized device with physical buttons installed—an old-fashioned whack-a-mole. Every time a mole surged, a specific button lit up. I'd seen those when I was young; my mother's cousin kept a few as antiques. They were powered by batteries. The girl soon became bored of the toy. She found a glowing spinner in her father's pocket. The stripes formed a beautiful pattern of lights in the semidarkness.

"We should have gotten one of those," I said to Alicia.

"Hello." The girl waved at me. "Do you want to play with it?"

The mother immediately shushed her and put her arms around her small body as a gesture of protection.

"Thank you! But I'm all right," I said gently.

The girl sighed at her mother. "No one likes my things."

"May I see it?" Alicia asked.

The girl stood briefly to hand over the spinner, then immediately sat back in her old spot.

"Wow. It's very pretty."

"Thank you. I made it in our mechanical engineering class."

"Sorry for bothering you. She's just getting a little restless." The mother glanced at me.

We rode in the back of the truck quietly. The trip itself was not the definition of comfort. But we could have been crossing rivers hand in hand, walking long distances under the blazing sun.

Alicia couldn't fall asleep, and neither could I.

Chapter 41

I t was seven o'clock. The truck's headlights provided very minimal lighting for those sitting in the back. The terrain underneath turned slightly smoother, though I wasn't sure if it was my imagination or if we were already driving on a coarsely paved road.

I heard the door open and close. Max's harshly white flashlight startled everyone who had adjusted themselves to the pitch blackness.

"Is this a bathroom break?" someone said.

"No, not yet. We need to switch tires and grab some supplies from the cabin."

"What cabin?"

I couldn't see anything besides the cylindrical sphere of light cast by Max, let alone a building.

"Are we staying the night?" Alicia called out to Max.

"Nearby," he answered as the people rustled in the back. "I need the men to grab the tires and a few others to grab the other things."

People began to stand.

"Stay here and be good with your mom," the girl's dad said before leaving the bench seat.

A man tried to take his backpack with him, but Max told him to leave it on the truck since we were coming back shortly. Alicia followed me to the edge of the truck. I jumped off first before trying to guide her down. Max suddenly raised his flashlight to her face, causing her to cover herself with her hands.

"What are you doing?" he asked sharply.

"You said you need people to carry stuff."

"Do you look like you can lift things?" Max said condescendingly. "Get back in there."

She looked at me one more time before turning back.

"I need someone else," he yelled. "You!"

He was pointing at an Asian woman who was a lot shorter than Alicia. She was about fifty years old and stick thin. Her hair was dyed to a brownish-gold color, though the gray shoots were at least two inches long and largely exposed.

"Me?" The woman pointed at herself. "I have, um, osteoporosis and heart problems."

"I don't care," Max said coldly, then shouted at a piercingly high volume, "Get the fuck down!"

"Okay, okay." The woman stood on shaking legs. She walked her frail body to the edge but was unsure of which leg to put down first, or where she should grab onto to safely maneuver off the platform. A man wearing a neon-green hoodie quickly helped her off.

"Where is the cabin?"

"Look this way." Max gave light to a seemingly random

spot in the dark. In the distance, a triangular-shaped roof emerged.

Behind us, the truck's engine had shut off. I heard the driver's door open and then close; perhaps he was taking a stretch break.

The smaller group marched forward to the cabin in the dark. It was a medium-sized hunting lodge made of wood. The door used a traditional metal key, which hung on Max's waistband. Inside, it was furnished with a round coffee table, two full-sized couches, and even a fireplace.

Max reached for a gas lamp on the wall and switched it on. The room was lit with a yellowish hue, just enough to make clear the surroundings. There were no boxes or tires. A smaller door was attached to the wall leading into another space in the cabin.

The man in neon green walked toward it.

"That's the bathroom," Max said without looking. He sat in the middle of the couch facing the ashy fireplace. He then pulled out a small vape from his pants pocket, inhaling deeply.

"Where is the storage unit?" I asked.

He rolled his eyes. "When did I say anything about a storage unit? Stay put, everyone. We're staying here for the night."

I scanned the room. Every man from the truck was inside. Out of the three women who were there, two were over the age of fifty, and the other one was close to Meemaw's weight.

A chill ran down my spine. When I made my way outside of the cabin, no one followed me. I didn't know if

I had reacted faster than the others or if everyone else had been completely careless.

With a compact flashlight, I searched the area where the truck was parked. All that was left was a broad and empty wilderness filled with nothing but rocks and sand. I found myself glued to the ground, unsure of how to problem-solve or if it was time to give up, though I didn't know what the definition of *giving up* meant in the current situation. I couldn't outrun a moving vehicle in the dark. I couldn't be forceful with Max, as he was likely armed; I'd be shot before I could get within arm's reach. At the same time, without him, the group could never make it out of the desert.

Suddenly, it made perfect sense why Ian's coworkers, especially the wife, spoke so little about their journey and acted extremely reluctant to give details of the trip. And Chris too. All of them had known about this. They were worried—rightfully so—that I might not have wanted to proceed if I knew the women were going to be taken.

I recalled all the strangeness since I'd first made contact with the middleman. I should have dug deeper. I should have let Alicia know. She would have realized the discrepancies from early on and perhaps we'd have avoided the problem entirely before we even left for the road.

The desert night felt more excruciatingly freezing than it was. Being from the other side of the country, southern California's desert weather could never be cold to me, but without a thick woolen coat, the wind freely punctured my body.

Before long, I turned back for warmth.

The cabin's front door wasn't locked. Everyone had settled inside. The three women formed a triangle in the corner. All of them were silent.

"See, I told you he'd come back." Max inhaled again from his vape.

The calmness of the rest of the group shocked me. They had to know about this beforehand. I wondered if they had a heart at all.

"You missed the briefing, brother," Max said.

I saw a spot nearby and dropped myself in it.

"Hey. Stop being all mopey." He kicked my leg with his dirty boot. "Do you see anyone else acting like you?"

I turned to the girl's father. He was quietly chewing on a granola bar. He didn't look happy but was able to contain himself like everyone else.

"Sorry," I muttered without knowing why I chose to apologize. I wiped under my eyes with the tips of my fingers. "Can I please know what I missed?" I asked.

"Nothing much." Max scooted his body forward. "We are spending the night here. The others are joining us tomorrow morning."

"Where are they?"

"Not here."

"Who are they with?"

"Whoever we have."

"What?"

"He said they were right next to the border in a makeshift international brothel for important people," the man in neon green said impatiently.

"We had a former secretary of defense two weeks ago,"

313

Max bragged.

"Can I just ask you why? Why do this?"

"Why do you think no one has to walk a single step the entire time? Where do you think the bus money came from? When my grandfather came from the other direction, everyone walked. Doesn't matter if you are five or fifty. You can really use some gratitude. They are doing you a favor, by definition."

"You took a child . . ."

He stood and patted me on the shoulder. "Children are off limits. If we didn't have strong morals, we wouldn't be running this business."

"Prostitution is legal in Mexico. What sort of clients would need to come to you only to find unwilling people?"

"Because they're not prostitutes." Max slowed down his speech. "We value cleanliness."

I was lucky to not throw up on the spot.

"Guys, look at how good of an actor this guy is." He took a pointer finger to my face and laughed out loud.

"You think it's acting when someone genuinely cares about another person?"

"Whatever." He rolled his eyes. "All I'm saying is that your journey has directly benefited from what they are doing tonight. They do the work, we get more money to make sure we have cars, and no one has to walk. Here is how you should see it—a small group is sacrificing themselves for the greater good of the big group, which the small group is also a part of. Have I made myself clear?"

"You are totally right, and just—I have no objections,"

I said.

"Does anyone want hot dogs?" he yelled to the rest of the cabin.

Chapter 42

I sat in the same spot as others moved around me. I didn't bother to check the amount of time that passed on my watch. At first, people dragged various objects across the room. Some took beach chairs; others held rows of chopped wood in their arms. Max wasn't upset about my choosing not to help with their cooking expedition. Eventually, everyone left to go outside.

The man in neon green came back to fetch me. He shut the door behind him carefully.

"There's hot dogs and marshmallows outside. Max asked if you wanted to join us."

I shook my head politely.

"Look." The man put himself next to me; his voice was soft. "I didn't come with anyone. But um, assuming you didn't put anything in your jacket and everything we have is in the truck, we don't have food besides what they are having outside."

"I really don't think it's the right time for an outdoor barbecue."

"I think it's exactly the right time for some food. It doesn't mean you are being uncaring. The guy with the kid is staying strong for his family. Or, at the very least, he's not pissing off Max."

"Am I pissing him off?" I asked.

"I honestly can't tell. I think whoever you're traveling with will need you there for them once they come back. So you should go eat something, especially when you don't know when the next meal will be. Plus," he added, "they're not dead. So you don't need to grieve."

"I understand. Thank you."

"My name is JJ."

"Edward." I paused. "You said you were alone. Do you mind—what did you do?"

"I ran the Iditarod with Chihuahuas."

"Did you finish?"

"Red Lantern." He laughed. "Sorry, I'd rather not say."

A bonfire crackled against the dark. The travelers sat around it, each with a long skewer in hand. Some had hot dogs, others white and pink marshmallows. From afar, the scene looked exactly like a group of friends hanging out on a weekend night.

Everyone's shoulders touched except for the two people next to Max, who kept a slight distance between themselves and the leader of the pack. A few feet away from the fire was a medium-sized cooler. It was in the exact same style as the one they used on the bus. People scooted around to find a spot for JJ and me. Without words, Max handed me an empty skewer.

We walked over to the cooler and stabbed a hot dog

each. It was the most generic type: thin, pink, and smelling of fish. I copied everyone around me, turning the skewer back and forth above the top of the flame.

"Stop shaking," Max said to the three women who were huddling together. "And you." He nudged me with his elbow. "Be happy."

"How do you keep the women there safe?" I asked in the hope that he would be talkative.

"Horse tranquilizers. Sometimes. I'm not sure. I mean, I've never had anyone not come back or come back hurt or anything. I've seen some people upset, but them being upset is not really my concern."

"Have you been in the business for long?"

"Yeah, it's my uncle's. I've been helping around it since I was fourteen. Started doing the trips at sixteen."

"They didn't let you go to school?"

"Dropped out. I got my GED, which does absolutely nothing, by the way. Even servers need a master's degree."

"Do you get a cut, or do you get a salary?"

Max scoffed at me, then shifted his focus back to his half-eaten hot dog.

"What did you do for a living?" a man sitting across from me asked.

"I was a product manager," I lied.

"You in tech?"

"Gaming. It's just a startup."

"Startup my ass," Max said loudly. "I looked him up. This guy is a lawyer leader at this gigantic law firm. The girl he knocked up is his brother's wife. My dude couldn't stand it anymore and killed himself over it."

Depleted of energy, I didn't care to explain, so I let him be. He folded and extended his fingers into a makeshift gun, casting a flawless silhouette upon the ground. He positioned his hand against his temple and flicked it upward, accompanied by an improvised sound effect.

"Oh," he added, "and this guy went to an Ivy League school. Isn't he so smart and different from the rest of us peasants?"

"His head is bigger than ours!"

Someone burst into laughter.

"How much student loans you got?"

"I didn't have any," I said.

"How come?" Max raised an eyebrow.

"I—" Once upon a time, my school offered need-based assistance until the corporation elected a new president. It was what I should have answered with. However, whenever my education was brought up, I had always made sure to differentiate myself from the nonlegacy students. It was arguable that our academic merits were comparable, but their struggles were far more severe. I couldn't let myself claim the same amount of credit, even in the eyes of pure strangers.

"My dad paid for it," I said.

"No shit?"

"Which bank did he rob?" another man asked. "I'm gonna go for the same bank."

"He didn't rob a bank."

Max tilted his head to one side, then glued his gaze on me. "You mean you had parents who paid your tuition?" he said softly.

"Yeah."

The intrigue in his eyes dimmed. His expression turned completely blank. It was the same unwarranted blankness that Henry looked at me with inside the dorm room. It wove together a multitude of different emotions I couldn't possibly understand. All I knew was that none of them were friendly in the slightest.

I felt the cold rim of a metal tube pushed against the back of my neck, where my skull and spine met. As my body tensed, I heard the women gasp, the men looking away.

If he decided to pull the trigger instantly, I wouldn't have any complaints.

"Go find something to tie him up with," Max said to the group.

At first, no one moved. As a droplet of sweat ran down my forehead, a man wearing a blue jacket ran back to the cabin. Everyone followed him quietly.

A few different pairs of hands worked on me at the same time. They bound my arms behind my back and wrapped a coarsely textured rope around my wrists. The knot was then tightened to cut into my skin. The pistol was long gone. Max dragged me up by the collar as everyone else took a sidestep to make way for us. We walked out to an open area away from the swaying flame. He shoved me forward. Unable to use my arms, my body plunged. I took a few long strides before falling.

I had no words. When I tried to stand, I was kicked in the back of my knees. It wasn't the shooting pain but the momentum that knocked me over again. My face planted against the ground, and small particles of bitter dirt and sand seeped through my teeth. As I coughed, Max pulled me up backward by the longest part of my hair.

From the corner of my eye, I saw everyone else circling us.

Max switched hands, holding my head up. He fished out a pocketknife. The blade reflected no other light but a small slice of flame in the distance. He rested the tip against my face with bizarre gentleness. He hesitated slightly, perhaps indecisive about where to make the first incision. A sharp pain spread down from my cheekbone in a nearly straight line.

"Damn it." Max stopped the slash before going through my jaw. "I thought rich people bled green instead." He slapped the other side of my face harshly as he dropped me. I rested my head against the ground, my ears ringing. "Riding on Daddy's coattails," he spat. "Everyone! Come over!"

The entire group rushed to me as Max walked away slowly.

Punches and kicks landed throughout my body. Some were testing the waters; others were forcefully directed onto my stomach and back. I crouched, then straightened like a crawling worm that, unfortunately, wasn't going anywhere. Even the women had joined the act. The older Asian woman pinched my thigh with raging hatred in her eyes.

People muttered various phrases, most of which were cuss words.

"Fuck this mooch with no loans."

"Who the fuck does he think he is?"

"Lazy bum who sits on his ass all day long."

"Is he gonna cry and call Daddy for help?"

"Useless piece of shit who's never worked a day in his life."

"Too bad Daddy isn't here."

Through the blurry motions, I saw JJ standing in the distance in neon green. He was not interested in letting his anger out on me, nor was he mitigating the situation. A part of me was thankful for him.

"He's free game for five more minutes!" Max yelled. "Just don't go for his brain."

Each second, a new spot of pain hit me. Eventually, I lost awareness of where I was being assaulted. I contemplated begging for mercy. If I apologized with enough sincerity, they might feel pity and let me off the hook. But what would I be apologizing for? My father's wealth? My inheritance? Was I simply abominable for growing up with my parents? I never knew these people who had led hard lives. I'd never harmed them, nor did my privileges involve them.

I was confused by the amount of hatred they carried. I possessed no aristocratic nor meritocratic hubris. I had not taken credit for what I did not work for. Were they upset by the lack of absolute fairness? Was absolute fairness truly necessary? My mind ventured toward a world where newborn babies left their parents the second they made their first cry. They would then be taken into a caring facility. Everyone had the same crib, wore the same clothes, and was given the same amount of food. When they reached school age, they were given the same amount of attention from the teachers, and no tutors were allowed. Then there would be a standardized entrance exam to colleges and universities, which would be run in the same way. When they graduated and entered the job market, no one would have any undeserved privileges. Everyone's achievements would have been the sole result of their personal merit. The hardworking ones were rewarded, and the lazy ones were punished.

But it didn't make sense. What if, in the facility, some infants were placed closer to the windows and received more sunlight? What if the time they were fed and changed wasn't exactly the same? Would that disrupt the principle of equality? What if some children had allergies to certain foods? What if they unfortunately got bullied by their neighbors while others didn't? What if the teaching methods of the teachers didn't match the learning styles of some of the children? And what if, when all circumstances were made equal, the world became an unadulterated competition of genetics that embodied an absolute form of *unfairness*?

I failed to think of a solution. I failed to understand.

As the pain in my body began to numb itself, the face of a middle-aged man appeared clearly in my sight. He was looking down at me. I couldn't tell if he was bald or had an extremely short buzzcut. He lowered his eyebrows and squinted. His gaze wasn't focused; it was as if he were looking through me and into another dimension. It didn't last long.

I recognized the look from the past—and from an entirely different person. One summer, when I was either in first or second grade, our apartment was going through some small renovations. My father checked us into a suite at his university's alumni club. Chris and I got up early every morning. By eight o'clock, we were ready and hungry for breakfast. We played in the hallway as my mother dressed herself and put on makeup. Our suite was in a corner; I remembered chasing Chris down to the other end of the building. I knew I was laughing about something, but I couldn't remember what made me so happy. Children had the superpower of laughing out of pure joy; adults didn't. We passed by a maid pushing a cart slowly. As we almost ran into her and tripped ourselves, she looked at us with slightly squinted yet disoriented eyes. It was jarring how two different faces could hold an expression in the exact same manner. After we passed her, I wanted to keep on playing. But Chris fell silent and barely spoke to me for the rest of that morning.

"Is the jaw okay?" I heard the man ask.

"If it's not the brain."

The second time his head appeared over mine, a row of knuckles hit my mouth. My head slanted to the side. I tasted blood from where the edges of my teeth cut into my lips. He climbed on top of me and held my head up by the hair. The second swing came from the same direction. The third came from a different angle. I felt excruciating pain shooting from under my cheekbone, followed by a quiet yet crisp crack. I howled. I begged with all of my strength for him to stop. I apologized over and over, using whatever phrases I was capable of mumbling at the moment. He swung at me another time. A stream of warmth ran down from my gums. The night sky spun around me as I lost consciousness.

324

Chapter 43

I woke up on the couch inside the cabin. The sky dawned through the small window next to me. A shade of orange hit my eyes. There was a dull but consistent pain inside my mouth. It was pulsating, making a small jump every time my heart pumped blood within my chest. With my tongue, I found a large area of swelling on my gums. It was near the root of an upper premolar or canine; I couldn't pinpoint which one it was without the help of a mirror. It could have been both.

Max rolled himself inside a sleeping bag. Others lay around on the floor.

I clung to the armrest of the couch and pulled myself onto my feet. Each small movement required extra effort. Each fiber of my muscle protested with every twitch. The various spots of soreness were likely bruises across my body. They hid themselves well under my long-sleeved clothing. The room swayed in the same rhythm as the throbbing ache in my temples. A wave of nausea hit me as I shuffled my steps to the bathroom as quickly as I could.

I knelt in front of the toilet. A damp piece of bath tissue was stuck on the side of the bowl. I didn't have much in me to reject in the first place. Acid ran out of my mouth, along with the very little meat I'd chewed on last night. As I continued to gag from the smell of feces reeking throughout the small bathroom, the sourness in my mouth turned bitter. I rested my head against the rim of the bowl. Eventually, what was once a blur came into focus, and the discomfort died down.

I wished for a sink with running water, but there was none. The toilet had a switch that flipped the content into a storage bin underneath after each use, hence why the piece of bath tissue wasn't able to go down.

There was a small mirror glued to the wall, no larger than the size of a standard paperback book. I lifted my upper lip with my right hand; it was a first premolar. The tooth structure was still intact despite how severely slanted it was toward one side.

I decided in that moment that the tooth must come out. With my limited dental knowledge, I could easily have been wrong. It was going to be stupid, yet I knew it was the sole reason behind the throbbing pain. Until it was pulled out, I was going to stay incapacitated. I longed for agency over my body.

I reached for the roll of toilet paper nearby. The layers were thin and fragile, like the ones provided in public restrooms. They quickly absorbed the sweat on my fingertips and stuck to my skin. With shaking hands, I wrapped the tooth with more of it.

My mother told us that the first premolars were an

interesting set of teeth. Some people had a singular root underneath, while others had two. I would have needed an X-ray machine to know, although even then I wouldn't have known how to look properly at the images. Dentists used a tool that resembled a screwdriver. Its bladelike tip was meant to squeeze into the tight area between the tooth and the surrounding gum tissue. After prying the area open, the tooth was loosened enough to be wriggled out of the socket by a pair of forceps. As a result of the beatings, my tooth had already been loosened. The mechanism couldn't be too complicated—swaying it back and forth until it was almost completely detached, then going in with a slight tug. It should come out entirely with the tip of the root still attached.

The loosened tooth was on the left side of my face. I went in with my nondominant hand. As I opened my jaw to make room for my fingers, the cut near my cheekbone began ripping. The newly formed blood clot stretched further and further, then eventually popped open as I fully widened my mouth. The pain worsened with each millimeter. Fresh blood ran down my face.

The amount of it was dismissible in comparison to what poured out from the empty hole in my upper jaw. I was embarrassed to have wailed at least once loudly. There was no knocking outside the bathroom door. I was glad no one decided to check on me. I couldn't let them see me in a state of weakness.

I bunched up a thick stack of toilet paper and placed it over the oozing hole. I pretended like it was a piece of clean gauze and bit down on it harshly. In my other hand, I held onto the freed tooth. Strangely, it looked like a plant, the gradually thinning root attached to the crown. I smiled in relief.

The toilet paper was soaked through almost immediately. I replaced it over and over until it was able to stay in the shape it was originally shoved in. When I didn't feel like swallowing the taste of iron, I lowered my head and leaned my body forward. Blood strands mixed with sticky saliva stalled long in the air before dripping onto my boots.

Pairs of wandering eyes stared at me when I came out of the bathroom. JJ stood beside the door. He handed me a small bottle of painkillers and a cup of water.

Max was the only person who didn't bother to look at me. He sat on the very edge of the couch, agitated. JJ took me to his spot. He fished out an energy bar from his pocket. He didn't hand it to me or eat it himself. He grabbed another cup of water sitting around on the floor. He dunked the energy bar into it, and when it was softened enough and began crumbling like a piece of cookie in hot milk, he nudged me with his elbow. I chewed on it slowly with my good side. My socket, which stemmed from my upper jaw and was made apparent by my gums, could stand very little movement. I ate my own blood as if it were sustenance.

We waited until my bleeding completely stopped, even without biting on the temporary "gauze." Max had never specified what his definition of *morning* was. By noon, he was vaping frequently and cussing left and right. The third time he went outside to check for the truck, he didn't return empty-handed. He ran to the bathroom and pounded on the door, making sure it was empty.

I didn't know how he was able to see the truck coming from such a long distance away. When we gathered ourselves on the front porch, it was still nowhere to be found. Yet a few seconds later, a brownish dot came creeping at us through the wind and dirt.

Max immediately climbed into the front once the truck made its stop. The door slammed hard. I heard muffled yelling through the barrier.

Alicia sat at the very front, leaning against the metal board separating the drivers and the passengers. She was wrapped in a blanket. Her eyes stared directly forward at the woman across from her, who was staring back at her too. She didn't see me.

I pulled myself onto the back of the truck as fast as I could. The other women made way for me to get to her. The group felt smaller, perhaps missing two to three members. However, I wasn't sure if it was just my own experience painting the coyotes in a bad light.

Alicia spoke to me, seeming not to notice the cut on my face.

"It's me," I said.

"I know." She put her head against the barrier again and closed her eyes.

The scent of chlorine traveled up my nose. Her hair was clumped together and formed thick strands that had hardened. The little skin uncovered by the blanket was chapped greatly. She had no clothes on underneath. The scent grew stronger as I leaned her body against mine.

"Cold," she murmured.

I put the back of my hand against her cheeks. It didn't require a thermometer to identify her intense fever.

"I'm gonna go find you some water." I poured out two pills from the bottle of painkillers JJ had given me. "Where are the backpacks?" Her head lulled to the side as her body slumped. "Alicia?"

I called out her name again, but she remained unresponsive. I looked around us; everyone else was conscious. Some were quiet but were still fully sentient.

"Alicia, please," I panted.

I hoped for any signs of discomfort—a fuss or a moan. Her face was completely drained of color, except for her rosy-red cheekbones. I felt like I was going to suffocate to death myself. The world around me blurred. I wiped away my tears forcefully. In the process, the back of my sleeves rubbed open the cut on my face for the second time. It was bound to scar now. I held my blood-smeared fingers against her wrist. After I failed to find a pulse, I shook her body as hard as I could. The blanket slipped off. Her head bobbed back and forth, but her eyes remained shut.

"Stop!" a woman's voice commanded nearby. Who was some stranger to tell me what to do?

"Please look at me," I begged over and over until a harsh slap landed on my face.

"You need to stop before you actually shake her to death." The woman across from us was now standing directly above us. Her face was stern. She put her fingers under Alicia's nose. "She's still breathing. Dead people are cold. She's warm as fuck."

Despite her shallow airflow, Alicia was indeed still breathing. She had likely fainted due to the fever, which was also not a good sign, but it was a semi-merciful answer I was willing to accept.

"What happened?" I asked.

"She fell backward into a pool. She crawled out by herself, but then they forgot about her for a good chunk of the night."

"She can't swim."

The woman rolled her eyes at me.

"Did she hit her head?"

"I didn't see the whole thing. I don't know if she got pushed in or if she slipped."

I wanted to ask if the pool was heated. But that would have been a stupid question. Even if it was, she was left to freeze in the night wind, the same one I had felt, which was harsh enough when it brushed through my dry and properly clothed body. "Do you know where the backpacks are?"

"They took them. Here." She unzipped her own jacket and handed it to me. "Take yours off, too, and put it around her."

"Won't she overheat? She's already burning up."

"If you can get her to sweat, then her temperature might go down afterward."

"That doesn't make any sense. Doesn't she need ice instead?" I frowned.

"Do you *have* an ice pack?" the woman lectured. "She can get brain damage if this fever keeps up. You might as well try."

I followed her directions immediately, adding two layers of jackets over the blanket.

As the woman spoke, a stream of unexplained tears rolled down her face. She sniffled, then looked away. I decided not to bother her. She continued to cry silently. Instead of removing her glasses with thick lenses, she took a piece of tissue and wiped her eyes from underneath the frames.

I scanned the rest of the truck. Everyone else had climbed in. The fight in the front grew louder. The three women from the cabin avoided me. They sat as far away as possible, perhaps in fear of retribution. I soon noticed what obviously made the group look different.

After the trip to the brothel, the little girl was gone.

Chapter 44

E ddie," Alicia said breathily, "what's wrong with your face?"
"I was happy to see her gaining consciousness again.

"It's nothing," I whispered.

I wanted to hold her longer, but the woman across from us interrupted again, "You should probably get the pills in her while she's awake. She's been in and out of it the whole way here."

I half ran, half limped to the passengers' window in the front of the truck. Max was now conversing more quietly with the driver, though his expressions were still fueled by anger. I knocked on the glass gently. His gaze softened when it landed on the wound carved by him last night. He gestured for me to stand back, then opened the door slowly before stepping out of the vehicle.

"Do you have water?"

He handed me a half-empty bottle. "Someone else messed up at the club's end," he called out suddenly before

I turned around. "It wasn't planned."

"Are we going to get going soon?" I asked.

"Yeah." He sighed. "But we're gonna have to walk now."

Alicia was in no shape to walk.

"Get the fuck out!" Max yelled to the driver. "And get everyone else out!"

"Bro, it's not my problem," the driver mumbled, but still began putting a few small loose items into his backpack. "Z was supposed to fuel the truck. And Josh was supposed to keep the time."

"I know that! But you're the one actually driving the car! Would it kill you to pay attention for five seconds?"

"Bro, I just get paid by the hour."

"Come with me," Max said to me.

"Do you know how long it could take?"

"Just a couple of hours. Trust me, I don't want to walk either."

"Can I ask you something?" I paused. "Would that be the final stop?"

"Yes. This is it."

The driver was hurrying people off the truck. I went against the direction of the crowd and climbed back inside.

"Here."

I handed Alicia two pills. With what was left in the bottle, there was more than enough for both of us. Her hand wriggled under the covering, trying to find her way out to grab the water. I loosened the blanket just enough for her arm to slip out.

Thank you, I mouthed to the woman who had kept an eye on Alicia.

She nodded back, then looked down immediately.

I waited until everyone else was off the truck before carrying Alicia to the edge. I sat her down on the platform and got off myself before reaching for her from the ground. For the first time, I was taken aback by how much she weighed. In my mind, I tried to find the best way to carry her. The blanket had to be wrapped up completely to keep her warm. When traveling long distances, the easiest way to carry someone was on their back. I couldn't do that, in this case. Eventually, I decided to pick her up horizontally in my arms. A few people silently offered their help, the same ones who had beaten me the night before. I didn't want their madness around her.

"Everyone! The truck is staying here. We're walking the rest of the way," Max said.

The group began to fuss. Max didn't speak further. He ignored the stares and began walking in an indistinct direction. The driver tagged along closely. The rest of us followed.

"Are you really leaving the car here?" someone asked loudly.

"Do you wanna push it instead?"

"But shouldn't we drive it as much as we can to walk less?"

"Walking a mile isn't going to kill you," Max lectured, then pointed at Alicia. "Maybe her, but she's not walking herself. A car costs money. You can't lose it."

He looked toward the unknown spot in the distance

again and kept on moving. His pace was slow but consistent, accommodating those who easily fell behind. It gave me a sense of peace.

When I wasn't paying attention, a gray shadow came charging at Max at full speed.

The girl's father grabbed his neck from behind using his elbow and dragged him backward. Max choked during the unexpected movements; he lost his balance and fell directly onto the man, who quickly flipped himself on top. Their bodies strangled each other on gravel and pebbles.

Fueled by rage, the girl's father had a disturbing amount of strength over the skinny teenager. His eyes were dark. His lips were slightly parted. He repeatedly mumbled a few words. From the distance, nothing was audible. Both of his hands were locked on Max's neck, attempting to cut off his air supply.

Max resisted as much as he could, his fingers trying their best to pry off the offender's grip.

We stalled and watched in silence. The driver, who was supposed to be on his side, remained where he was. It wasn't in his job description to help a coworker out.

"Where is she?" the girl's father asked. "You said you wouldn't touch her!"

Max looked like he wanted to answer, but all he could utter were a few hoarse moans.

The girl's father yelled and cried at the top of his lungs. He squeezed tighter on Max's neck but soon gave up. Seeing how he couldn't kill him off immediately, he began throwing relentless punches at his face and chest.

I slowly let Alicia onto her feet. She buried her face in

my chest. As much as I disliked Max, I contemplated intervening, but the girl's father was no longer sane enough to be reasoned with. He had every right to lash out. Even though Max wasn't the one who had taken the child away, he was part of the situation.

"Please. Let me explain. Please, I'm sorry—I can explain. I'm sorry. It wasn't me. It really wasn't me." The moment his throat was released, Max began begging for mercy. With glistening tears trailing down his cheeks, he looked nothing more than an innocent, sincerely sorrowful boy pretending to be an adult. As he cried, he gave up all resistance. Fists landed on him. His hands fell to his sides, no longer trying to lessen the damage.

The girl's father paused to stare at Max. He was out of breath himself. "Just tell me where she is."

The sound of metal clashing was followed by a muffled crack.

He still hovered on top of Max, except his head was now slumped downward. A bullet had traveled from one side of his temple diagonally to the back of his head on the other side. The hole was sizable. His emotions finally drained as blood oozed from both ends of the wound.

Max shoved the man off like a sack of meat. He held the gun in his right hand. He stood, cleared his throat, then spat out a large glob of pink mucus onto the body. "Fuck." He glanced over it and shot it two more times in the chest. "Fucking wild shit," he scoffed, then walked on as if nothing had happened.

"Bro, you just killed someone." The driver stood in front of him, blocking his way.

"He was trying to kill me first."

The driver looked down at his feet. "I mean, what are we going to do with him now?"

"I'm not dealing with it." Max spat again. "Hopefully the birds can come eat him soon."

The girl's mother was surprisingly calm. She didn't stare at her husband any more than the rest of us. She quickly made her way from the back of the group to where Max and the driver were.

"Excuse me," she said, "I need your gun."

"What? No." Max shook his head dismissively.

"I don't want to go to Mexico anymore."

He shoved her away. "I'm really sorry about your daughter."

"What am I gonna do there?"

"That's none of my business," Max responded quickly, irritated. "I'm a compassionate person. I don't shoot innocent people."

I didn't know if he intended to sound humorous.

"Please?"

"No."

The girl's mother scanned the area around us. Was she looking for a cliff to jump off? She turned back to Max and went to unbuckle the handgun sitting on his belt. Max pushed her off. She landed on the ground but stood back up quickly.

"Fuck off," he said. "You're wasting everybody else's time."

She lunged for the gun again. This time, Max watched impatiently from above. When she finally gained her grip,

Max kicked her in the stomach. As she crunched her body in pain, he shot her twice in the middle of her neck.

I covered Alicia's eyes as best as I could.

An uncertain amount of time passed before Max spoke again. "What are you waiting for?" He looked at me. "Hurry up!"

"What?"

"You want her to have clothes, don't you? Hurry up!"

I couldn't move an inch.

"Get the clothes or we leave without them. It's your choice," he said.

No one volunteered to help me. I put Alicia down. A numbing sensation ran down my fingertips prematurely. I felt the ground softening with each step I took to get to the woman. I wobbled to the side, tripping over the laces on my boots.

I looked back at the group. They were waiting for me.

She was lying on her back. One of her knees was awkwardly twisted at an upward angle. The two shots in her neck blended into one. I couldn't see the opening due to the stream of blood running down her shirt. Her chest pumped up and down in a strenuous manner, trying its very best to keep its owner alive. A series of guttural noises sprang from her as if she were about to cough, yet her airway had been obstructed. She attempted to propel herself along the gravel. She moved a few inches, diagonally, closer to where her husband had fallen.

"She's still alive!" I ran back to the group, waving my hands in the air.

Max followed me. He examined the scene quickly.

"She's done. There's no saving her. Stop wasting your time."

"I can't." I shook my head with my eyes closed. "She's in pain."

He shot her again multiple times in the face and chest. I caught a glimpse of her glasses shattering; small pieces of the lenses dug into her cheekbone. The sight of her injuries became a blur. I looked away, yet I felt like I could see the bullets breaking through her skull, different tissue matters surging out one after one.

When she was finally still and lifeless, I unbuttoned her jacket. I loosened her shoes, socks, and pants. I ran back to the group, leaving the body almost entirely naked under the blazing sun.

***

Alicia's arms draped over my shoulders, resting calmly on my back. I tightened the strings on the pants and managed to prevent them from slipping. The general discomfort in my body became concrete pain. It sprang from the right side of my stomach and radiated with every step I took. Despite this, I couldn't let go of her. Thoughts and memories gradually exited my head. I planned on forgetting about them all.

The coyotes talked about a rectangular building protected by a long line of towering brown fences. The posts would be thin, like the spaces in between them. They would stretch on endlessly. Lots of cars would be parked both inside and outside the gate. We would part ways then.

I failed to see it. I tried squinting and tilting my head at multiple angles. The others began letting out mumbled cheers. They seemed so happy. It made sense; the family had no relations with them, so they had very few reasons to care or to mourn for them.

"Do you think they're getting married?" Alicia said.

"Who?"

"Your mom and her boyfriend."

"Maybe."

"Should we go to their wedding together? Or are you going by yourself? For the robotics finals, are we sitting together? Your dad's friend invites us every year. Chris can't come this year, of course, but we should visit him more often."

I was worried about the fever destroying her brain. I let her down. I checked her face and neck. Her temperature had lowered drastically and was perhaps even cooler than my own.

"Can you walk by yourself for a little while?" I asked.

"Yes."

"We'll get you a doctor as soon as we get there."

She nodded, took a few steps forward, then waited for me to follow. I told her to go on, that I was right behind her. When she had traveled an insurmountable distance, she stumbled back toward me, panicked.

I caught a break where the insides of my stomach burned a little less. She tried to pull me off the ground but failed pathetically.

"I want you to talk to my mom," I said to her.

I thought about what I wanted her to relay. I didn't know if I was in a position to declare forgiveness to my mother or to issue an apology. I didn't like the way things

341

had ended when we'd last seen each other. I wished I'd never had the opportunity to find out who she was, or who I was.

"What is it?" Alicia screeched at me.

"Never mind." I shook my head.

She left me temporarily. From afar, I saw her conversing with others. She spoke to several different people. Some turned their heads to look at me; others pushed her away.

I knew that she needed to go on without me. Yet, in a way, I wished for her to turn back. She eventually stopped trying. I saw her look in my direction two more times. I never knew what she was thinking. It had all happened too fast and had not been monumental enough.

She walked on, wearing the bloodstained clothes of another, much less fortunate woman. The redness had turned into a dark shade of brown. It had hardened in front of her chest. The once free-flowing liquid formed unique, pressed-on patterns on her sleeves. When she caught up with the rest of the group, she blended in. I desperately tried to hold on to her with my eyes. But soon, I couldn't differentiate her from the others.

ABOUT THE AUTHOR

KIMBERLEE LIU is an aspiring best-selling author from Southern California, now based in New York City. When she isn't writing, she enjoys hand-lettering and exploring local bakeries.

She can be reached at authorkliu@gmail.com

ABOUT THE AUTHOR